**'Master Dudgeon t**
**against the Armad**

'Master Dudgeon tall
short answer.

'I told him, most strongly, I didn't believe you
could be an ordinary anything.' Kate paused. She
was going to say something daring and she didn't
know how he would receive it. Oh, to Hades with
caution, she would speak her mind: something her
uncle rarely allowed her to do.

'I don't believe that you are an ordinary seaman
now.'

This jolted Martin's mind much as a crossbow-
bolt would have jolted his body. Now why did she
think that?

His reply was mysterious. 'Perhaps,' he said.
'Perhaps not.'

'I have already observed that you frequently talk
in riddles.'

She was observing far too much. He did not
think it wise to tell her so.

Kate decided that if she were to inform him of
her true feelings about this proposed marriage,
now was the time to do so.

# Author Note

Elizabeth I lived to what was a great age in the sixteenth and seventeenth centuries. As a result she outlived all her strong, powerful and wise advisers, and Gloriana – as she was often called – lost the power to entrance men by her beauty and her wit. It was the winter of her years, but for the young men surrounding her it was their spring, and England's defeat of the Armada and Elizabeth's part in it had faded into the past.

The court had always been a hotbed of intriguers, but she had been above them and had never been their target. Now they even began to question her right to rule. The Earl of Essex, who had been her favourite, overreached himself and started to call her authority into question. It is against this background that Lady Kate Wyville and Martin Chancellor, the Black Sheep, find themselves faced with an arranged marriage that neither of them wants. Their efforts to resolve this problem, and at the same time fend off the enemy who threatens them, run parallel with the ageing Queen's attempts to fight those who would destroy her.

Throughout the centuries, love, sex, power and politics have been intermingled, as they are in THE BLACK SHEEP'S BRIDE.

These are the novels which make up **The Elizabethan Season:**

| | | |
|---|---|---|
| *Spring* | – | MAID OF HONOUR |
| *Summer* | – | LADY IN WAITING |
| *Autumn* | – | THE ADVENTURER'S WIFE |
| *Winter* | – | THE BLACK SHEEP'S BRIDE |

I hope you enjoy reading this quartet of books about this fascinating period in history.

*Paula Marshall*

# *The* Elizabethan *Season*

# THE BLACK SHEEP'S BRIDE

## *Paula Marshall*

MILLS & BOON®

*MILLS & BOON and MILLS & BOON with the Rose Device are registered trademarks of the publisher.*

*First published in Great Britain 2004 by Harlequin Mills & Boon Limited, Eton House, 18-24 Paradise Road, Richmond, Surrey TW9 1SR*

© Harlequin Books S.A. 2004

Special thanks and acknowledgement are given to Paula Marshall for her contribution to The Elizabethan Season series.

ISBN 0 263 84088 3

*148-0604*

*Printed and bound in Spain by Litografia Rosés S.A., Barcelona*

Paula Marshall, married with three children, has had a varied life. She began her career in a large library and ended it as a senior academic in charge of history in a Polytechnic. She has travelled widely, has been a swimming coach, and has appeared on *University Challenge* and *Mastermind*. She has always wanted to write, and likes her novels to be full of adventure and humour.

*Other novels by*
**Paula Marshall**

JACK COMPTON'S LUCK
RINALDI'S REVENGE

*and in the Regency series*
**The Steepwood Scandal**

AN UNCONVENTIONAL DUENNA
THE MISSING MARCHIONESS

*and in*
**The Elizabethan Season**

MAID OF HONOUR

# Chapter One

*Early Autumn, 1600*

'Sing it again, Maister, sing it again!'

Martin Chancellor, buccaneer, merchant and poet, was roistering in a tavern in Deptford known as the Bull, not far from the lodging-house where Christopher Marlowe had so mysteriously died. He had not shaved for days and was wearing the well-worn clothes of an ordinary seaman. The only valuable thing about him was the lute which he had been playing to entertain the grimy and crowded room.

He was lying back in the room's one armchair, his booted feet on a stool. He had a tankard of ale in one hand, and the other was busily waving acknowledgements to his audience. When at last it fell silent, he said, 'I usually make it a habit, gentlemen, never to repeat myself, so, in a moment or two, after I have wet my whistle, I will favour you with another song, this time one of my own invention.'

His hearers particularly liked being addressed as gentlemen, seeing that they were so patently nothing of the sort, and allowed themselves to fall silent on being promised further amusement. For the moment Martin occupied himself by drinking his ale and examining the faces of the crowd. On his way to the Bull he had had an uneasy feeling that he was being shadowed, or watched, but every time he had turned round to try to find out who it might be, if anyone, he had seen nothing.

Which did not, in his world, mean that there was nothing to see. However, he was not going to allow his enjoyment to be spoilt by such whim-whams. His ale finished, he hammered on the table, lifted his lute from where it rested beside him, and made ready to play and sing. He possessed a good, baritone voice, with which he had enlivened more than one dull moment on the different ships in which he had sailed.

'As promised, gentlemen,' he announced, 'my offering to my own truly fair,' and began, without further preamble, to sing.

> A sonnet to my mistress' eyes
> Avoids the parts I really prize.
> So I will celebrate instead
> Those that we enjoy in bed...

The entire room sent up a howl of mirth on hearing this. Tankards were banged on tables, cheers rose to the dirty rafters, and most of the rest of the ditty was lost in the uproar. Several complaints were made by many furthest away from him, that the later verses of the song had been lost in the applause created by the first, but to no avail: called on to repeat it, Martin refused with a grin.

'It's too late,' he told them, rising, 'and I'm too tired. I'll be off to my bed now.' He offered his audience a highly suggestive wink, while slinging his lute round one shoulder and making discreetly sure that the poniard he always carried was ready for him to use if aught went amiss on his journey home. Before leaving he flung some coins to the landlord, to treat those who were nearest to the bar and had made the most noise.

Once outside, he took a deep breath and made for the nearest steps down to the Thames, where, despite the lateness of the hour, a wherry might be waiting to row him back to his temporary home, a small house in one of the City of London's back streets.

Before he reached the riverside he heard running steps behind him. He turned rapidly just in time to see a burly man, wielding an upraised knife, ready to attack him. The lifted knife was a mistake, although it might have put paid to most of the would-be thief's victims, for Martin, skilled in dirty fighting, chose instead to use the poniard which he had rapidly drawn, not to stab the fellow but to strike him hard in the face with its heavy hilt.

He had chosen the fellow's nose to aim at: streaming blood, the thief blindly staggered away, dropping his knife. Martin caught him by his left hand, twisted his arm behind his back and, reversing his poniard, now drew it gently across his prisoner's throat, saying, 'Can you offer me any reason why I should not slit your throat on the instant?'

'Aye, master, for it was only your purse I meant to cut, not your throat,' he managed to gasp.

'Now, why do I not believe you?' Martin told him, negligently sliding his poniard once again across the thief's neck, so that it drew a little blood. 'For you were busy watching me in the tavern and before that I thought that I saw you in the street on the way to it. Were you hired to kill me? Speak up before I decide to finish you off at once, and then I might spare you.'

'Your word on it,' gasped the thief.

'For what it's worth, yes. Now talk, before I change my mind.'

'To tell truth, master, I know not who the man was. He was a little fellow, richly dressed and gave me a couple of groats if I would kill you after such a fashion that it looked like a robbery on a drunken man. As God is my witness that's the truth on't.'

It might be, and it might not. Martin had no wish to kill the clumsy fool, even if he might be doing the state some service by ridding it of such a clodpole, so he privately decided on mercy, but also decided to let his attacker stew for a few moments before he released him.

'And that's it? Someone unknown points you in my direction and for a few trifling pennies, and the small sum in my purse, you will cheerfully dispose of me? You sold yourself uncommon cheap!'

'Aye, maister, so I did. I'm but a poor man. Now will you let me go?'

'Only when you hand over the groats your unknown master gave to you.'

'You said yourself they was only trifling…'

'You,' said Martin, tightening his grip on his would-be murderer, 'are trifling with me. Hand over the groats and think yourself lucky that I did not call the watch.'

Now this was an empty threat because, for a variety of reasons, Martin did not wish to involve the law in his business, but the thief was not to know that.

'Aye, if that will save me.'

Martin released his grip a little so that his assailant could pull the groats out of his purse and hand them over, moaning under his breath while he did so.

'Now, your name, and where you may be found,' asked Martin, resuming his iron grip on the fellow.

'You may find me at the Bull, they know me there. I'm hight Wattie Harrison, an it please you.'

'Oh, it doesn't please me at all, but life being what it is, I might need your incompetent services one day. Life is full of such surprises, as you are finding out. One word of warning before I let you go. Try this trick, or any other, on me again and I shall not spare you a second time.'

'Aye, aye, maister.'

'And don't take your knife with you.' This last instruction came as Wattie bent to pick it up. 'I've a mind not to be attacked after being merciful—I shouldn't like to have to kill you after all.'

'By Satan and all the devils you're a hard man, maister,' offered Wattie admiringly.

'Never mind that. Be off with you—and if your paymaster complains because you didn't kill me, tell him that.'

Wattie pulled a grudging forelock. 'Aye, so I will,' and ran lightly down the path, away from the river.

Martin bent down to pick up the knife. He looked at it and gave a wry smile. 'Now was I a complete fool to let him go? But I do hate to kill a man for nothing—even though I might regret it later.'

He was still pondering on this when, after his journey in the wherry, he reached his small home in an alley just off Forge Street. As he expected when he let himself in by the back door, Rafe, his lieutenant and his best friend, who had sailed with him many times, was waiting for him in the kitchen.

'You are back earlier than I expected, Master.'

Martin put his lute carefully down on a shabby settle before he answered with, 'I grew bored with low company, I must be getting old. I am ready for bed and the night is still young.'

'Never say so, but you cannot retire yet. Two hours ago a high-nosed sort of clerk—or lawyer—arrived, demanding to see you if you were one Martin

Chancellor. I told him to come again tomorrow at a more Christian time, but he said that his master had bade him not to return until he had met you, since the matter was urgent. He would not tell me what it was so I put him in the parlour to await your arrival.'

Martin gave a great yawn. 'I suppose I ought to see him, if only to find out who the devil he can be and why he is here. You told him nothing of me, I trust. He thinks this is my one home? And that I have but the one name?'

Rafe put a finger by his nose. 'Take me not for a fool, Master. He thinks me one—which is all to the good. He asked me about you, but I wittered to him some nonsense which had you working down at the docks and having gone to the Bull in Deptford for the odd dram after a hard day of it—which seemed to surprise him a little.'

'Excellent. He may be friend, or he may be enemy, but a confused man waiting for me can only be to my advantage.'

'So, I thought, Master. May I go to bed now?'

'Certainly, if only to stop hearing you call me Master. I am Martin to you, Rafe, ever and always.'

Rafe laughed softly at that. 'D'you know, Martin, I have the strangest feeling that we may be sailing into waters where the old rules which guided us no longer apply.'

'Dear God, I hope not,' Martin riposted.

And now to find out who the devil it was who

needed to speak to him with such urgency that he was willing to wait so long to meet him.

The parlour which he entered was a small but clean room, furnished with the minimum of cheap possessions, except for a rather splendid clock on the shelf above a primitive hearth. A well-dressed young man with a clerkly air was seated in the one armchair before the fire. He had been reading a book which he had obviously brought with him and which he put down on the small table beside him. A leather satchel stood by his chair.

He rose as Martin entered and stared at him. At his rough clothes, at his heavily bearded face, his unruly black hair, and his blue eyes, startlingly bright against what could be seen of his brown skin. His lip involuntarily curled a little. He made no effort to speak and it was Martin who finally broke the silence by asking, 'Who are you? And what business brings you here, sir, that you were willing to wait so long for me to come home?'

The young man picked up the satchel, saying, 'My name is Thomas Webster, and you, I hope, are Martin Chancellor?'

'And if I am?'

'Then I also hope that you can prove to me that you are the man of that name for whom I have been looking.'

'But why have you been looking for me? That is, if I am Martin Chancellor.'

'More strictly, it is m'lord the Viscount Bretford

who is Martin Chancellor's father and who has the most urgent need to speak to his son.'

'Has he, indeed! You surprise me greatly, since I could scarcely describe such an act as sending for me after fourteen years' absence as an urgent one.'

Martin had often wondered whether he would ever see his father again. He might once have thought that he might seek him out, but never that the first overture would come from his father.

'So, you need proof that I am the rightful Martin Chancellor!' He gave a short laugh before saying, 'Oh, I can prove that—if I need to. The marks of the flogging he ordered for me two days before I left home are still on my back—as well as the brand on my shoulder marking me as thief and rapist. Will that do for you and m'lord? Would you have me strip here? And if I told you to take yourself back to him with the message that I have no desire ever to meet him again, what then?'

'That he is old, lonely, like to die soon, and wishes to see you, and yes, the message is urgent.'

'Yet you may not tell me of it.'

'No, he wishes to speak to you himself.'

'You say that he is lonely. He has my brother John. Is he not enough for him?'

Webster's face grew shuttered. 'M'lord has said little to me of his reasons for wishing to speak to you, but of your mercy, I would beg you to do as he asks.'

'He showed me little enough when I lived with him as his son, so why should I trouble with him now?'

'I know nothing of the past, but I would ask you to reconsider. We are all sinners who need mercy, either from God or our fellows, you, I, and m'lord.'

Martin turned his back on him and stared into the fire as though he could read the future in its flames. To go, or not to go? What had he to gain or to lose? No talk of mercy moved him, and as for God, he was one with Sir Walter Raleigh, since they neither of them believed in such a nonsense. If he gave way and agreed to accompany Webster to Bretford House at this unwonted hour, it would be out of curiosity, simply to find out why in the world his father wanted to see him so urgently.

'Very well,' he said abruptly. 'I will return with you—and I will bring my friend, Rafe Dudgeon, with me.'

'Oh, I am sure that m'lord will agree to that. May I say how pleased I am that you have made this decision.'

'No, you may not. It is no affair of yours, and I do not yet know whether it is any affair of mine that my father should, after so many years, seek me out. I go to find out what bee is buzzing in his bonnet and for no other reason. Now, sit down for a moment while I speak with Rafe and make ready to accompany you. Have you been offered any refreshment during your long vigil?'

'A little—but a pint of ale would be welcome before we set out.'

'That you shall have—and at once. I will see to it myself.'

With that Martin took his leave.

Some instinct told him that neither he nor Rafe would return to Forge Street that night, so after he had fed Webster, they both packed small satchels with a change of linen before accompanying him to Bretford House, that magnificent palace on the Strand, so different from the small cottage where Webster had tracked him down.

Late though it was, there were footmen on duty. It was apparent that they had orders to admit him to m'lord at once. This they did, after staring at Martin's appearance—as the butler later said to the staff, 'It was hard to tell which was master and which was man.'

Despite Martin's protests, Rafe was detached from him, to accompany the butler to the kitchen where, Martin later discovered, he was wined and dined. Once he had gone, a footman led Webster and Martin up the great staircase to m'lord's bedroom and not, as Martin had expected to the downstairs withdrawing-room, the latest word for a place where a gentleman might be private, far away from the chambers of state.

His father, propped up by many pillows, was seated in his great bed, with its Viscount's coronet mounted at the top of the green and gold curtains. Martin scarcely recognised him. He remembered him as a large man of great presence, ruddy of face, hale and hearty, with a voice which could, as his retainers were fond of saying, be heard half a county away.

Now he was shrunken and withered, his face was as grey as his hair and his hands were ceaselessly plucking at the sheets. His voice was still cold and severe when he spoke at last, after his faded blue eyes had ceased to roam over Martin's face and figure. It was, however, low and hoarse, quite unlike the commanding bellow of old.

Martin offered him no bow, no filial deference, merely stood there waiting to be spoken to.

'Martin?' his father said, and the word was a question not a statement.

'Unfortunately so, m'lord.' He would not call the man before him father.

'I've had you sought by my agents for the last six months. I was beginning to think that Martin Chancellor had disappeared from the face of the earth.'

'Did you indeed?' Martin was quite determined not to initiate any subject of conversation with his father. He would not tell him that his existence as Martin Chancellor had ended on the day he had fled from his home, until he had revived it in mockery of what he had once been.

'Yes, and the matter which I need to raise with you has become more and more urgent.' The man on the bed fell silent as though speaking over-much tired him.

Still Martin said nothing. What he found surprising

was the raging anger which was beginning to overcome him. At first when he had run away, hatred of his father had ruined his days and nights, but gradually, as time passed, he had left it behind. It was of no consequence: he had created a life for himself far from the one which he might have led before that fatal night.

Perforce his father spoke again. 'I have only sent for you out of necessity. Nigh on six months ago your brother, John, died of the great pox—something which only my physician and I knew he had contracted. His death left you, my remaining son, as the one person who could get an heir to ensure that the Chancellor estates do not revert to the Crown—with all the ills that such an act might entail.

'Some months before John's death Lord Clifton and I had arranged that he should marry Lady Kate Wyville, his ward. She was his dead sister's daughter and the heiress of the late Earl of Wyville's estates and fortune. John fell ill shortly afterwards and the marriage was postponed pending his recovery. After his death I asked Lord Clifton if he would agree to my other son, Martin, who would become the new Baron Hadleigh, replacing him as Lady Kate's future husband—if you could be found, that was.

'Lord Clifton, who has been my friend for many years, was most agreeable, provided only that you were found before six months were up. That period of time ends in ten days. In short, you have become

my heir and the future husband of one of the richest
heiresses in England.'

Martin began to laugh. He laughed so hard that he
started to stagger, and only saved himself from falling
by seating himself on a bench before one of the windows. His father and Webster, who had been standing
near to the door, stared at him in astonishment.

Lord Bretford said, frostily, 'I fail to see why what
I have just told you should have caused you so much
amusement.'

'You do?' Martin stopped laughing, rose and advanced to the foot of his father's bed. 'Your brain
must have become addled since you have grown old
if you do not find it a subject for comedy that your
good son should have died of the pox and that the
bad one should then be desperately searched for in
order to save the family fortunes by marrying the so-
called good son's leavings.'

His father's grey face turned even greyer. Martin
heard Webster behind him give an involuntary gasp
after he had finished.

'You have not changed,' his father finally achieved.
'You come here looking like a piece of scum from
the gutter and when I make you a grand offer—which
you do not deserve—you choose to insult me.'

'A grand offer? I have a life of my own. So why
should I choose to live the one you have so belatedly
offered me?'

'A life of your own! And pray what might that be?
I understand from Webster that you are living in a

hovel in a dirty back street and you come here looking like a beggar. Yet I still stand by my offer. Accept it—and I am ready to forget the past.'

'*You* are ready to forget the past! I, however, am not. I shall not remain here this night, but will leave immediately. I would bid you goodnight, but that I do not wish to bid you a good anything.'

He moved towards the door, to walk past Webster, except that the man followed him out and shutting the door behind him took him by the arm.

'A moment,' he said abruptly. 'I would speak with you.'

Martin felt a deathly tiredness overcome him. 'Whatever can you have to say to me?'

'This: you are throwing away a fortune, a rich and clever wife, and the chance to allow the old fool in there to die happily. Now, I must inform you that I have also discovered your many secrets. I know that you do not need his fortune, that you have another name and that it is a good one and an honoured one, even if you occasionally amuse yourself by enjoying yourself as you did when you first went to sea. Moreover, what have you to lose by obliging your father?

'Those whom m'lord employs, the estate itself and all its dependants will lose everything. I do not name myself as one of their company, since I shall still have my good name to sell—but they will have nothing. Why are you doing this? To satisfy your taste for revenge? M'lord thinks that you are a penniless ne'erdo-well and I have not disabused him of that false belief. Can you not see that your best revenge would be to accept his offer? And, saying nothing of your own truth, laugh at him while you deceive him, and at the same time save those unfortunates who cannot help themselves?'

'You know the truth of me—and have not told him?'

'Why should I? His judgement is poor: he worshipped his so-called good son, and he believes that he is doing you a favour by forgiving you, the so-called bad one. Do yourself a favour—go back and tell him that you have changed your mind—with one condition only.'

Martin was fascinated. The previously anonymous man before him had changed colour like that odd animal the chameleon—or like himself, for that matter!

'And that condition is?'

'That you will be allowed to employ me to assist you in your new life. After all, he believes that you will not be accustomed to such grandeur.'

To Martin's amusement, the wily fellow had the audacity to offer him a wink when he had ended his sentence. 'I had not believed you to be a rogue,' he said at last.

'No? As you must well know, we are all rogues when it comes to acting on our own behalf.'

Should he do as Webster had suggested? Did he really want a wife to be chosen for him by two old men? On the other hand, as Rafe had so often told

him, he ought to marry, and in the class from which
he had sprung most marriages were arranged ones.
And since he no longer believed in love, he might as
well marry without it.

Was the fellow trying to blackmail him? Almost as
though he had read his mind, Webster leaned forward
and said confidentially, 'Have no fear that I shall use
my knowledge of your true self to gain a hold over
you. After all, it would be a strange sort of power to
use against a man—that you knew that he was a success when everyone else thought that he was a failure!'

'True enough.'

The more Martin thought about it the more attractive Webster's advice became. To pretend that he was
virtually a beggar by allowing his father to believe
that, in accepting him as his son again, he was doing
him the greatest favour, was indeed a joke. Life had
grown dull lately, which was why he was masquer-
ading as Martin Chancellor, a poor seaman, to try to
enjoy himself as he had done when he had been a
poverty-stricken lad trying to make his way in the
world.

'Very well,' he said at last. 'I will do as you suggest, but if I should choose to tell him the truth at
any time, I shall do so.'

'Oh, that is your choice, and if the lady does not
please you—then that is your choice, too.'

'Amen to that.' Many women had pleased Martin

Chancellor since he had fled the family home, and he doubted that this one would be any different.

He walked back into the bedroom to tell the old man that he had changed his mind. 'I will agree to become your son again,' he said, 'on one condition— that you allow Webster to be part of my household in order to help me to behave as Lord Hadleigh should.'

To which Lord Bretford said, smiling a little, 'At last, the prodigal has returned. Of course you may have Webster to serve you; I can think of no better task for him.'

Webster, still in the background, had a hard time of it trying not to laugh aloud. Martin's face remained impassive.

'First of all,' said his father, his face alive with interest for the first time since his son had arrived, 'you must consent to live here for a time, ready to meet your future bride when I have informed her guardian of your return.'

Martin shook his head. He might have guessed that his father's attempt to control him would begin im- mediately and he intended to have none of that. 'Not so. I have a home of my own, and duties connected with it to which I must attend. I will visit you when- ever it is convenient to do so.'

He was lying, of course, for the home to which he was referring was not that in Forge Street. It struck him that he and the truth had rarely been friends since he had ceased to be Lord Bretford's son, and being restored to that position had certainly not changed matters. If anything it had made them worse!

His father's hands began to pluck at the bedclothes again. 'It is a bad omen, Hadleigh, that you have begun your new life by defying me, but if you must, you must. I am prepared to allow such a course of behaviour, but for a short time only.'

'Most gracious of you, sir. And now you must allow me to retire. I am tired, so I must believe that you, being bedridden and old, must be even more so. We will discuss matters further in the morning.'

By using the word 'discuss', he was telling his still tyrannical father that he would not blindly obey every whim and fancy which the old man might care to wish of him.

'Very well,' said m'lord, 'in the morning, then. Webster, see Lord Hadleigh and his servant to the rooms which have been prepared for their use.'

Martin bowed, not a low bow, but it was the first act of courtesy which he had offered his father since he had met him again. Despite himself he was shocked by the old man's frailty—and what it told him of his own mortality. Again, on the other hand, the past fourteen years could not be ignored as though they had never been.

'I agreed, uncle, to be betrothed to the late Lord Hadleigh to oblige you and not myself. It was wrong of me I know, and quite un-Christian, to be pleased that his death relieved me of that marriage. You know perfectly well, for I have often told you so, that I have no wish to marry. Yet, knowing that, and behind my back, without any form of consultation, you have arranged yet another marriage for me. This time with the new Lord Hadleigh, whom I have never even met because he ran away from home fourteen years ago and no one has seen, or heard from him since then. You must cancel this proposed marriage at once, for I will have none of it.'

Lady Kate Wyville was speaking to her uncle and guardian, the Earl of Clifton who had just informed her of his and Lord Bretford's decision—that she should exchange the dead Lord Hadleigh with the live one. As always, even when she was angry, she was speaking in a quiet and measured voice, totally in control of herself and all her emotions.

'Now, now, my sweet child,' murmured Lord Clifton in an attempt to placate her, 'you know as well as I do that you must marry. You are a woman, and women need a husband to protect them and their lands. Yours and Bretford's run side by side, so to marry his heir is a most sensible arrangement. Fortunate it is that the missing young man has been found so that he, too, may do his duty to his present name and his future title.'

If Kate had been a different sort of young woman she would have said, 'To the devil with *his* future title—it is my present one that I wish to keep!'

Instead, maintaining her iron self-control which was at such odds with the cool and classic beauty of her face, where only her bright green eyes told of the passion which lived somewhere inside her, but which she never revealed for the world to stare at, she said, 'Uncle, if our Queen could remain unmarried and rule this kingdom with such success without marrying, then I can see no reason why I should not follow her example.'

'But you are not the Queen, my dear, and look how she is ending her life. She is an old woman with no chick nor child to comfort her and all the friends of her youth are dead and gone, including those whom she might have married. Her beauty has gone, too, and such upstarts as Essex seek to defy and demean her, since she has nothing to control them with any more. Oh, she may punish and disgrace Essex for his incompetence and his various follies, but that leaves her even more alone, a creature to pity.'

Kate could not deny the truth of this, yet she still clung to her wish to be independent, to rule her own lands as the Queen had ruled hers, and hope that the end of her life might be different from that of her monarch's.

She shook her head, saying, 'Even so, but at least she had the right to choose. You have not given me that. I would take the chance of suffering a lonely old age if I could but once do something as remarkable as the Queen's behaviour when she defied Philip of Spain and his Armada.'

'You may say that now—but what might you say or think when you have reached that old age? Is it possible that you might look back and wail, "Had I but known, I would have done thus and so, rather than what I actually did."'

Kate rose and began to pace the room. 'None of us can guess what the future might bring, but in the present in which we live I would wish to be my own mistress, as a man is his own master, rather than have another make my decisions and rule my life.'

Her uncle sighed. He thought that she had never looked more beautiful, more fit to make some fortunate man's life happy, but the questioning intellect which ruled her was preventing her from choosing to follow the path which most women were wise enough to take.

'My dear,' he said, still gentle, so gentle that Kate wanted to rage against him for sounding so reasonable, 'I fear that you have no choice in the matter. Like it or not, you signed a binding contract of *verbis de praesenti* to marry one Lord Hadleigh, and it is Lord Hadleigh who has told the lawyers that he is willing to fulfil that contract and marry you.'

'But he is not the Lord Hadleigh that I was willing to marry. He is Martin, the younger son, not John, the elder.'

'As the contract was drawn up on his side, merely in the name of Lord Hadleigh, then that argument cannot hold water.'

'Oh!' Kate sat down, frustrated, fearing that her hard-won composure was in danger of flying away altogether. 'I don't know him, and since he returned

there the servants at Bretford House have told ours
that he is a savage, totally unlike his elder brother.
How could the contract have been worded so loosely?
Could it not be broken?'

Lord Clifton, who knew the truth behind John
Chancellor's sudden death and was of the private
opinion that Lord Bretford had cunningly allowed it
to be drawn up after a fashion that would enable the
next heir to take the marriage over, muttered, 'Very
difficult, my dear. No, the die is cast, as they say—
and the result will work to your benefit. It is likely
that after the marriage, given the increased size of the
Bretford estates, Her Grace will elevate the
Viscountcy of Bretford to an Earldom and you will
become a Countess.'

For some reason this last piece of information was,
so far as Kate was concerned, the very last straw. Her
green eyes flashing fire, she whirled on her uncle with
such force that he started back.

'Oh,' she exclaimed fiercely, 'I have not the
slightest desire to be a Countess, and I wish most
heartily that you would stop calling me *my dear* in
an attempt to wheedle me into doing what I would
rather not—particularly since it seems that I have no
choice at all in the matter because of some clerk's
stupid mistake. If I must go to what I regard as my
execution then I must, but do not expect me to like
it—or him. More than ever I wish that I had been
born a man.'

Suddenly appalled by her own behaviour, she sat

down and tried not to burst into tears, tears which would merely serve to reinforce her uncle's opinion that every weak woman needed a man to protect her.

'Now, now, my dear,' said her uncle tenderly, 'I am sure that all will be well. You will look back on this day and agree that you were right to do your duty, marry Lord Hadleigh and live the life for which you and all women were born. Forget the Queen; you are not royalty and her example is not a good one for you to follow, as you will agree yourself when you are older and wiser.'

'And resigned to my fate,' muttered Kate, tears banished. 'I suppose that I am to meet my future husband before we actually stand at the altar.'

'Of course, my dear, we are not barbarians. We are to visit Bretford House when Lord Bretford sends for us—at the moment he is unwell.'

My dear again! It was the sort of phrase with which one handed a child a sweetmeat. Well, from the gossip, Lord Hadleigh was far from being a sweetmeat. He had run away from home at the age of sixteen after some unspecified piece of misbehaviour and nobody had heard any more of him until the other day when it had become common knowledge that his father had tracked him down.

And what did that tell you about him?

Nothing good for sure.

But she, God help her, was to be his wife.

Unless, of course, he found her undesirable and indicated that he did not wish to fulfil the contract—

and she, equally of course, would be only too willing to oblige him.

Her smile broadened. Lord Bretford and his new-found son would be unwise to count their chickens before they were hatched...

# Chapter Two

'So your father's minion has come home with us. Why?' Rafe Dudgeon asked Martin on the following morning when they were at last alone together in his Forge Street home.

'Because he is my minion now—or as much as he is anybody's. I suspect Master Webster to be ambitious. He probably feels that I am a better prospect for the future than that tired old man, my father.'

'Aye, no doubt. The servants were full of gossip. The one piece which they didn't tell me, and which might have interested me, was why you ran away all those years ago, when by staying you could have lived a life of luxury and ease instead of ploughing such a hellish difficult furrow—even if you did find success at the end of it.'

'I doubt that anyone but myself knows the truth of that,' replied Martin dryly.

'And does this Webster fellow know the truth of you now?'

'Yes, which is why I asked for him to join my camp—that way I have at least some chance of knowing what he might be plotting. I should have had no notion at all of his activities if I had left him with my father.'

'He did not tell your father what he had discovered?'

'No, but it might not be long before he knows. London, though growing larger, is still too small for anything happening in its boundaries to remain a secret for ever.'

'One thing,' said Rafe. 'Webster cannot live here. There is barely room for the two of us.'

'True, and the pair of you will return to Saxon Hall this afternoon. I shall remain here—old Mother Laurence from next door will look after me. I have gained a few days' grace before I move into Bretford House. You and Webster will, of course, come with me when I go there—and Jacko. I can't leave him behind. We might need him.'

'Your friend, your brains and your muscle,' grinned Rafe. 'All three of us covering your back, as usual.'

'Oh, I learned that the hard way,' Martin told him, stretching. 'In any case, this house is too small for me to live in long anyway. I shall keep it, though. Who knows when one of us might need a hiding place?'

'Very true,' agreed Rafe, 'we live in dangerous times.'

'All times are dangerous, only some are more dangerous than others, especially now that the old Queen is slowly dying and so many are plotting for the future with Tower Hill possibly waiting for the failures.'

'You scarcely need to plot for yours, though. Marriage to a great heiress—it is exactly what I have been advising for you—but you dismissed everything I had to say. It took that old man to bully you into it.'

'It was my decision, not his, and I could scarcely listen to you until you had followed your own advice and found a wife yourself.'

'Never,' exclaimed Rafe fervently, beginning to laugh at the mere idea. He stopped only when Webster came in, carrying a large satchel.

He bowed to Martin. 'I have left Bretford House and am at your service, m'lord.'

'In that case I would wish you to accompany Master Dudgeon to Saxon Hall, where he will find you accommodation. I have an excellent library there, where you may entertain yourself before you accompany me to Bretford House. Rafe, of course, will arrange his own amusements. I shall remain here, alone, for the time being. We shall eat together before you leave.'

'Indeed, m'lord. As your lordship wishes. I am always at your service.'

It was very strange to be called m'lord, a title which he had never expected to possess. For a moment there, while he had been sparring with Rafe, it was as though yesterday had never happened and the world had not turned upside down, to leave him with yet another identity and one which he did not want.

Was he right to have agreed to be reconciled, to become Lord Hadleigh and to accept his late brother's betrothed, sight unseen? By so doing he had not only obeyed the father whom he had sworn never to oblige again, but had also appeared to fall in with his demand that he marry Lady Kate Wyville.

Only appeared to fall in, though, because he could surely manage matters in his behaviour towards her after such a fashion that the wench would wish to cry off. He had no desire to marry. Women, except as bed-partners, bored him these days. He had been continent for some time: if truth were known, ever since Mary and her child had died...

Martin tried not to think of them, to put them to the back of his mind, while he informed Webster that he would be leaving Forge Street to move to his true home, Saxon Hall, near Bishopsgate, where many of London's *nouveaux riches* were building houses in which to display their wealth.

'By the by,' he ended, 'I would prefer it if you did not constantly m'lord me. As you know, at Saxon Hall I have quite another name, which is Andrew Martin, and that is how you will address me when I am there. In Forge Street I am Martin Chancellor, and only when I am at Bretford House am I Lord Hadleigh.'

'So noted,' and Webster bowed, his face impassive. After they had gone, Martin sat down, and for the first time thought carefully and slowly about what he had done and what he ought to do. One thing was imperative: somehow he must organise the different strands of his life so that, for the moment, they did not become tangled.

Bevis Frampton, old and ailing, but his vicious will still intact, sat alone, as always, in his palatial home. He was musing on the past and the strange and secret power which he had wielded throughout the old Queen's long reign. A power which no one knew of, or even suspected, since he had always lived in the shadows, rarely in the public eye.

It had become the most supreme pleasure for him to arrange matters in such a fashion that those who had crossed him, those whom he disliked and those of whose politics he disapproved, always paid for it dearly, either through loss of life or through ruin and shame.

Even if that old woman, the Queen—whom he so greatly detested—still ruled England, he had made her life miserable by his machinations. Although he had been unable to achieve his greatest ambition by helping her enemies to succeed in having her killed or dethroned, he had made sure that she had lived for most of her reign in fear of both fates as a result of his plotting.

His next move against her, designed to bring her down at last, was in train at the moment. He was preparing to join my Lord of Essex and to take part in the rebellion against the Crown which the Earl intended to mount as soon as he had sufficient supporters.

Best of all, none of the many whom he had sent to their doom had been aware that he had been the author of their misfortunes. They might curse the unkind gods, or the monarch, but never that meek creature, Bevis Frampton!

Recently, though, he had had nothing to gloat over. His latest victim, the son of the man who had wronged him long ago, but whom he had never directly attacked because he preferred to watch him suffer instead, had, by some mischance, escaped from the trap which had been laid for him. His hireling had failed to kill him. His first impulse had been to have the bungling assassin disposed of, his second was to have the fool try again, since these days reliable henchmen had become hard to find.

Only when he knew that Lord Bretford was lamenting the untimely loss of the second of his sons would his vengeance be complete. To have secured the death of both brothers would be enough to make the thought of his own end pleasant, since he would be going to his grave a happy and satisfied man.

He called for his assassin to be brought to him from the ante-room, where he was doubtless waiting in fear of what his punishment might be for his failure. This time he would be pardoned for it, but if he should bungle his mission again, he would be shown no mercy.

* * *

On the morning that they were summoned to Bretford House, Kate had herself dressed slowly and carefully. So elaborate were her clothes that it was virtually impossible for her to be dressed without the help of her maid, Jennie Johnson. First of all she was attired in a simple linen shift and a pair of knotted silk stockings, fastened just above the knee with ribbons to act as garters. Next she was laced at the back into a bodice whose ornamental embroidered front was heavily padded with canvas—Kate disliked whalebone stiffeners, finding them uncomfortable. She also disliked heavy and ostentatious ruffs, so hers was a small cream one.

The bodice ended at the waist in a vee which showed above the kirtle which was draped over her skirts. Like her skirts, it was embroidered, but not heavily, and they were both draped over what was known as a Spanish farthingale, a framework of hoops, which allowed them to fall into soft and elegant folds, thus creating a cone-shaped effect.

After that, since they were separate from the bodice, came the tying on of the padded sleeves, which were of the same material as the skirts. Shoes of the most delicate and expensive leather, with very high heels completed the picture.

Jennie next combed and brushed her glorious, lightly waving chestnut hair and, since she was still a maiden and unmarried, tied it loosely back, without putting on it a cap or a chaplet of pearls. Kate refused the sleeveless over-gown she was offered, since the day was warm and the clothes she was already wearing were heavy. Jennie then hung round her neck a thin chain from which a golden rose depended. It had a tiny pearl at its centre.

Lastly, a scented pomander was placed at her waist to repel the unwanted and unpleasant smells which filled central London and were thought to cause infections.

When she was finally fully dressed, she stared at herself in the Venetian mirror which adorned one wall.

'Oh, m'lady,' gushed Jennie, standing back to admire her handiwork, 'you look splendid.'

'Perhaps,' sighed Kate, 'but I much prefer living in the country where I needn't be burdened with such a quantity of clothing. A knight in armour scarcely wears more than we ladies do.'

'But think how much it becomes you. You're sure that you don't want me to whiten your face a little and put some red on your lips to look like a real lady fit to go before the Queen?'

'I could scarcely be more of a real lady than I already am,' was Kate's weary reply. 'I am not going before the Queen today, and as you well know I am not over-happy about meeting this man whom his father and my uncle have chosen for my husband, so I'm quite enough of a painted maypole as it is.'

'Go to, m'lady,' replied Jennie with the cheekiness

of long service, 'you are certainly not tall enough to be a maypole.'

'But taller than most women—and quite a number of men.'

'Perhaps Lord Hadleigh will be taller than you are, which ought to make you both happy,' said Jennie, still daring. 'Now you are fit to join Mistress Saville and your father, who will doubtless be waiting for you.'

Would Lord Hadleigh care that he was taller or shorter than his future wife? Somehow Kate doubted it. She walked downstairs, to find that her Aunt Jocasta, her late mother's youngest sister, who acted as her attendant lady, was waiting for her in the entrance hall.

'The coaches are come, but your uncle has not,' wailed her aunt. 'He always keeps us waiting.'

'That is his prerogative,' said Kate, 'since he is Earl.' She had had this unnecessary conversation a hundred times before; unnecessary because her uncle always kept his women waiting.

Her aunt sniffed, but fortunately on this occasion Lord Clifton chose not to leave them standing about too long, but arrived with his usual servants in attendance.

'Let us not keep the horses waiting,' he announced, as though Kate and her aunt had turned up late, instead of it being the other way round. Neither of them said anything, and Kate decided, quite resigned to her fate, that if she married Lord Hadleigh she would be merely exchanging one tyrant for another, so in a sense accepting Lord Hadleigh as a husband would change very little.

They emerged into the early September sunshine to find the two Clifton coaches already standing on the gravel sweep. Their owner was one of the few noblemen with two such equipages and he liked to display his wealth by using them together as often as possible. Kate and her aunt were to travel in the first, while he followed in the second.

Kate was driven towards her doom, as she was beginning to think it, at a slow pace, frequently held up by herds of cattle, sheep and other animals being driven towards Smithfield market, as well as numerous carts carrying into the city the mountains of food which were needed to fill the Londoners' bellies. It was as well that she could not hear the curses which her coachman flung at the passing show whenever it ceased to pass.

She did not know whether she was glad or sorry that it was taking so long to reach Bretford House.

Earlier that day Martin had returned to Saxon Hall, a noble red brick mansion in the style of Wolsey's Hampton Court, but smaller, where he soon found that Webster and Rafe were living in a kind of armed truce. It seemed that the most strife was caused by the question of the division of their duties.

He met them in the library, which opened off the

Great Hall, and soon solved this problem by a few brisk and trenchant words.

'If you can't agree to behave like sensible folk and not like fools, you leave me no recourse but to dismiss the pair of you,' he bellowed at them, as though he were back on the quarterdeck of his own ship again. 'I don't expect to have to negotiate a truce between two supposedly clever men.'

That did the trick, and no mistake. The pair of them banded together to defy him and not each other. Neither of them wished, for their own reasons, to be dismissed. They grumbled off, to sit down in the room which Webster had commandeered for his office—or his bureau as he called it—and worked matters out for themselves before being summoned to be ready to accompany Martin to Bretford House, where they were to meet the Lady Kate Wyville and her guardian.

They grumbled still more when he came downstairs and met them in the entrance hall.

'You're not going dressed like that, and without having shaved or arranged your hair,' they exclaimed together.

Martin, who had arrived in what he thought of as his shabby Forge Street garb, and had not changed out of it, said, 'Why not?'

'As Lord Hadleigh and Lord Bretford's heir,' announced Webster pompously, 'your present appearance when you are about to meet your betrothed, who is a great heiress, is neither fitting nor proper.'

'I agree,' chimed in Rafe, at one with Webster for the first time. 'What is good enough for Forge Street will not do for Bretford House.'

Martin glared at them. 'When I ordered you to agree with one another it was not so that you might join together to instruct me in matters of etiquette. I shall wear what I please.'

'Well, it won't please anyone else,' muttered Rafe, 'least of all your future bride.'

'What makes you think I want to please her?' roared Martin. 'To horse, both of you, and don't waste time. I employ you, you don't employ me.'

Webster opened his mouth to say something then, seeing the expression on m'lord's face, shut it again.

Neither of them were to know that Martin did not mean a word of his reprimand: that he was baiting them for the pleasure of watching them agree with one another and be disciplined as a pair, rather than separately. It was a bit hard on Rafe, whom he had always indulged, but now that Webster had been added to his household that might have to change a little.

'I thought Jacko was coming with us,' Rafe said more deferentially than usual.

'So he is, but he is doing a necessary errand for me and will be arriving later. Now let's be off.'

They trotted slowly down the drive, delayed by the packhorses with them which carried their clothing and other personal possessions. Unaware that he shared these thoughts with the Lady Kate, Martin was not sure how soon he wished to reach their destination and rather relished the numerous stoppages for traffic on their journey.

By the time they reached Bretford House he was certain that this whole business was the first mistake he had made since he had run away from home. Only a perverted sense of honour kept him from ordering their little procession to return to Saxon Hall, from whence he would send his apologies to his father for reneging on his promises and announce that he was immediately renouncing the title of Lord Hadleigh.

Reluctantly he dismounted in the stable yard, ordered their possessions to be taken to the rooms assigned for them, and strode into the house determined to try to make the best of things, but doubting whether he could.

Somehow he survived, but only just, his first encounter with his father, who was now downstairs, seated in an armchair in the withdrawing-room off the Great Hall. He stared at Martin and his feral appearance when he entered it.

'Body of God, Hadleigh,' he exclaimed, to the secret amusement of Webster and Rafe, who had followed their master in. 'You're surely not proposing to greet your betrothed looking like the wild man of the woods! Go and make yourself presentable. I will offer your excuses to the Lady Kate if she arrives before you have done so.'

'By no means,' Martin retorted. 'I have been a working seaman these many years, these are the clothes I wear, and I don't propose to change them now.'

It took Rafe all his strength not to say, 'You haven't been a working seaman these many years either, and your normal garb is exactly what m'lord would wish you to wear today.' Once he would not have hesitated to do so but, judging by this morning's outburst of wrath, times had changed and not for the better. Martin, amused, could almost feel Rafe bristling behind him, and that his father was evidently about to reprimand him, saying more or less what Rafe would have done.

In order to stop this sorry argument from developing further, he said briskly, 'I have a mind to take a walk about the grounds, sir, before I resign myself to spending too much time indoors—with your permission, of course.'

For a moment Lord Bretford was tempted to say him nay, but an unseemly verbal brawl before his son's servants was the last thing he wanted.

'Very well,' he murmured ungraciously, 'but do not be too long about it. Lord Clifton and his party are already late.'

Martin sketched a bow. 'Most kind of you, sir. My staff will arrange for our possessions to be stowed away. I will see you all later.'

He was grinning to himself while he walked around the neat garden, full of the scents of early autumn before rounding the corner of the house to see Lord Clifton's two coaches arrive, the first well before the second. Curious, he slowed his pace in the hope of gaining the first glimpse of John's—no, his—betrothed.

'Here at last,' exclaimed Aunt Jocasta unnecessarily.

No one emerged from the oaken front door. One of the Cliftons' accompanying footman stepped down to throw the coach door open so that he might help Kate, then Aunt Jocasta, to step down.

'I will inform the steward that we have arrived,' he said, 'and ask for some assistance in carrying in our luggage.'

Before he could do so a man walked round the corner of the building. He was uncommonly tall and broad, and dressed, not in the uniform of a house servant, but in shabby clothing which tallied well with his unkempt hair and beard. He was obviously one of the gardeners, or perhaps a stable hand not sufficiently important enough to be given a uniform, or livery, of any kind.

Kate was suddenly impatient. Here she was on an errand not of her making, only to arrive to find that apparently no one was ready to receive them. She advanced beyond the footman before he could address this great bear—it was the only word which she could think of to describe the man who was walking towards her. He really did look very like the one she had seen on her visit to the Tower of London.

'Come here at once,' she called imperiously—quite

unlike her normal quiet and pleasant self. 'Pray begin to take our luggage into the house and inform your masters that Lord Clifton and Lady Kate Wyville have arrived.'

Martin stared at her, bemused. So this dominant creature was the Lady Kate Wyville, whom he was shortly to marry. She was fair enough, with her creamy complexion, green eyes and chestnut locks, and her splendid clothing which must have cost the equivalent of a year's pay for a simple merchant sea-man. She obviously had a temper, and he was about to reply in kind when the devil tempted him.

'Certainly, m'lady,' he said, pulling his forelock, and using the accent of the common sailor which he had adopted to avoid mockery in his early days as a lad on board ship. 'Indeed, m'lady, at your service.'

He picked up some of the luggage which was al-ready being unloaded by the footmen, just as Lord Clifton's coach, which had been held up by cattle blocking the road half a mile from Bretford House, also arrived. At the same time the front door opened and a herd of apologetic servants swept out to greet the visitors, apologising for their tardiness.

Martin swept by them, deposited the luggage in the entrance hall, and, laughing to himself, returned by the backstairs to the room where his father was wait-ing before he could be scolded for arriving after the guests.

In the usual rituals which took place before the front door, all the more elaborate because of their necessary apologies, since Lord Bretford's staff had been too busy preparing for their guests to notice that they had arrived, Kate failed to notice that the bear had not returned. If she thought about him at all, it would have been to assume that, when the indoor staff had taken over, he would be swiftly returned to his menial duties outside.

Once inside, she was led up to the rooms prepared for her so that she might rest a little after her journey before she was introduced to Lord Bretford and his heir. The house's furnishings were splendid, but ill-cared for, and Kate, used to a hard-working indoor staff, could not help but be aware that Lord Bretford's servants were slack in their duties.

Her Aunt Jocasta came out with several more of her unnecessary remarks while pointing out the staff's deficiencies, although her final conclusion was a reasonable one. 'If you are to reside here, my dear,' she ended magisterially, 'a number of changes will need to be made if your life is to be comfortable.'

Kate knew that Lord Bretford was reported to be constantly ailing these days and doubtless that was the reason for inefficiency everywhere. Before she had been shown upstairs she was introduced to the housekeeper, Mistress Cray, a stout woman who seemed pleasant enough, but looked rather harassed.

Finally it was time to go down to meet his lordship and her future husband. Would he be like his brother John? He had been a handsome man, always beautifully dressed, charming and pleasant to everyone, and

his early death had to be regretted, since, like the
footman who escorted her and Aunt Jocasta downstairs, it was leading her to an unknown and unwanted
bridegroom.

She was shown into the withdrawing-room, which
opened off the Great Hall, with great pomp and ceremony. The first person she saw was Lord Bretford,
who was strangely altered from the time when she
had first met him, since he now looked so old and ill.

What was surprising, though, was that the great
bear whom she had encountered outside stood at a
little distance behind him on his right. Perhaps,
though, since m'lord was reputed to have difficulty in
walking, he was there to use his undoubted strength
to assist him. If so, why was he not wearing livery?

Two other men, both well dressed in the latest fashion, and whom she had never met before, were on
m'lord's left. One of them must surely be her betrothed, so she eyed them as carefully as she could
without appearing to be impolite. Neither of them
took her fancy, although both might be considered to
be handsome, nor did they resemble in the least the
late Lord Hadleigh.

The one nearest to her was tallish and blond, with
a clever, if rather cold face. The other, equally tall,
possessed a humorous and knowing one. It was difficult to tell which of them was her future husband.
All this time her uncle and m'lord were going through
the droning rituals which persons of their station

thought necessary on such important occasions as these.

The preliminary courtesies over, her uncle called her forward and re-introduced her to Lord Bretford, to whom she curtsied before standing back again after he had greeted her warmly and she had said all that was pretty to him.

Now it was his turn to introduce his son to her and her father.

'M'lady Kate Wyville and Clifton, my old friend, I present to you my new-found son and heir, Martin, Lord Hadleigh, long-lost to me. Hadleigh, I bid you come forward.'

When he did, it was neither of the two handsome young men who obeyed him. Instead, it was the great bear who sauntered towards her, bowing and saying, 'My pleasure to meet you, Lady Kate,' in a voice in which mockery was predominant.

This! She was to marry this hairy and unkempt creature. To her horror Kate found herself on the verge of fainting, partly as a consequence of her tight clothing and partly as a result of her fear of meeting the new Lord Hadleigh, which had caused her to eat little in the last two days. How much more would she have feared this meeting if she had known exactly what he was going to be like? A man who resembled a bear—and whom she had insulted by treating him as a servant. Near to, he proved to be even larger than she had remembered him to be.

He was bowing to her and somehow she was curtseying back, her head swimming. He was saying, what was he saying? 'I am sure that you will be relieved to learn that your luggage reached its destination safely, even if your servant was not quite who you thought he was and, besides that, had never been properly house-trained.'

He was mocking her, yes, he was. Perhaps she deserved it. She had not been her usual courteous self when she had first met him. Come to that, *he* had not been his usual self either. Persons of the station of Lord Hadleigh did not walk around looking like a cross between a chimney-sweep and a bear. Perhaps it was not only unkind, but untrue, to call him a chimney-sweep, since his hands, and what could be seen of his face which wasn't covered in hair, were clean.

Strangely enough, while all this internal monologue was going on she was talking, apparently sensibly, to the bear, saying lying things like, 'It is a pleasure to meet you at last, Lord Hadleigh.'

To which, of course, his reply was, 'Not at last, Lady Kate, this is our second meeting. You have apparently forgotten that we met once outside before we enjoyed our formal introduction.'

Kate had recovered her senses enough by then to say, in as poisonously sugary a tone as his, 'Oh, but you were not Lord Hadleigh then, although I was certainly Lady Kate Wyville.'

'A fact of which, by your manner, you left me in no doubt.'

'*Your* manner and your speech left me in no doubt

that you were the servant which your clothing proclaimed you to be.'

They were so close together, their voices were so low, and they were both wearing such lying smiles while they spoke that their watchers were deluded into believing that Lord Hadleigh and Lady Kate Wyville were already on exceedingly good terms with one another. Something which pleased the two old men immensely.

So, m'lady has a nasty tongue, too, was Martin's genuine response to her, which was only matched by the reaction to him of his unwilling future bride. For some reason he was quite certain that she was unwilling. Well, so am I, he reflected, which leaves us quits. If we both dislike this proposed match then we might be able to find a way out of it.

Not yet, however. At the moment all between the parties—with the exception of the inner feelings of the future bride and groom—was honey. Even Lord Clifton's dismayed disgust at Martin's appearance remained unspoken, since he believed that his ward's marriage to the Bretford heir took precedence over any qualms about the fellow's eccentricity. He was prepared to swallow more than that to attain such a prize as the joining of Bretford and Wyville lands. As for Martin's father, he was more than willing to acknowledge and favour his unruly son in order to keep his estate out of the clutches of the Crown when he died.

After some further pleasantries in which Martin

spoke to Lord Clifton and Kate was introduced to Webster and Rafe, the whole party adjourned to the Great Hall where a sumptuous meal had been prepared—one of its main delicacies being a boar's head with an orange in its mouth. It was perhaps fortunate that no one overheard Martin murmur on passing it, 'I know exactly how you feel, old fellow,' before sitting down in the place of honour, next to Kate, and preparing to eat some of it.

Food and drink being great lubricants of the tongue, it was not long before the room resounded to the noise of gossip. The Lords Clifton and Bretford spoke of the scandals associated with Lord Essex, who, from being the old Queen's prime and pampered favourite had been brought low by illness and disgrace, following his disastrous campaign against the Irish, who had completely out-manoeuvred him.

As a result of his subsequent wild behaviour in the Queen's presence he was at present under house arrest at his London home, and was, Lord Bretford said censoriously, fortunate in that he had not been sentenced to imprisonment in the Tower until he was tried.

Lord Clifton, who was friendly with many of those nearest to the Queen, expressed surprise that Essex had gathered a large number of supporters at Essex House, among them Master Francis Bacon and Sir Walter Raleigh.

'It has also been remarked,' he said, between drafts of good hypocras, 'that he is being greatly influenced by that old man Bevis Frampton, who has been on

the edge of matters ever since the Queen succeeded
to the throne. The word is that Master Bacon does
not trust him and thinks that his advice is poor, since
he is encouraging Lord Essex in his wilder flights of
fancy.'

Martin leaned forward to say something to the effect that he knew for sure that Sir Walter Raleigh was
no longer a fervent supporter of the Earl, since he
believed that he had become overbearing and rash in
his opposition to the Queen and his refusal to recognise the faults of his Irish campaign. He checked
himself before he could say a word, remembering that
someone who claimed to be as lowly as he was would
not be in a position to know someone as grand as Sir
Walter. Of Frampton he could say nothing, since he
could not recall ever having met him.

And yet, and yet. The name rang a bell in his mind,
but why it should do so remained, for the moment,
unexplained. He sat back again and allowed his sen-
iors to hold the floor.

Since those eating and drinking heartily in great
comfort feel safe in discussing bad, rather than good
news, because it enhances their own feelings of being
favoured by fortune, the next topic raised was that of
the reports of a poor harvest. It was even rumoured
that it was going to be worse than that of the previous
year. As for the war with Spain, it was certainly not
being a repetition of the great days when the Armada
was defeated by Britain's heroes, and by a westerly
gale in the Channel.

No one at table was aware that one of them, the new Lord Hadleigh, who had taken part as a humble seaman in the Spanish fleet's destruction in 1588, was sitting there, mumchance, amid all the noise. His future bride, who was as silent as he, sat beside him. He had been eating and drinking sparsely and was watching Lady Kate do the same.

He could not resist leaning over towards her, picking up her goblet and saying, 'The belief is, my future wife, that those who are greatly enamoured with one another are unable to eat, being quite deprived of appetite, which means that by our behaviour, we are among that happy few if our conduct at table is any guide. Pray drink this toast to our future with me, and let us be noisy, too. We must not deceive others into thinking that we have fallen into an instant passion for one another such as Messer Boccaccio has often written about.'

Kate waved the goblet away, a little surprised by his knowledge of the Italian master. 'By no means, m'lord. Moreover, since I believe that it is your habit to deceive others, I would not have you act against your true nature. To pretend that you and I were half-way to being lovers would be deception indeed.'

'So after such a short acquaintance you already know what my true nature is,' remarked Martin, drinking the wine himself from the goblet he had proffered her. He was a little surprised that she had begun to read him correctly—but he had given her that opportunity by his foolery on the gravel sweep.

Not only that, but she had proved again that she possessed as forked a tongue as he did—and from whom had she acquired it? Not from her simple-minded aunt, that was certain.

Perhaps all women were following the example of the Queen in being mistresses of wit, learning and cunning devices. What would his late brother have made of such a creature—and what would he, if he were to marry her?

Was she fooling him as he was fooling everyone? He knew very well that sooner or later most of his secrets would be, perforce, revealed, and he was not quite sure what the consequences of that would be. In the meantime he would enjoy himself.

The lengthy meal came to an end and the guests returned to the withdrawing-room. Some of the men, who had drunk heavily, retired to relieve themselves in the new jakes which had been installed in a small room off the Great Hall. The women in similar need were ushered upstairs to the suite allotted to Lady Kate by one of the women servants who attended on them as they left the Hall.

Martin wandered away to find the library, which was larger than he had remembered it. He was tired of being perpetually on show and was relieved when the only person who followed him was Rafe, a worried expression on his face. He had come to nag him as usual.

'Sooner or later,' he began without preamble, 'you are going to have to tell them the truth.'

'Tell me something which I don't know,' replied Martin, not lifting his eyes from the book he had taken from the shelves. 'It's what I pay you for. Or have you handed that task over to Webster?'

Rafe was unmoved. 'He'd simply say the same thing. What profit do you gain from all this foolery?'

'Amusement,' said Martin, not raising his eyes from his book.

And power, he thought, power of an odd kind. Years ago I was helpless and powerless in this house, and it pleases me that I can deceive those who had control over me then.

'So you are going to marry the Lady Kate?'

'So it would seem.'

'Only seem? What kind of an answer is that?'

'The only one I am prepared to give you at the moment. Do run away and leave me in peace. When the time comes I shall tell you all.'

Now I don't believe that, I really don't, was Rafe's rueful thought as he did as he was bid. What the devil's irking him at the moment that he should be so short with us when he never has been before?

Martin hardly knew what was wrong with him. He closed his book and prepared to rejoin the betrothal party—for that was what it was. He seemed doomed, however, to be badgered by others as to his intentions. This time it was Lady Kate who entered, without her attendant lady.

'One of the footmen told me you were here,' she

said. 'I hadn't thought…' and then she stopped lest what she had to say might be thought discourteous.

'That I might adjourn to the library?' he said, his eyebrows raised and, by what could be seen of his mouth through the hair, amused. 'I can read and write, you know. My education before I left home was a strict one.'

'Is that why you ran away?' she asked him before she could stop herself.

'Not exactly. Incidentally, who told you that I ran away?'

'My uncle. He thought that I ought to know.'

'Did he indeed? What is it that I ought to know about you? Pray tell me.'

'That I never had the opportunity to run away. Master Dudgeon told me that you sailed against the Armada as an ordinary seaman.'

'Master Dudgeon talks too much,' was Martin's short answer.

'It's as well worth knowing as that you ran away. I told him, most strongly, I didn't believe you could be an ordinary anything.'

Kate paused. She was going to say something daring and she didn't know how a man who looked like a bear would receive it. Oh, to Hades with caution, she would speak her mind: something which her uncle rarely allowed her to do.

'I don't believe that you are an ordinary seaman now.'

This jolted Martin's mind much as a crossbow-bolt would have jolted his body. Now why did she think that?

His reply was mysterious. 'Perhaps,' he said. 'Perhaps not.'

'I have already observed that you frequently talk in riddles.'

She was observing far too much. He did not think it wise to tell her so.

Kate decided that if she were to inform him of her true feelings about this proposed marriage, now was the time to do so. Whether he was truly like the bear he resembled or not, she must throw down the gauntlet, as it were, and take her chances.

'I do not believe that you wish to marry me, and I'm sure that I do not wish to marry you.'

There, it was out, and before he had time to determine how he was to deal with the shock which her frankness had produced, Webster arrived in search of his master—only to find him closeted with his betrothed, who had left the anteroom with the excuse that she wished to retire upstairs in order to refresh herself. It was beginning to seem that the lady was as devious as her future husband.

He thought this even more when he found them standing face to face, eyes aglow, talking busily to one another. From their manner one might deem them to be a pair of eager lovers but, somehow, Webster doubted that very much.

So intent on each other were they that he finally gave vent to a loud cough to tell them that he had arrived. As a result they both turned together to stare at him. Face masked, eyes hooded, he gave a small bow and said, 'I must present my excuses for disturbing you, but I came to ask m'lord whether he had any further instructions for me.'

'Oh, yes,' Martin retorted, 'I certainly have. Leave us at once. I will send for you when I need you, which is not now.'

Webster, trying not to stifle a laugh despite this curt dismissal of him, offered them another small bow, and muttered, 'So noted, m'lord,' and took a dignified leave.

Without waiting for Martin to speak to her again, Kate said indignantly, 'That was most discourteous of you, m'lord. The man was only doing what he saw as his duty—and, as a matter of interest, what did he mean by *so noted?*'

'Do you,' retorted Martin glacially, 'wish me to reply to the reprimand at the beginning of your little speech, or to the demand for information at the end of it?'

Kate did not know whether to laugh or to cry when he came out with *his* little speech. It really was the oddest conversation in which she had ever taken part.

'After you have accepted my reprimand, you may answer my question.'

'I don't accept the reprimand. Webster is my servant and must do as he is bid.'

'He is not your slave, though, and he did as he was bid, most politely.'

Kate did not know why she was so determined to chop logic with the bear. Only that after some strange fashion it was exciting to tease him, wondering whether he would merely growl at her—or, perhaps, try to eat her. Metaphorically speaking, of course.

She was delighted to notice that his voice deepened into a growl when he riposted, 'He only obeys me so promptly because I was severe with him. As for his reply, so noted is what a secretary, or a lawyer, says to the man who employs him to show that he understands the orders which he has been given.'

'I must remember that,' Kate said, without thinking. 'Only I don't think it would have much effect on Aunt Jocasta. Of course, she's neither a lawyer nor a secretary, but she is supposed to obey me—which she rarely does.'

Martin began to laugh. He was amused to find that he had become trapped in an extremely inconsequential dialogue with a young woman who was rather more clever than he had supposed her to be. His laugh was further intended to be a diversion for himself: a much-needed one, since, faced with a pair of flashing green eyes and a pretty mouth offering him clever nonsense, his wretched body had begun to respond to his betrothed after a most alarming fashion.

Fortunately the heavily padded breeches which he was wearing were sufficient to disguise his surprising arousal. Surprising because for the last year his continence had been easy to sustain; so easy, indeed, that

he had begun to worry a little that he was losing his
male potency.

The biggest irony of the whole business was that
of all the women in the world, the one who had
caused it to awaken again had to be the only one
whom he had no wish to marry—mainly because it
would please his father if he did. So what would become of his campaign to have Lady Kate Wyville
hate him when what his wretched body most desired
was to stop her mouth by kissing it, then have her
beneath him, gasping her pleasure while he made sure
of his own?

Martin shook his head. What the devil could be
making him behave like a green boy faced with his
first woman? He really must tell his errant body to
behave itself—which he did to no avail. All this was
shooting through his mind at top speed, so that it was
fortunate that Kate's reply to his laughter was to begin
to laugh herself.

They were both still very merry when Rafe came
in—to stare at the pair of them. What the devil was
it that had made his usually dour master so cheerful?
Webster had returned from his interview with Martin
speaking and acting so mysteriously—Rafe had never
seen him laugh before—that, frustrated, he had decided to find out what m'lord, as he had begun to
think of him, could be up to.

'What in Hades do *you* want now?' Martin roared
at him, after using his linen kerchief to wipe from his
eyes the tears which his laughter had brought on. 'Are

the pair of you never to allow me five minutes' peace?'

'Oh,' Kate could not prevent herself from offering a gloss to that, 'was it peace that we were enjoying? Besides, I must point out that you are being as unkind to Master Dudgeon as you were to Master Webster, and for very little reason.'

'It was not a peace, but a truce,' Martin threw at her over his shoulder. 'Except that it won't last if you continue to provoke me. If ever a man was so beset by those around him...' And he shook his head at them both.

Rafe was daring. 'Forgive me, m'lord, you didn't seem very beset to me. Most people usually laugh only when they are enjoying themselves,' he added mildly, 'but if I am *de trop*, then I will leave.'

'Not for my sake,' said Kate sweetly. Baiting the bear was more enjoyable than she had thought it might be.

'If he knows what is good for him,' growled Martin savagely, 'he will leave at once.'

'Willingly. I always do what is good for me— though I thank m'lady for her kind invitation to remain.' After bowing slightly more deferentially to his lord and master than Webster had done, he took his leave.

So Martin Chancellor, or Lord Hadleigh, had found his match in the demure-looking Lady Kate and did not quite know how to deal with her. Life, which, like his master, Rafe Dudgeon had lately found boring, was suddenly growing more interesting.

'He took his time in leaving,' Martin growled meaningfully at Kate, his recent laughter, as well as his arousal, having disappeared.

'Well, he didn't say so noted,' returned Kate, 'so it seemed that he had no real wish to leave us.'

It was useless. If they started sparring all over again he was in danger of becoming aroused to the point where he could not keep his hands off her. Cold courtesy must be resumed so that they could return to the safety of verbal distance when they met. Without that, all his plans would be overset.

Kate saw the bear's face and manner change. The momentary rapport which they had so recently shared had disappeared. To remain would be a mistake. Rafe's entry had ended something which had promised to bring them together.

'It is time,' she said, 'that I left you, lest the rest of the company feel that it is their duty to corner us in the library.'

Martin, almost unable to speak because of his conflicting emotions, nodded his head in agreement.

The Lady Kate Wyville walked upstairs with the feeling strong in her that a marriage with Lord Bretford's bear might not be the disaster which she had first thought it—even if she still hoped that she could avoid becoming his, or any man's, wife.

# Chapter Three

Martin's verbal duel with Kate Wyville had the oddest effect on him. Not only had she roused him with her flashing green eyes and her naughty tongue, but all his other senses had been heightened. The first consequence being that he remembered where he had heard of Bevis Frampton before—something which had evaded him when Lord Clifton had spoken the man's name.

That night, before sleep claimed him, he recalled that earlier in the year he had been at a meeting of the Friday Club at the Mermaid Tavern, off Friday Street, not as Martin Chancellor, but as his other self of which Bretford House knew nothing. Sir Walter Raleigh had been there and, his tongue loosened by drink, had conversed more freely, perhaps, than was wise.

Martin recalled how little some of the others spoke, in particular the playwright Shakespeare, who invariably sat in a corner, listening, always listening, to what the great men like Raleigh had to say, doubtless so that it might end up in one of his plays. More than one man had ruefully recognised himself in the mummer who was entertaining the mob by his quirks and follies.

That night, Raleigh had been cursing some of those around Lord Essex, who had just arrived back from Ireland in deep disgrace. 'And no wonder at that,' he had concluded, 'since lately he has taken to listening to that old fellow Frampton, who privately hates all of us because of the knighthood which he has never been given.'

'Essex is like Edward II,' Ben Jonson had said, 'he listened to bad advice, too.'

'To say nothing of King Richard II,' Shakespeare had offered quietly; he was always quiet. 'M'lord Essex is only different in that he is—or rather was—Her Grace's favourite, but while those monarchs listened to their favourites and were destroyed by them she seems to have avoided that fate.'

Those around him knew that Shakespeare had written a history play called *Richard II* which had been staged in 1597 and had caused a great deal of excitement, since the Queen had let it be known that she disliked intensely the notion that a monarch could be turned off the throne by a successful rebellion if his courtiers and the country grew tired of him.

'Aye and therein lies the old woman's greatness,' Sir Walter had said, 'for she may have her favourites, but she never listens to the stupid ones, something which Lord Essex failed to remember.'

They had all laughed at that, for the gossip about how scurvily she had treated him when he had returned home from Ireland a failure, instead of forgiving him as he had expected, had run round London, growing in the telling. Not only had she banished him to the confines of his own home, but she had caused many of his revenues and monopolies to be cut off, thereby reducing his fortune greatly.

'At least,' Sir Walter had ended, 'she didn't order him to be executed, so he kept his head on his shoulders—for the time being, anyway,' which unkind sally had provoked yet another laugh.

So that was where Bevis Frampton's name had been mentioned in his presence, but echoes of it still rang in Martin's head. He had surely heard of him before, if only briefly, but to his annoyance, he could not recover that further memory which still eluded him.

For some reason sleep that night was long in coming. To begin with he could not keep Kate Wyville out of his head, nor, try as he might, could he think of any convincing plan by which he might avoid marrying her nor how, if marriage became inevitable, he could bring the two opposing parts of his life together. Looking back, it might have been better if he had told his father the truth about himself straight away, but the desire to trick him had, perhaps, overwhelmed his common sense.

In the end he punched his hot bolster vigorously and virtually commanded sleep to release him from the snakes writhing round in his head until, at last, it reluctantly obeyed him. But his dreams were many and various, and although he forgot them when he awoke the next morning, he knew that they had not been pleasant.

Which, after all, was no new thing for him.

Kate was faring no better. Meeting the bear had served not only to excite her, but to present to her a whole new world. She was beginning to feel as though she were one of the European explorers when they had first set foot in the Americas. Like them she had no notion of what the next day might bring— except that it would probably prove dangerous.

After she had broken her fast, her uncle visited her in her room.

'I have been trying to discover where you and your husband-to-be are to live once you are married. Lord Bretford appears to believe that you will lodge here, but your future husband, when I questioned him myself, was most brusque. He left me in no doubt that he does not wish to settle at Bretford House. As to where you might dwell instead, he shrugged his shoulders and made no answer, other than that you would undoubtedly have a roof over your head somewhere. Which is no answer at all.'

'No, indeed,' agreed Kate. 'He is a most disoblig-

ing fellow, is he not, who never offers one a straight
answer.'

'And with a quarterdeck voice when he is annoyed.
When I remember his brother's charming civility...'
and Lord Clifton shrugged his shoulders in disbelief.

'Yet you still wish me to marry him?'

'Oh, one does not marry a man for his manners.'

Kate could not resist the pun. 'Unless, of course,
he possesses plenty of manors—and their rents.'

'Precisely,' returned her uncle, resisting her intended joke and taking it seriously.

Perhaps the best way to think of her wedding was
as a joke, rather like that play she had seen two years
ago where the principals, Beatrice and Benedick,
sparred with one another all the way through it, before
falling into one another's arms at the end. Only a fool
would not have seen *that* coming.

'*Much Ado About Nothing*,' she murmured aloud,
confusing her uncle still further.

'Eh, what's that, niece?'

'Nothing, uncle, just a stray thought.'

Would Martin Chancellor allow her to have stray
thoughts? Did he have any stray thoughts himself, or
was he strictly practical? She ought, for sheer self-
preservation, to try to discover more about the man
he really was behind all the flim-flam and humbug
she was sure he was serving up to everyone. What
was the true man really like? For no reason at all she
believed that he was otherwise than he seemed to be.

A line from the play she had recently been thinking

of shot through her brain. 'A star danced and I was born.' Could she possibly be as constantly witty as Beatrice—and thus transform Lord Hadleigh from a bear to a ... To a what? She could not really think what kind of man she wished to marry, since she had always consistently refused to think about marrying.

'You are attending to me, niece, I trust,' her uncle was saying, while she wool-gathered.

'Oh, yes,' Kate managed, although she had not heard a word of her uncle's lengthy speech and did not know what she was agreeing with.

'I was saying that I will have a word with Lord Bretford himself. Since, by Lord Hadleigh's dress and manner, his father is the one who controls the purse-strings, he might bring particular pressure to bear on Hadleigh to settle at Bretford House—in a place that your rank should demand as of right—rather than in some hole in the corner where I gather that he has hitherto been living.'

Kate, remembering the bear's determined face and the brisk fashion in which he had treated his subordinates, prevented herself from saying, Must you, uncle? She had no doubt that however much the two lords might bully him, Martin Chancellor would do exactly as he pleased.

There was one question which she had hitherto refrained from asking and now felt that she ought to. 'How soon will my marriage take place?'

'As soon as possible—which we hope will be in a fortnight. The ceremony will take place in St Paul's.'

St Paul's, that gloomy cathedral which she had always detested.

'Not in the local parish church?'

'By no means. Your rank—and his—demands no less.'

Her rank seemed to be demanding a great deal which she did not want. By her uncle's manner it was useless to complain. After all, this was how most women were treated—as though their opinion and wants were of no matter—always excepting, of course, the Queen.

It was perhaps unfortunate that when she went downstairs, the first person she saw was her future husband. He was as untidy as usual—except for his boots, which were spotless.

'Well met, lady,' he told her, bowing.

'Why should that be?' she asked, deliberately trying to provoke him.

'Why?' Martin considered for a moment before saying, 'I have just been told by Master Dudgeon that my manner to you is not sufficiently flattering or courteous, and so I am trying to please two people, you and him, by improving it. Do I understand that I was not successful?'

What witty answer would Beatrice have made to that? 'Not exactly. I was merely wondering why we were well met when all we had done was encounter one another, quite by chance, at the bottom of the stairs.'

This might not be witty, but it had at least the merit of being the truth.

Martin's smile was rueful. 'I'm sorry it didn't please you. It was merely one of a small selection of apt remarks which Rafe suggested I might use when I told him that my life had not prepared me for making the kind of compliment which ladies seem to expect. I chose that one because I thought it rather more apt than most.'

It was Kate's turn to consider.

'I suppose,' she said slowly, 'that once you *had* made it I should have simpered at you and offered you something equally meaningless in return, such as, "Indeed, sir." You could, of course, if you will accept a suggestion from me, have offered me an even more flattering remark.' She paused to think for a moment before adding. 'Yes, I have it. "You look remarkably fine this morning, Lady Kate," would do very well.'

'Would it? And what would your answer have been to that?'

'Another simper, or perhaps a toss of my head and the words, "You flatter me, m'lord," which would have given you the opportunity to reply, "Indeed, not."'

Martin asked, as though he really wished to know, 'What would that have earned me?'

'A giggle and a hand before the mouth, like so,' and Kate gave a remarkable imitation of an empty-headed beauty. 'Of course, if I were carrying a fan at the time I could have struck you gently with it—or not so gently if I were feeling frisky.'

'Frisky, eh?' and Martin began to laugh. It was safer so, because even at this early hour the sight of Lady Kate Wyville making mock of him was having its usual dreadful effect on his self-control.

Before Kate could laugh back at him they were interrupted by Rafe Dudgeon entering and saying impatiently to his master, 'I thought that you were in a hurry—the horses were ready for us some time ago. Oh, I do beg your pardon for interrupting you, Lady Kate. I must say that you are looking remarkably fine this morning.'

Whereupon Kate tossed her head and simpered at him, saying, 'You flatter me, Master Dudgeon,' which, to the bemusement of Rafe, set Martin laughing again.

Rafe forgot that while they were at Bretford House they had privately agreed to avoid the easy camaraderie which he shared with Martin away from it—and with which Webster had begun to join in—and said, his tone a bantering one, 'What's the joke, Martin, I mean, m'lord?'

'I'll tell you later—if the horses are waiting I must immediately take my leave of m'lady with a suitably apt phrase.'

'May I, perhaps, suggest something in the order of the following, "I can scarce wait to rejoin you again—but duty calls,"' was Kate's swift reply in her most teasing voice.

'Oh, I can't speak of duty since Rafe and I are merely going for a gallop to clear our heads and we don't want to be back too soon.'

Kate shook her head at him. 'No, no, that won't do at all. Forget the truth and remember that gallantry is all. I suggest that you say it to me before you leave— and I promise to be equally untruthful in return.'

Martin, Rafe's wondering eyes on him, did as he was bid, and in return Kate laughed confidingly back up at him and said, 'Ah me, pray do not be too long, I can scarce wait for you to come back to me.'

Martin leaned forward and said, very quietly, so that Rafe should not hear him, 'Minx—you speak more truthfully than you know.'

And then, after Rafe had left them, it struck him like a hammer blow— What was he doing? He was in danger of forgetting his campaign against his father by succumbing to her charm. If he did so, he would merely succeed in obliging him. He must, at all costs, disillusion her. So he said, his voice and manner as cold as he could make them, 'Are all women the same? Virtual courtesans who offer any man only the words that they most wish to hear?'

He had the dismal satisfaction of watching the colour leave her face before she turned away from him. He cursed himself and fate before leaving her and walking to the stables where Rafe and their horses waited for them.

Rafe said, 'What was all that about? You surely didn't tell her of my advice to you!'

'I surely did—and the lady had the goodness to offer me some pithy phrases of her own which she thought rather better.'

'I can see that she is beginning to come to terms with you—and perhaps you are both not regretting this marriage over-much as a consequence.'

'Coming to terms with *me*! No, she is arranging it so that *I* come to terms with *her*. Every remark I make is taken up and embroidered by her to her own advantage. The woman has the tongue of the devil.'

Then you are well matched, was Rafe's unspoken gloss on that, before they mounted their horses and set off for a tavern in the city where Martin hoped that Webster would be waiting for them with some information which he had earlier required of him. The formidable Jacko had been in attendance on Webster not only to protect him in the deep waters of the criminal underworld in which he had been trawling, but also to point him in the right directions.

'You never told me that you had been attacked,' Rafe said reproachfully to Martin. They were all drinking warm ale of poor quality in order not to look out of place in an alehouse and listening to Webster's report, given in low tones so that he might not be overheard. He was amused to note that, today, the usually immaculate Webster looked nearly as untidy as his master. Doubtless Jacko had told him that it would not do to look too much like a member of the Queen's court.

'I wasn't sure whether it was the result of an accident or by design. Jacko and Webster have been busily making enquiries for me and, as he has just said, it seems that the attack was definitely by design.'

Webster nodded. 'Jacko knows of several assassins who can be hired for a goodly sum and the fourth man we questioned—or rather,' and he started to laugh ruefully, 'whom Jacko threatened, told us all that we wished to know. What now remains is to give you the name of his paymaster and ask you, Martin, what you know of him. He is Bevis Frampton, an old fellow who has been hanging around the court since the Queen's accession. I thought it most unlikely that he was the one who wanted you dead, but the fellow was adamant—even gave me a description of him.'

'Bevis Frampton,' said Martin wonderingly. 'Why the devil should he want me killed? So far as his appearance is concerned, I was told by Sir Walter Raleigh that he is a little man, stooped and grey, with a servile manner. Is that how your informant described him?'

'Exactly.' It was Jacko speaking at last. 'To the very word, master.' Of the three of Martin's henchmen he was the only one who spoke to him as he thought a man of his master's station ought to be addressed. 'Once I convinced him that it was in his interest to tell me the truth he could scarcely stop talking.'

'Which doesn't surprise me,' remarked Martin dryly. 'What does, is his motive for wanting me dead.

I scarcely knew he existed, although my father mentioned his name the other night.'

Webster leaned forward. 'But that establishes a connection with your family, does it not? Could he be trying to attack your father through you?'

'But the attack was *before* you had found me for my father. Who else could have known that I was my father's son? After all, I only recently started to call myself Chancellor when I bought my Forge Street home, and so far as the world knew I was dead and gone long ago.'

Rafe said, 'That is truly a mystery, but—forgive me for saying so—under the name you have borne since you left home, there are places you might have frequented recently where this Frampton fellow might have seen you, but you might not have noticed him. Beneath the disguising hair that you are sporting at the moment, do you resemble your late brother at all?'

Martin considered, 'A little, perhaps, but your theory, I must say, consists of drawing a giant bow at a venture.'

'But it could be true for all that,' put in Webster. The other two nodded their heads in agreement.

'The only real truth we possess, though, is that for some reason Frampton wants me dead. Webster, I think that you ought to begin discreet enquiries about the fellow and Jacko, you can come back with me to Bretford House and watch my back. He might yet try again and at present I have so many other distractions that I would find it difficult to guard myself.'

Distractions like Lady Kate Wyville, Rafe thought, but did not say aloud.

'Another draught of ale before we go, Master, seeing that we shall have missed dinner at Bretford House,' was Jacko's contribution to the conversation, 'and the bread and cheese is better than the ale.'

They all said Amen to that, and as Martin remarked while waiting for their order to arrive, 'It's as well that we have, at last, found something on which we can all agree.'

Martin was still thinking about Webster and Jacko's revelation when he arrived back at Bretford House with his three henchmen in tow. If the butler's eyebrows rose when he saw Jacko enter, that was the only comment which he allowed himself. On Martin's instructions he sent him off to the servants' hall and wondered what they would make of him.

Kate, Aunt Jocasta nearby, was seated in the withdrawing-room when Martin came downstairs after scrubbing himself in an effort to remove the smells of the tavern from his person. He had left Webster demanding a bath before he consented to resume his usual clean and decent clothing again. 'I wonder that you can bear wandering around looking so unkempt,' he had moaned at Martin. 'Remember that I have seen you in your usual habiliments.'

Trust Webster to use a long word when a short one like garb or clothing would have done, was Martin's reaction to that—but the man was turning out to be trustworthy and reliable and must be allowed his little freaks of speech. He was still grinning when he sat down on a long bench opposite to Kate.

She was working at a tapestry and did not greet him until she had reached the end of what appeared to be an everlasting line of stitching.

'You are late back and have missed your midday meal,' was all she said. 'Would you care for me to order something for you to eat?' Her manner was so different from the lively one which she had adopted earlier that day that Martin was a little troubled by it, until he remembered his last harsh and cruel words to her.

Aunt Jocasta was also glaring at him, probably because she distrusted all men—and who was to say that she was wrong. His conscience pricked him again and he said, 'Thank you, but no. We all had a meal at a tavern on Bankside.'

'And ale, too?' was Kate's response.

'Of course, rather more ale than food, I regret to say.'

'You were on some sort of errand, perhaps?' Kate asked, her curiosity aroused by the *we*. 'I gather that the butler informed your father and my uncle that you had brought home some kind of bravo.'

'Not a bravo, but my friend who has saved my life in the past. It is his wish, and not mine, to use the servants' quarters rather than associate with us.'

He heard Aunt Jocasta snort. 'At least *he* knows his proper station,' she said coldly.

'As I do not?' Martin could not help riposting.

'If the cap fits,' she told him.

He could see that Kate was troubled by this exchange. 'You forget,' she told her aunt, 'that Martin is Lord Hadleigh and thus Lord Bretford's heir.'

'Then let him behave and dress as though he is.'

For some contrary reason her frankness pleased Martin. At least she had the courage to be honest. Everyone else, even his father and his future uncle-in-law, tiptoed around him saying nothing of his untoward appearance, although he suspected that it was the cause of a lot of gossip behind his back. He was beginning to find it tiresome himself, but he judged that the time had not yet come for him to abandon it and display his true self.

One of the things which surprised him most was that, for all his recent hard words to her, he wanted Kate Wyville to accept him as he was. Rafe had passed on some servants' gossip which said that Lady Kate, when speaking to her tiring-maid, had once referred to him as a bear—supposedly because of his hairy appearance. As he had been contrary in his appreciation of Aunt Jocasta's honest appraisal of him, he was contrary in his sudden wish that Kate would accept him as the bear he seemed to be. Not because he was handsome, or had perfect manners, or wore the correct, beautiful clothing of a nobleman, but because she would like him as the man he truly was, not because of his trappings either as a nobleman or a bear.

'Beneath our clothing,' Martin had once told Rafe, 'we are all at one with Adam. And if the old sayings have it that manners and clothing make the man, then those sayings are wrong, because despite my present untoward appearance I am the same man that I ever was. I am simply Adam's brother or his distant descendant, call me what you will, but I am nothing else.'

It was something which he had come to understand when he had served on his first ship in the battle against the Spanish Armada. He had still been Lord Bretford's son and Lord Hadleigh's brother, and felt little different from the man he had been when all around had deferred to him. Then they had bowed to him, pulled their forelocks, obeyed him and attended to his slightest wish, but on board ship he was the one who carried out these humble duties—yet he still remained the same Martin Chancellor underneath.

It had been hard at first to become the slave and not the master, but he had learned that to be true to one's self was the only thing that mattered. He did not know whether or not he had been a good master before his flight, but his pride demanded that he cease to hanker after the lost past and become the best servant that there ever was—which he had done.

If he had succeeded in life—and he undoubtedly had—it was because he had learned these necessary lessons. He had already discovered that Kate Wyville was a strong woman. Bear she might think him, but she was baiting him, throwing buns at him in the form of witticisms, not showing any fear of him, and when they were sparring nothing mattered but that. They were man and woman together, Adam and Eve before the fall—which would be their marriage—if they married, that was. More and more, though, he was coming to accept that he was ready to make her his wife after all. There was some time still to live through and she might yet find a way to refuse him, but Martin was starting to relish the challenge which the lady presented to him. Did she feel the same about him?

Kate had quietly resumed her stitching, Aunt Jocasta was scowling at him over the top of hers, and he was sitting there, mumchance, staring blankly at the tapestry on the wall behind Kate, which showed Paris carrying Helen off from Greece and thus starting the Trojan War. It all went to show how much love and passion ruled the world if an empire like Troy could have fallen because of it.

The mere idea of behaving like Paris, snatching up Kate and making off with her, attracted him, which was stupid since he was being offered the lady legally, on a platter as it were—so there was no need for him to have fancies about abduction.

With some difficulty a highly aroused Martin rose, saying, 'I forgot that I have need to speak to Rafe. I trust that you two ladies will forgive me if I leave you.'

'With pleasure,' said Aunt Jocasta tartly. Kate said nothing, but her rather sad smile for him was enough.

The memory of his last words to her still hurt her, but she told herself that she must always remember how hard his life had been and forgive him a little if he were occasionally savage with those around him.

She was not to know that Martin went out to cool himself down. He wished that he could find a lake where he might strip to the buff, dive into the water and work off his thwarted lust—except that he was beginning to wonder whether lust was the right word for what he was starting to feel for Kate.

In the meantime he was compelled to live at Bretford House, from which Kate was to be married since Lord Clifton's London home was being rebuilt and was in no fit state to be used for wedding celebrations. At least this had the advantage that he could get to know his future wife a little more than if he had been compelled to wait until their wedding day before he met her—something which many bridegrooms would have welcomed.

All too often the first sight of their bride had been in the church where they were to be married.

# *Chapter Four*

Kate was being dressed for the day by Jennie. She was in a curious state where, at one and the same time, she was either welcoming her future or fearing it. The previous evening her uncle had informed her that her marriage was to be celebrated in a fortnight's time, a special licence having been granted. Kate was not sure whether celebrated was the right word to use of a union to which neither the bride or groom seemed to be looking forward.

Jennie, as usual, was passing on to her the gossip from the kitchens. 'They do say, m'lady, or that man Jacko says, that m'lord Hadleigh and Master Rafe lived in a little house in an alley off Forge Street before they came here. I thought as how you ought to know. Just fancy what a change in life it must have meant for them when Master Webster brought them here.'

'An alley off Forge Street—where is that?'

'Some hole-in-the-corner place not far from the Tower and the river.'

So that had been his home, poor man—no wonder he looked like a bear! The thought of it intrigued Kate so much that she decided to ask him about it. How fortunate his life had become—even if it had taken his brother's death to allow him to return to his true place in society.

Downstairs she found that Martin had broken his fast early and had gone riding with his three hench-men, as his father had contemptuously dubbed them, not knowing that his son always thought of them as his friends. There was nothing for it but to wait for him in the withdrawing-room. When they finally re-turned, the happy noise they made in the entrance hall set Aunt Jocasta sniffing again. Her sniff seemed to have taken up permanent residence since Martin Chancellor had returned home.

How did Kate know that the noise that they were making was happy, that it was the sound of men who had been enjoying themselves? Neither of them had ever heard that kind of commotion before—except at the theatre. She remembered the ease and pleasure with which the bear always talked of 'we' whenever he referred to the three men who were his constant companions.

They must all have gone upstairs to his rooms, for the noise died away and no one repaired to the with-drawing-room. Shortly afterwards she heard Martin—

she was sure it was Martin—run downstairs, but again
he never came in to see her.

Kate sighed and put down her tapestry—her everlasting tapestry. She said, as apparently idly as she
could, 'I am tired of stitching. Perhaps a visit to the
library would be pleasant change.'

Her aunt sniffed again. 'Hiding in the library for
most of the day is not the way to a man's heart.'

Since this trenchant remark came from a spinster
past her last prayers, Kate was unkind enough to
think: if you knew the way to a man's heart so well,
why did you not take it? But she was not sufficiently
unkind to say so. Instead, she rose and walked as
swiftly as she could to the library. She did not expect
to find Martin there, but she didn't want to tell a complete lie. An incomplete one was quite enough for one
day.

Sure enough the library was empty, except for
Webster, writing busily in a ledger. He looked up and
gave her his rare smile.

'Looking for him?' he offered.

Now how does he know that? thought Kate crossly.
Am I so easy to read? But, of course, he had seen
them laughing together and had doubtless drawn his
own conclusions. She did not answer him, so he volunteered helpfully, 'M'lord is in the garden. He says
that all his memories of it are happy ones.'

He did not add, 'unlike his memories of being in
the house', something which he had guessed from
Martin's behaviour indoors.

'Thank you,' Kate said, and made off again.

Custom demanded that if she were to go to the garden to find him she ought to take Jennie, or Aunt Jocasta, with her to act as a chaperon, but since she was so soon to be a married woman, she decided that she could dispense with their unwanted presence. Somehow, ever since she had met the bear she had begun to break all the rules dictating the expected behaviour of young ladies of good, if not to say great, families. He really was being a bad influence on her!

She found him at the far end of the garden, hidden from the house, seated on a bench from which he could look out on to the Thames, where the Bretford barge was moored at an ornamental jetty. He was leaning forward, his chin in his hands, and did not hear her coming. It was the first time that Kate had seem him inactive. Always before he had been talking, laughing, forever in restless motion.

For a moment she was able to study him from the vantage point of a small archway formed from intertwining trees. In repose his face was stern, and the habitual mockery which was always present in his expression, or his voice, was missing. He was obviously lost in thought, so much so that Kate decided not to interrupt him.

Unfortunately, just as she had made this decision and had turned to go, she must have caught her stiff petticoats against the leaves of the arbour's trees, for on hearing the slight noise he immediately swivelled round, exclaiming, 'Who's there?'

His voice was so stern and hard that Kate scarcely recognised it. Worse than that, the command in it was so strong that instead of fleeing, she stammered out, 'It is I, Kate.'

Martin's face changed immediately. It softened into one of his masks which she knew, the mocking one.

'Have you come to find me, I Kate?'

For some unknown reason she felt compelled to lie to him. A complete lie this time, God help me! I shall never reach heaven at this rate.

'No, I have never been further down the garden than the lawn behind the house. I wanted to see the river.'

Perhaps what she had just said could be counted as only half a lie, since she *had* wished to see the river, but had never found the opportunity to do so. If it were only half a lie it meant that, added to the other one, she had told merely a whole one, not one and a half—which was bad enough.

'Allow me to believe that to be true,' he told her, mocking again. 'Come and sit by me, Kate, and let us admire the river together.'

She needed no second invitation. Gathering up her skirts, she walked across to take her place by his side, wondering whether Webster would later expose her untruths by reporting that she had been looking for him. It was the closest she had ever been to Martin and she became immediately more aware of his great size and strength. Far from shocking or frightening her, it gave her a feeling of security as well as the oddest sensation of breathlessness.

They sat there for some moments in silence. The sun was casting a golden light on the river and the many boats and barges which plied up and down it. For once, he seemed unwilling to initiate conversation, and the peaceful scene before them was enough for Kate—for the time being at least. In the end she offered him the most banal remark she could think of. 'Do you come here often?'

'Every day,' he said tersely. 'The peace comforts me,' and fell silent, his usual flow of speech absent for once.

What a strange thing for the bear to say! It was almost monk-like. Encouraged by his difference from the man whom she thought that she had come to know, Kate asked him, 'Jennie tells me that your home is in an alley off Forge Street. Is that true?'

Martin, taken by surprise, nearly replied, truthfully, 'One of my homes.' Instead he merely muttered, 'Yes.'

'What is it like?' and then boldly, the words flowing out of her unbidden, 'I wish I might visit it.'

Martin swivelled round again. 'You do? Why?'

Tell him the truth for once and thus try to cancel the lies you have already told to him, and to others, this afternoon.

'Because I am shortly to marry you, and I would like to see the place which you call home, before I do.'

'Why should you wish that?'

'I think that it would tell me something about the man I am about to call husband.'

For some strange reason Martin began to laugh. Kate could not think why. He said, between gasps, 'Do you, indeed? Well, so you shall. Now, if you wish.'

'Now? How might we do that?'

He pointed to the highly decorated barge lying in wait before them.

'We can be rowed down river to a stairway near the Tower, leaving the barge there to await our return. After that we can walk to my home, which stands in an alley off Forge Street. Are you prepared to make such a journey?'

'Certainly, but I would have to take Aunt Jocasta with me as my chaperon.'

'Good God, no,' was his first response to that, his deep-blue eyes flashing mockery at her. Then, with a laugh, he added, 'Wait but a moment, I will consent to her coming with us, only if you will allow me to take Jacko with me as mine.'

'Jacko!' Kate thought of the burly bravo whom she had seen briefly once or twice after his arrival at Bretford House. 'Why Jacko as your chaperon, not Webster or Rafe?'

'Because Jacko is my bodyguard, always ready to save and protect me.'

A bodyguard? Why did Martin need a bodyguard?

What had he been doing which required him to be protected?

'But what would Aunt Jocasta think if she were required to travel in close quarters with Jacko?'

'It doesn't matter what she might think—she merely has to obey your orders, does she not? In any case, it would do her good to travel with Jacko. It might cure her of her perpetual sniffing.'

Kate gave a little laugh. 'It may be cruel of me to agree with you—except that, on the other hand, it might bring on a worst fit of it than ever.'

'I'm inclined to risk such a catastrophe! Jacko has more tricks than a fine lady like yourself might think. It's possible he might try them on her.'

Kate bridled a little at this. 'A fine lady! Is that how you think of me?'

'Of course, for that is what you are.'

'If so, then I must tell you that the one thing of which I am sure is that you are not a fine gentleman!'

'You ought to be pleased that I am not, for if I were we should not be having such interesting conversations. I would be reduced to a constant repetition of the phrases which both Rafe and Webster assure me is all that fine ladies require from their gallants.'

'Webster! So he is helping you now?'

'Oh, yes, and being rather more of a fine gentleman than Rafe, he has greatly enlarged my vocabulary. Would you like me to offer you a few elegant but meaningless words—or would you rather I tried them on Aunt Jocasta?'

Kate began to laugh, no ladylike titter, and Martin joined her until she gasped at him, 'Why does any speech I have with you end with both of us laughing heartily?'

'Because I think that I would rather you laughed than cried heartily. I know which I would prefer.'

This set Kate off again—as he had intended.

'If we carry on like this we shall never visit your home this afternoon.'

'True; let us both walk back to the house and make ready for our jaunt.'

Which they did, but on the way back Kate remembered Martin's different face and made a resolution to uncover the man who lived behind it.

'Go in a barge with him and Jacko to his hovel near the Tower! Have you run mad?'

'No, dear aunt, but I have a great desire to see him in the place where he lived until he came back to Bretford House. I shall then know a little more about him. What I do not know—which intrigues me greatly—is how he gained his living before he came here.'

'I shall speak to his father and your uncle about this. They are sure to refuse you permission to do such an undesirable thing as visit a back alley in the City.'

Kate, for the first time in her life, used her rank to defy her aunt.

'You will do nothing of the kind, aunt, or I shall

ask for you to leave my service. If we were going into the City to shop it would be perfectly reasonable for us to take a footman with us to protect us. Jacko, by his size and strength, will take the place of the footman, so I do not understand why you are making such a fuss. If you do not come with us then I shall take Jennie in your place.'

For the first time they had reached the state known as nonplus, and for the first time also her aunt gave way.

'Oh, very well. But do not expect me to like it.'

'No, aunt, I don't, since these days you never like anything. Pray try to endure it—for my sake if not your own.'

'How can you speak to me like this?' her aunt wailed at her, threatening to cry.

'I really think that it was long past time that I did,' Kate told her. 'Now go and make ready for our journey.'

'I shall not call him Jacko, that would be too much.'

'Call him what you will, so long as you come with us,' were Kate's last words.

Later, when, without telling the two lords of their journey, they were handed into the barge, already manned by stalwart oarsmen, Kate was amused to notice that her aunt had dressed herself rather more richly than usual, as though to emphasise her rank. Kate, however, was attired modestly, as befitted one who was visiting an alley off Forge Street. Martin and Jacko looked pretty much as usual—unkempt.

They had scarcely left the jetty behind them when Aunt Jocasta addressed Jacko in a melancholy voice.

'Pray, sir, I understand that you are usually known as Jacko. But I cannot believe that it is your true name—which I would prefer to use.'

'My true name is Jackson, Joshua Jackson...' he began, but Aunt Jocasta was quick to interrupt him.

'That is much better. I shall address you as Jackson, or Master Jackson, whichever you prefer,' and she actually offered him a small and fearful smile, for she found his sheer size intimidating.

'Nay, mistress, that won't do. For, sithee, if you were in trouble Master Jackson would be a rare long mouthful for you to call for help from me. Jacko, now, that's short and sweet. Besides, I doubt me if I would know who Master Jackson is, seeing that it's so long since anyone called me that. Therefore Jacko it must be.'

He even offered her a very yellow toothy grin at the end of this little speech—the longest which the amused Martin had ever heard him utter.

'Very well, then,' she quavered at him. 'I can see that Jacko it must be.'

'Aye, mistress, and then we shall all be happy.'

This was yet another doubtful statement, since Kate, Jacko and Martin were all happy but Aunt Jocasta wasn't sure how she felt—only that in some tricky fashion Jacko had bamboozled her. She remained silent, staring at him all the way to the Tower stairs. Kate was silent too, but she was admiring the view of London from the barge, in the intervals of covertly watching Martin, who, for once, was also silent, and was affecting her again by his nearness. No one expected Jacko to speak and he didn't let them down.

He helped Aunt Jocasta out before Kate and Martin and fell behind them while they walked the short distance to Forge Street, whose timber-fronted houses were slightly more desirable than those in the unnamed alley off it. Aunt Jocasta gave a muffled cry when Martin put his key in the door of one which was no more distinguished than the rest.

Kate was not surprised. She had expected nothing better than this. She was even relieved that Martin's home was not so bad as she had expected it to be. Jacko still behind them, they found themselves in a room which served as a parlour, with a ladder at one side of it which led to the two small rooms upstairs. Facing them was a hearth with a fine clock on its mantelpiece and beside it a door which opened on to a kitchen.

Aunt Jocasta gave another small moan and sank into the only armchair in the room: one long bench and two stools made up the rest of the seats. In its cramping smallness and lack of luxury the room, nay the whole house, was so unlike every place she had lived in that she felt oppressed by it to the point of being ready to swoon. It made Martin and Jacko look even bigger than they were.

'Feel a bit faint, mistress, do you? Not accustomed to the way in which we poor folk live, I suppose,' Jacko said solicitously. 'I'll wager there's something for you to drink in the kitchen which'll make you feel better. I'll go fetch it.'

Aunt Jocasta stared after him. 'I think he means to be kind.'

'To be sure,' said Martin, amused by the tactics which Jacko was employing to get round his, so far, implacable enemy. He would have her eating out of his hand shortly. He hadn't long to wait. Jacko emerged from the kitchen carrying not only a tin mug containing Madeira wine, but several small biscuits on a pewter plate which he offered to the bemused Aunt Jocasta.

'How very good of you to take such care of me,' she quavered at him.

'Oh, I'd do the same for me old Mam—if she kept Madeira in the house, that is.' And he winked at her.

This was as good as a play, Kate, thought, fascinated by the big man's cunning in his handling of Aunt Jocasta, a cunning which she had not expected of him. She had not expected her reaction to Martin's home, either, since it was such a strange mixture of feelings. On the one hand, like Aunt Jocasta, she was shocked at the thought of people having to live in something so small and sparsely furnished. On the other hand, by some magic, the little room gave her the feeling that it was a happy place whose occupants always felt at ease in it, unlike the stately mansions to which she was accustomed.

She could imagine Martin sitting here, before the fire, his long legs stretched out in front of him, a flask of Madeira at his elbow which he was sharing with either Jacko or Rafe, or both. It was not a scene in which she could picture Webster. They would be talking merrily together after the fashion of men in the absence of women...

'You are very quiet, Lady Kate,' Martin said, his voice gentle for once. 'Has the room distressed you as well as your aunt?'

'Oh, no,' she told him quickly, 'not at all. It's very unlike Bretford House or Lord Clifton's home where I have been living recently, but it hasn't shocked me in any way. I have to remind myself that more people live like this than in the ease and comfort in which most of our great families do.'

'True,' said Martin, and thinking that he might carry Kate's education a little further, added, 'but you must understand that most people in England live in much worse homes than this one off Forge Street. Many come to London to better themselves—and most succeed.'

On hearing this new, and somewhat unwelcome, knowledge, words flew out of Kate's mouth almost without her willing them.

'Men know so much more than women about the world outside their own home and family, which cannot be right. I can speak two languages well and two passably, but I was not aware of how most people live, and have never reproached myself for my ignorance. Is the Queen equally unaware of the nature of all those whom she rules? I'm aware that she is knowledgeable about war and diplomacy and how to govern us—but what does she know of the lives of the people whom she governs—apart from those around her, that is?'

It was Martin's turn to stare at her when she ended her passionate little speech.

'Men like to think that they protect their women from such knowledge.'

'Which men? Great men like you and those in our families? The men in the poor families cannot protect their women from anything.'

She was so serious, her green eyes flashing at him, her whole body vibrating, because by bringing her to his retreat off Forge Street he had opened up a whole new world to her. He had to confess that when he had agreed to bring her here, he had done so in order to give her a sharp lesson by showing her how the urban peasantry lived, but he had not expected her to be so powerfully affected by it.

He had originally believed her to be as selfish and spoiled as most of the women he had met whose lives were spent in the great world, as he thought of it, but she was quite unlike them. This discovery was doing strange things to Martin. Mixed with his feelings of respect for her unexpected compassion were others, far more earthy.

He wanted to take her in his arms and kiss her until her questing mind ceased to quest and her beautiful body took over, so that she was responding to him as powerfully as he might wish. Of all the strange things which had happened to him since he, the black sheep, had returned home, this was the strangest.

He had thought that Mary's sad death had robbed him of the ability to want another woman, either as mistress or wife, but meeting Lady Kate had proved that he had been wrong. Not only had he come to desire her beautiful body but he also admired her lively tongue, so much so that he was constantly provoking her to use it on him.

He would not provoke her over this, though. Instead, he found himself saying, 'Jacko brought your Aunt Jocasta refreshment. Would you like some?'

No doubt if he retired to the kitchen for a moment or two, absence from her disturbing presence might serve to cool down his errant body.

Of all the things which he might have said to her after her last speech, Kate had not expected this.

'You agree with me?'

'About poor women, yes. I have lived among them, and hard though their men work, they work harder and die sooner. You have not answered my question, though.'

'Now that you have answered mine, I will answer yours. I will gladly drink Madeira with you, but only if you and Jacko share it with me. I see that he is hiding in the kitchen, which he would not do if he were alone with you. Since we are shortly to become one, as the Prayer Book says, then it is only proper that he join us.'

Aunt Jocasta was sniffing again—this time not at Martin or Jacko, but at her because of her forward conversation. Never mind that, Kate had achieved what she had wanted. Martin put his head round the kitchen and bellowed his orders. Shortly afterwards, Jacko, a great deal of Madeira, three more mugs and an even larger plate of biscuits all came into the parlour together, where Jacko immediately asked Aunt Jocasta to join him in a toast to m'lord, m'lady and their coming marriage, to which she happily agreed.

If, a fortnight ago, anyone had told Kate that she would enjoy herself so much while sitting in a tiny room in one of London's back alleys, with a minimum of furniture around her—and what there was, extremely simple—she would not have believed them. Even more would she have refused to believe that her Aunt Jocasta would be manifestly revelling in the attentions of Martin's hired bravo, Jacko.

When Martin slyly winked at her while Jacko solicitously cared for her aunt's comfort, she could scarce refrain from laughing out loud—remembering her indignation when this jaunt was first proposed. Later, when they were back in the barge, a strong wind rose and Jacko was all consideration for her aunt when she began to shiver, immediately removing his jacket and inviting her to put it around her shoulders.

'Most kind,' she almost crooned at him. 'River journeys can be treacherous and the result is nearly always a fit of the ague. Are you sure that you will be warm enough?'

'Oh, I'm a hardy beast, mistress, never fear for me.'

'Would you like to wear my jacket?' Martin asked Kate soulfully. 'I would not care for you to contract an ague so near to our wedding.'

Kate, again trying hard not to laugh, shook her head at him. 'I like the wind, it is not too cold. I find it most refreshing.'

Martin, looking at her, could believe that she was telling the truth. Her green eyes were shining, her cheeks were flushed and her whole body was vibrating with pleasure. Anything less like the cold and haughty piece he had first met he could not imagine; with the result that, of all inconvenient things in this narrow boat, his treacherous body was giving him trouble again.

Kate was having similar problems. Seated next to Martin, feeling his warm body so close to hers, smelling his unique smell, which despite his beggarly clothes was a pleasantly musky one, was having its usual strange effect on her. The flush on her cheeks was the result of excitement, not warmth.

If she felt like this on the open river, with a strong wind blowing, several rowers around them, and Aunt Jocasta and Jacko facing her and Martin, what extraordinary effect would being alone with him on her wedding night have on her?

No, don't think about that. Think about the book you have been reading—but that would not do either, because it was about Abélard and Héloise, two lovers who had broken all the rules of good conduct, with dreadful results. The trouble being that ever since the bear had walked through the door, every hero of every book she had read turned into him—and she, of course, turned into the heroine.

To say nothing of how he had suddenly appeared in her dreams last night. Given all that, how could she be cold and haughty with him? Besides, it wasn't his fault that her mind was wandering so much when before she had always been in complete control of it.

'You are very quiet this afternoon, lady,' Martin whispered in her ear. 'Does something ail you, after all?'

A truthful answer would be, 'Yes, you,' but that Kate could not tell him. The only trouble was that she was amassing untruths at such a rate that she must surely be on the primrose path to Hell of which the parson had so often warned her.

'Am I troubling you?' came his next insistent whisper.

Oh, dear, he must be reading my mind! How can I reply?

'No, of course not,' she ventured.

'We are rather near to one another, I fear.'

What kind of answer could she make to that? A

silly one apparently, because all she could come out with was, 'Are we? Yes, I suppose we are.'

Dear God, she was losing her wits, as well as her breath. It had undoubtedly become difficult to breathe.

Her colour must be disappearing, too, for Martin's next whisper was, 'You do seem to be feeling the cold after all. If you do not care to borrow my jacket, allow me to take your hand and chafe it.'

Whatever would he suggest next? The thought of him chafing her hand was almost too much for Kate— and why should that be? She could scarce refuse him without making a fuss, though, so she allowed him to take her small right hand in his two large ones.

The only thing about allowing him such a liberty was that before he chafed her hand, he tickled its palm gently with his right hand, and if Kate had been excited before, then this last favour he was doing her nearly over-set her quite. So much so, indeed, that when his hand-chafing began she started to wriggle, unable to check herself.

'Oh, you *are* cold after all,' Martin exclaimed, letting go of her hand. 'I insist that you allow me to lend you my jacket.'

Well, that was some relief, that he was no longer touching her. But when he took off his jacket, and slipped it around her shoulders, it involved him in so much tender handling of her that Kate's wriggling grew rather than diminished. What made it worse was that she suddenly saw the sly grin on Jacko's face as he watched his master's manoeuvring.

What Kate did not know, but Jacko did, was that Martin's love-making to Kate—for that is what it was—was having an even more disastrous effect on Martin himself, particularly since he did not seem to be able to stop teasing her! The only innocent party in the barge, except for the rowers, who were too intent on their task to notice anything else, was Aunt Jocasta, who was prattling merrily to Jacko about the splendid views from the barge.

'London is so large,' she kept exclaiming. 'I am sure it was not so big as this when I was a young thing.'

'Which could not have been very long ago,' said Jacko.

It was many years since Aunt Jocasta had been so flattered. She gave a little cry and looked away from him. Kate wondered which of the two men was being the most forward in their treatment of the two women in the boat with them, Martin or his servant. At least Martin, still holding her hand, although no longer tickling it, had ceased to trouble her. And there was another fib—since lie was too strong a word for it— because she had begun to enjoy the sensations which his tickling had created and was missing the pleasure it had given her.

Such treacherous thoughts disappeared, however, when Lord Bretford's steward met them in the entrance hall. He bowed to Martin who had Kate on his arm.

'M'lord, your father ordered me to ask you to be good enough to attend on him as soon as you had returned from your journey on the river. He is in the study off his bedroom.'

Except at mealtimes Martin had spent very little time with his father since he had arrived back at Bretford House. When he had met him it was merely to discuss the details of his marriage to Kate, and any legal business connected with his own succession to his brother's honours. By his manner his father made it plain that it was only because of necessity that he spoke to his black sheep of a son at all.

He was seated at his desk when the steward ushered Martin in. M'lord looked up, threw down his quill pen, and said, his face hard and his voice severe, 'Do I understand, for so I have been informed, that you took the barge down river on some jaunt to the Tower, where you left it while you and that bravo of yours took Lady Kate and her aunt Jocasta for a walk in the back alleys of the City? Can it be true that you did such a thing without taking a suitable escort with you?'

Martin, who had not been offered a seat, leaned back against the wall which was opposite to his father's desk, crossed his arms, and made no effort to speak.

'Answer me, sir!' his father roared.

'I need not,' said Martin, smiling slightly, 'since it

is plain that you know that I did exactly that of which you have accused me. I could, of course, reply by saying that since Joshua Jackson and myself were all the protection which the two ladies needed, and I did not wish to draw attention to our rank in the said back alleys, I deemed it safer not to make our presence overt.'

'Then I must ask you why you took them there.'

'Lady Kate expressed a wish to see my home just off Forge Street, so I obliged her.'

'Then you should have had more sense. Your brother…'

He was interrupted in full roar by Martin, who uncrossed his arms, leaned forward and said, his own voice quiet and deadly, 'My brother, sir? That paragon of virtue—the manner of whose death proves quite otherwise—what has he to do with the matter?'

'I must speak to you of your home off Forge Street: you are surely not proposing to settle there with your wife after you are married. Your home will be here.'

'No, sir, it will not, nor will it be off Forge Street, but that is neither here nor there.'

'I shall not give you an allowance that will enable you to live anywhere other than Bretford House, and since Lord Clifton controls the trust from which Lady Kate derives her income until she reaches the age of twenty-five, he will allow you nothing, either—so live here you must.'

'Again, it matters not, sir. I have already made my

own arrangements, which I believe to be satisfactory, for her home with me.'

'Then I demand that you tell me of them—at once!'

Martin uncoiled himself lazily. 'No, sir. I have decided to follow your example and be as uncivil to you as you have been to me. I am no longer a child. I have been a grown man and my own master since I left this house fourteen years ago. From all the evidence available to me I believe my judgement to be sounder than yours. Were it not that I am legally contracted to marry Lady Kate, I would leave this house at once, never to return.'

His father, his face so red that Martin feared a syncope, glared at him. 'You were an unruly, ungracious child and you have not changed.'

'So you like to believe. I shall not waste breath trying to defend myself, it would be useless.'

'Be sure that I shall inform Lord Clifton of this.'

'Inform whom you please. It will not change my mind. I will take my leave.'

So saying, he strode from the room, leaving his father spluttering behind him. Nothing had changed. He was still the black sheep, the child whom ill-usage had driven from his home. John was still the paragon, and to try to disillusion his father by telling him some of the truth about his brother which he had discovered since he had returned to London would be useless.

Despite his brave front, his pretence that his father's demeaning of him could not affect him, Martin felt desolate when he ran lightly down the stairs. He made for the garden door. He needed air, needed to be away from everything inside the house which reminded him of the bitter past.

He walked briskly towards the Thames, to his favourite seat. The wind was stronger than ever, and although it was meeting him full in the face, he welcomed it since it felt like a cleansing thing. There were a few people dawdling along the river path before the jetties where the barges of the great were moored.

Gradually the simmering rage which had overwhelmed him died down. He had never been afraid to be alone, had welcomed it rather. There was a bird singing somewhere nearby, and peace enfolded him, to be shattered by the noise of something hitting the tree by his head.

Martin knew at once what had happened. Someone had shot at him and missed. He started to his feet, ran out on to the path, looked to his left, and then to his right—where he saw a man running away from him, holding something in his right hand.

His speed was no match for Martin's. He tore along the path, pushing a few startled walkers out of his way until he reached the man and wrestled him to the ground. The man's large pistol fell onto the path beside him. Martin kicked it away and tried to pin down his would-be assassin, only for the fellow to strike him in the face with such force that he reeled back.

This gave the assassin the chance to run down a jetty and dive into the Thames in an attempt to avoid capture and certain death. Alas for him, he surfaced in front of a huge, ornate barge and was struck on the head by one of its oars, so that he sank, semiconscious, to the river bottom. Death by drowning had superseded death by hanging or the axe.

Martin, holding his kerchief to his bleeding nose, picked up the pistol. It was a magnificent and costly weapon: a German wheel-lock, a breechloader of the latest pattern, something which must have belonged to whoever it might be who had hired the assassin. Its owner, most probably Bevis Frampton, would be sorry to lose it. Martin was even sorrier that the man had drowned, since it meant that he could not force from him the name of his employer, and confirm whether or not it was Frampton.

One thing was sure. He was not going to tell anyone—other than his own henchmen—of this new attempt to kill him. He stanched his bleeding nose and felt it gently to be certain that it was not broken. He would have to concoct some story to explain away any swelling or bruising.

Back at the house, not knowing which troubled him the most, this second attempt to kill him, or the knowledge of his father's dislike, he made several decisions, none of which would please the old man.

He met Rafe on the way in. Rafe was looking unhappy, he disliked living at Bretford House nearly as much as Martin did. He stared at the pistol in Martin's hand.

'Now where the devil got you that?'

'If we can find somewhere private I will tell you, after one of the footmen has summoned Webster and Jacko to join us. Until then, you must be patient.'

'Patient is my middle name these days,' grumbled Rafe. 'I can't wait to go home again—no matter whether it's off Forge Street or Saxon Hall.'

'We shall be returning to Saxon Hall sooner than you might think,' Martin told him when they discovered that the guardroom by the entrance, long disused since the coming of this Queen's more peaceful time, was empty, save for a table with long benches on either side. Presently the footman ushered Jacko and Webster in, and was told that he was not to inform anyone of where they all were.

'Why this secrecy, m'lord?' Webster asked.

'Call me Martin in here—and the secrecy is necessary.'

He had already laid the pistol on the table round which they were now all sitting, and, pointing to it, said, 'You see that murderous piece of craftsmanship? Not an hour ago a hired assassin tried to kill me with it when I sat on the bench by the Thames. It was the second attempt on my life in recent sennights.'

Rafe picked up the pistol and inspected it.

Webster said, 'Yet you still live. What happened to your would-be assassin?'

'His aim was poor and he missed me. I chased him, we struggled a little, he broke away, dived into the Thames to escape being caught, only to be run down by a barge—which was the end of him. A pity, since I would like to know for sure who wants me dead—and, if it proves to be Frampton, why.'

Rafe said, 'Frampton or not, it is someone rich. This is a rare weapon the like of which few possess. Almost certainly given by its owner to the man who tried to kill you. There is no name on it.'

Webster said, 'Your father should be informed at once and steps taken to find out who the real culprit is.'

'No!' exclaimed Martin. 'I want this matter to remain a secret between the four of us. Jacko can do more than the law, and more quickly, since he is not constrained by it. I have also come to another decision. Tomorrow, at first light, we shall return to Saxon Hall—I find this house stifling—and we shall prepare for my marriage there. I shall not tell my father where we are going, and the three of you will not tell him either—and that is an order.'

'He won't like it,' mourned Webster.

'I hope not.' Martin's voice was savage. 'It is one of the reasons I am leaving. I have no mind to oblige him any more than he feels the need to oblige me. I take my cue from him, as the actors say. I shall inform him, and Lord Clifton, of our departure after dinner, before I retire for the night.'

'He might think that you are reneging on the marriage,' said Rafe, smiling a little at the mere idea of his haughty lordship having to worry about something for a change, instead of worrying everyone else.

'Let's hope that he does—but I have every intention of turning up at St Paul's to marry Lady Katherine Wyville.'

'Have you told her so?' asked Webster, his lawyer's mind busy.

'Not yet—I only made up my mind to go home just before I sent for you all—but I shall do so immediately. Before we depart I shall need to reassure her that I don't intend to leave her at the altar, a bride without a groom. Now, do any of you have any sensible questions to ask me?'

They shook their heads. 'I have a comment to make,' said Webster. 'I'm not sure that I approve of your decision, but I am also certain that you believe that you have a good and sufficient reason for making it.'

'Then you know more than I do,' Martin told him with a grin, rising in order to leave them. 'But so long as you obey me you may think what you please.'

'And that's why I like him,' Rafe told Webster with a grin of his own. 'He always knows his own mind and I've seen him make decisions on the spur of the moment—just like this one—and he's usually been right. What does trouble me is not that, but that someone wants to kill him, and that we have no absolute certainty of who it might be, although the main suspect must be Bevis Frampton.'

'Amen to that,' sighed Webster, while Jacko nodded his head in solemn agreement.

* * *

Martin found Kate in the withdrawing-room again, Aunt Jocasta in attendance. He smiled at her aunt, saying to her, 'I have need to converse privately with Kate. You will excuse us, I'm sure.'

Prior to their excursion Aunt Jocasta would have argued with him. Instead, she graciously waved her tapestry needle in the air and murmured, 'Indeed, provided that you do not detain her over-long—we must not give the servants an opportunity to gossip about you both before you marry.'

'Goodness,' exclaimed Kate, when she and Martin were alone. 'Whatever has come over her to make her speak so civilly to you?'

'Jacko,' said Martin with another grin. 'We shall not go far—a promenade up and down the long gallery will suffice for what I have to tell you. Come,' and he offered her his arm.

She took it, and asked, 'What is of such urgency and importance, m'lord, that you need to converse with me alone?'

He smiled down at her. 'Nothing that need trouble you. Briefly, I and my three counsellors will be leaving Bretford House tomorrow morning to prepare for our wedding. Do not be afraid that I am about to desert you. I shall arrive at St Paul's prepared to fulfil the contract which I have signed. Do not allow your uncle, or my father, to worry you by suggesting that I might be about to leave you at the altar.'

'I think that you might do many things,' Kate said, slowly, 'but not that.'

'So you believe me.'

'That you will not betray me, yes.'

Impulsively Martin leaned forward and kissed her on her damask cheek. 'Bless you, my sweet. Not many have ever expressed such faith in me at such short notice—even if you did qualify it somewhat!'

*My sweet.* He had called her my sweet!

Did he really mean that?

Or was it the idle sort of remark which men made to women to keep them quiet?

And yet, and yet. She believed him, where many wouldn't have done. He would not humiliate her. She was a little frightened of him, because she thought that there was more to him than either her uncle or his father believed. She had no notion of what that more might be, only that it existed.

Would she find out after she had married him?

Or was she never to know?

For the moment it was enough to be with him, and what did that mean? Was she falling in love with him?

No, that could not be, she told herself fiercely, because was she not *that cold piece* Lady Katherine Wyville, as more than one man had called her, who could never, ever fall in love with the bear whom she had first encountered on the sweep at Bretford House? And what a surprise it would be if she did!

* * *

Predictably, Lord Bretford was more enraged by his son's news than he had ever been since he had discovered all those years ago that Martin had run away from his home in the middle of the night.

'What d'you mean by leaving Bretford House so soon before the wedding, to retreat to that alley off Forge Street which you call home? You might have had the goodness to remain here until the wedding ceremony was safely over. Do you intend to behave as you did fourteen years ago and disappear from home without warning—leaving the poor young thing at the altar?'

'You always did think the best of me, Father,' Martin murmured. 'I have every intention of keeping my word. I am leaving tomorrow morning and we shall next meet in St Paul's. This I promise you.'

'And what, pray, are your promises worth?'

Martin kept his temper with difficulty. If he lost it he knew that he would say or do something unforgivable, and for Kate's sake, not his own, he wished to avoid that.

'No more, and no less, than anyone else's. I shall be taking my men with me, and you may be certain that Webster, at least, will make sure that I do not stray from the path of virtue.'

'Webster! That fellow whom I took into my service to be my right-hand man and whom you immediately suborned. What does *he* know of virtue?'

'Only that he expects me to practise it.'

'Pah!' His father turned on his heel and addressed Lord Clifton, who had remained silent during this after-dinner wrangle, which grew more heated by the minute.

'It's your niece whose life he is playing with—what do you think of this notion of Hadleigh's that he must leave his home and disappear from view until the morning of the wedding?'

'That I am not happy about this proposal, but since Hadleigh is a grown man, not a boy to be controlled by word or whip, we can only hope that he means to keep his word and to marry Lady Kate as he is contracted to do.'

This was not at all the answer which Lord Bretford wanted, but it was the one which he would have to live with. That damned fellow, his son, was smiling at him, and bowing to Lord Clifton, saying, 'I am happy to see, m'lord, that you, as well as your niece, trust me to behave properly. Now, if you will allow me, m'lords, I will retire. I have much to do tomorrow.'

He had waited until Rafe and Webster had left the dinner table at a sign from him—Jacko always ate in the servants' hall—before he had told his father the news which he did not want to hear. All that remained when he arrived at his rooms was to inform them that the matter was settled.

'Not to his satisfaction, I'll be bound,' was Rafe's immediate remark, while Webster, more circumspect, echoed Lord Clifton's judgement of the matter. 'He might not like it, but all in all he is powerless to act. He has already discovered that he cannot blackmail you by cutting off your allowance which leaves him with no hold over you.'

Rafe began to laugh. 'I suppose he thinks that we are all bound for the alley off Forge Street. What a tight fit that would be! For a fact we shall be more comfortable at Saxon Hall than here. I really want to be present when he learns the truth of you, Martin. His face should be a rare sight then!'

And that was something which set even Webster laughing, until he noted that his new employer was not joining in the mirth which Rafe had provoked. As a man of sense, as well as being a lawyer, it was not for the first time that he asked himself what exactly had happened fourteen years ago to cause Martin Chancellor to leave his home and family behind him.

# *Chapter Five*

**M**artin arrived back at Saxon Hall just before his first visitor. He was still wearing the disguise which made Kate think of him as a bear. He was upstairs unpacking his own luggage for there were a number of items in it which he wished no one else to see. One of them was a small volume which he had found at the bottom of a chest in his bedroom at Bretford House—the room which had once been his brother's.

It was bound in vellum and appeared at first to be a commonplace book in which the owner entered in his own handwriting poems, sayings and items which had interested him. Written in faded ink on the title-page were the words *John Chancellor, his book*. Even a cursory inspection, however, showed that the book was more than that. After a few pages it turned into a diary, a record of his brother's daily life, and as Martin rapidly turned its pages he saw his own name mentioned several times.

Curious to find out what his brother might have

written of him—if anything—he had put it in his luggage in order to read it at leisure when he reached Saxon Hall. It was all that he had taken with him from the place which his father insisted on calling his home, and it was more than he had taken with him when he had fled into nowhere fourteen years ago with no luggage and nothing in his purse or his pockets. He placed it on a table beneath a window immediately before his steward entered the room.

'You have a visitor, sir. I think that he is one whom you would not wish to turn away.'

None of the staff at Saxon Hall yet knew that their master was Lord Hadleigh, Bretford's heir—hence the sir.

Martin said dryly. 'It would be useful if you told me his name.'

'It is Sir Walter Raleigh, and he says that it is important that he speaks to you as soon as possible. I have shown him into the withdrawing-room.'

'Good,' said Martin and set off to find out what it was that Raleigh thought was important enough to pay a morning visit to Saxon Hall. Never mind that he was still dressed in his beggarly seaman's clothes, and that Raleigh only knew him as his other self, he must oblige him at once. After all, it would not be long before all his secrets were in the open.

Raleigh's eyes widened in surprise when Martin entered the withdrawing-room. He was, as usual, finely dressed, with a pearl in his left ear. He also

brought with him a general air of power and consequence.

'I had not thought to see the wild man of the woods
come in,' he remarked, smiling. 'You look larger than
ever now that you are accoutred like one of your seamen—or was that what you wore when you helped
to rob the Spanish argosy?'

Martin was not embarrassed. He said coolly, 'There
is a good reason for my appearance. Had you arrived
a little later you would have found the man you have
always known.'

'Captain Martin, there is always a good reason for
everything you do—as I have long been aware. I have
called on no idle errand. I have been, as I need not
tell you, a friend of m'lord Essex, and I have come
to you with a message from him. What you must understand, though, is that I am only a messenger, a
postman of sorts, and that whatever I have to say to
you comes from Essex, not from me. I am not trying
to persuade you to join in any of his enterprises. You
must do as you think best when you have heard what
he has to ask of you.'

Martin began to laugh. 'You are then, a vocal letter,
no more and no less.'

Raleigh smiled at him. 'The very thing. I am as
impersonal as the piece of paper on which a letter is
written. Now this is the gist of the matter. Lord Essex
thinks that England needs a new, younger and better
ruler, not an elderly woman long past her prime. To
that end he wishes to rid the state of the relics of the

old guard who make up her advisers. Not only that, he wishes to rid us of the Queen herself, and replace her by appointing himself as the Lord Protector around whom he will gather new men, young men who will make England both rich and great. In short, men like himself—or like you—self-made men.'

Martin gave a short laugh. 'Then he doesn't want me. I'm not a new man. I am descended from the old men of power—as he is. You—and he—know me as Andrew Martin, the lowly sea captain who has made himself rich by helping to loot the Spanish galleons, the argosy which carries the treasure from the New World to the Old.

'The time has now arrived when I must tell you the truth about myself. My name is not Andrew Martin. I am Martin Chancellor, Lord Bretford's younger son who ran away from home. I became Andrew Martin, who sailed against the Armada and clawed his way from poverty up to riches. By chance, and the death of my brother, I have recently become Lord Hadleigh, my father having tracked me down after many years.'

He paused, and Raleigh, raising his brows, said, 'So you are the mysterious Lord Hadleigh of whom London's society has been talking. I wonder what your father makes of you seeing that you are not in the least like your brother John. He was so sleek and smooth, while you...' And it was his turn to pause and Martin's to laugh.

'While I am rough-spun and speak my mind. I will

do so now. First, I must tell you that my father does not yet know that I am Captain Andrew Martin—he thinks me a poor failure. I shall shortly enlighten him and I know that he will be as disappointed by my success as he was pleased by my failure. Second, I would not give Lord Essex the time of day, let alone join him in such a mad enterprise as trying to unseat the Queen would be. I don't believe, Sir Walter, that you wish to help him either, nor do I believe that Bacon, once his best friend, will support him. Bacon is a man who always looks after his own best interests—as a sensible man should—and therefore he will never encourage Essex in his folly.

'In my opinion m'lord Essex is a fribble, a fool who does *not* know how to look after his own best interests. A man who made a sad botch of his enterprise against Ireland and afterwards behaved in such a mad fashion as to lose the Queen's confidence, nay her love, does not merit my support.'

'Well said,' remarked Raleigh. 'It is exactly what I would have expected of you. More than that, I have to tell you that I don't respect the men who make up Essex's court. That nasty little hobgoblin Frampton is ever present these days.'

Frampton—this was the second or third time that Martin had heard Raleigh mention his name recently. 'What do you know of him?' he asked Raleigh, after the butler had brought in hippocras and a plate of biscuits and they were busy enjoying them.

'Very little; only that I always suspect those who

spend their time crawling and fawning around people like Essex and who also give me a cold grue whenever I see them—that's the Scottish description of a nasty shiver. I was told of it by one of Moray's folk when he visited the Queen.'

Trust Sir Wat to pick up an odd phrase—and then use it!

Martin said thoughtfully, 'So you won't be supporting Essex in any rebellion against the Queen?'

'No, even though I think that Her Grace's best times have come and gone. I was a very young man when I first met her and to see her now...' he shuddered, and said slowly, '...is to understand what time does to us all—should we live long enough.'

'True,' and they both fell silent. Raleigh shuddered again, before remarking with a slight smile, 'At least under Her Grace, unlike her sister and father, most of us have the chance to achieve a long life.'

Years later Martin was to think of this conversation and sigh, remembering something which Shakespeare had later written, 'We know what we are, but we know not what we may be.' At the time, however, he thought nothing of it, only laughed a little. His friend had always possessed a lively mode of speech, which he showed in the many poems he wrote.

Raleigh took another swig of his hippocras before saying, 'Lord Essex being disposed of, I must turn to Master Will Shakespeare. You haven't attended the Friday Club recently so he asked me to give you a message when next I saw you.'

'Playing the postman again?' grinned Martin.

'Anything to oblige. He says that he has read your play and is most impressed by its beginning, since it is plain that a true mariner wrote the first scene showing a storm at sea. Nevertheless, while he thinks that there is much promise in it, he also believes that it will need a great deal of reworking before it is fit for the stage. He asked me to tell you that you may either have the script back, or leave it with him to rewrite when he has time. He will then, of course, discuss his alterations with you.'

Martin was not sure whether this was good news or bad. 'At least he discovered something to praise in it. I think that I found it difficult to decide what to do next once the shipwrecked sailors reached the island.'

'Exactly what Will said. He's a shrewd fellow—busy making money in all sorts of enterprises which have nothing to do with the theatre. In his way he's as hard a man as you are. His only worry is that he might find himself in trouble with the Queen. She let it be known that she was most annoyed by his play, *Richard II*, because it showed an unpopular monarch being deposed, and now he has been warned that Lord Southampton—Essex's right-hand man—is talking about it being staged again, to raise support for Essex's policies.'

'Perhaps it's as well, then, that mine is not ready to be staged. At the moment I am too busy to spend my days dabbling in the theatre. Now that I am Lord Hadleigh, not only am I to marry the young woman who was betrothed to my brother, but my father's health is such that I don't think that he has long to live. I have two favours to ask of you before you leave. First of all, I would be pleased if you would not reveal my true identity to anyone until after my marriage, and secondly, referring to my marriage, I have something to ask of you.'

'Ask on.'

Martin told him what he wished Raleigh to do for him. Sir Walter clapped him on the shoulder, finished off his hippocras and left, but not before assuring Martin that he would be only too happy to assist his good friend. After all, he would be able to enjoy the joke of his changed appearance more than anyone.

Later that day, Martin went upstairs to his room to pick up his brother's diary. Once there, he paused to look at the portrait of his late wife Mary, which was hung in a small closet, away from prying eyes. She had been very small and sweet, quite different from Lady Kate in her gentle submission to him and to life. Distraught after her death—and that of his son—in childbirth, he had vowed never to marry again. Yet here he was, ready to stand, once more, before the altar. He could not help but feel that he was betraying her memory.

Before he had met Kate, it had been easy, not to forget Mary, but to prepare himself to marry her from a sense of duty, if for nothing else. Except that once he had come to know her, Kate had sounded some chord in him which Mary had never touched—with the result that his sense of betrayal had become even stronger. Once he had told Kate that he would not leave her at the altar, however, he felt compelled to honour his commitment to her, to his family and his name—even if to oblige his father stuck in his craw.

Finally he saw himself, briefly, in a Venetian mirror which he had won at cards from a young fellow who had been to Italy and had spent so much on beautiful objects there that he was virtually penniless when he arrived home. Yes, he did look like the wild man of the woods, or the bear which Kate had called him, and which she had been unaware was the motto which he had adopted on the coat-of-arms he had acquired after making his fortune—*Cave Ursum*, or Beware of the Bear.

Laughing a little, he picked up his brother's book and sat down to read it...

Bevis was trying to control his anger at being misused. He had arrived at Essex House with some plans anent a possible uprising which he wished m'lord to study. Until this visit he had always been ushered immediately into Essex's presence, but this morning the steward had informed him that m'lord would not be able to see him for some time. It seemed that Mr Francis Bacon was with him and even when he left, which might or might not be soon, his lordship had yet another great man to see before he had occasion to speak to Master Frampton.

Time passed. Bevis's anger grew. He would not have been so annoyed if he had not worries of his own to trouble him while he waited. He had given his hired assassin his most treasured and valuable weapon, a German wheel-lock pistol with which he could be sure of finishing off Martin Chancellor. He had told him to report to him immediately the deed was done, but several days had gone by, the fellow had not returned, and Martin Chancellor still walked the earth.

Either the fool had failed to kill Chancellor and he had then run off with the pistol which he had been stupid enough to lend him, or Chancellor had disposed of him, and he did not know which supposition he liked the least. All was to do again. Bretford had still not been punished sufficiently—that damned second son seemed to possess a charmed life, if all he had learned about his career since he had fled his home was true.

One ironic joke was that Bretford did not know what a powerful man the second son had become in comparison with that weak fool, his brother, whom he had found it so easy to suborn and destroy—without even needing an assassin to do it for him.

His musings were interrupted by the steward, who came to tell him that Lord Essex was ready to see him. Nothing for it but to go in, and try to persuade the fool which he knew Essex to be that if he were going to engineer a rising to depose Her Grace, it must be planned most carefully or it would not succeed.

The devil of it was that nearly all the human tools whom he had used in his long life to try to bring about his much desired revenges had broken apart in his hands, and he had the horrid feeling that Lord Essex was going to be no better than the rest.

Afterwards, closing his brother's diary, Martin was to ask himself whether it might not have been better to have cast it into the nearest fire rather than have read it. Even before he had turned a single page he had known what kind of weak and vicious fool John Chancellor, Baron Hadleigh, had become. Once Martin had become rich and, as his world knew it, powerful, he had hired agents to find out for him all that was known of his brother's life after he had left home.

The subsequent reports had made painful reading. John's life had been a series of betrayals of women and friends, as well as a record of cowardice which would have been unbelievable if the evidence of it had not been plain before him. One agent had discovered that there had been some dark influence on Martin's brother by someone whose identity he could not trace. 'Before a certain date,' he had written, 'm'lord's escapades had been, if not innocent, not particularly vicious. After that date he changed, and it was during the following year that he had contracted the Great Pox which had brought about his death.'

Martin sighed. Now, after reading John's book, he knew from what was written there that the first, and in some sense the most dreadful betrayal of all, had been of himself, his brother's younger twin, who had been innocent of all the misdeeds for which he had been so often, and so severely, punished, until in the end he had been compelled to leave home in order to save himself.

There, in John's diary, was recorded in detail the fashion in which, while pleasuring himself, he had been able to attach the blame to his brother. The brother whom he had envied because, even though he had been the second-born twin, he had been the larger, the stronger and the cleverer. The elegant body, the looks and the easy, outward charm had gone to John, but all else had been gifted to Martin.

And John knew that. By what he had written he had always known it, and he had allowed the envy which it had created in him to destroy his life while he was trying to destroy his brother's. After he had successfully driven Martin away by his lies and deceits, he had descended further and further down the primrose path to hell, unable to give up his vicious way of life.

No one who knew him had ever suspected to what depths he had sunk. To his father he had been, and still was, his paragon of a son. Even the manner of his death had been attributed to bad luck rather than a consequence of the debauched career of which neither his friends and family knew anything. Only 'my friend'—that vague shadow who had accompanied John on all his most vile adventures—knew the true man.

John had never given any direct hint in his diary of the friend's identity. Once, his writing disturbed and barely legible, he had complained bitterly that he was unable, for some reason he did not understand, to write down his 'friend's' name—other than that his Christian name began with B. That he trusted him was plain from what he wrote—except that now and then there was a hint of fear, a feeling that he was being led into adventures of a kind even he would once have flinched from.

Martin's one bitter thought was of how disillusioned his father might be if he were to hand him John's diary and allow him to discover what his favoured son had truly been like. But, little though he loved his father, he would never do that—unless it were needed to save himself, since in some of his worst escapades John had called himself Martin Chancellor.

What irked him the most was that his father had been willing to allow his pox-ridden pervert of a son to marry poor Kate. But he must try not to let what he had discovered disturb him over much. One thing was certain: he needed to remember to guard himself from any further attacks while he was waiting to marry Kate Wyville. He smiled ruefully at the surprising thought that this marriage, which at first he had decided to try to avoid, was becoming more and more attractive to him, so that he could hardly wait for the wedding day to arrive. What magic did she possess which had caused him to transform all his thinking about women?

Oh, be damned to that! He was simply lusting after her and trying to find excuses for why he should be doing so—but he knew that he was deceiving himself, for what he was beginning to feel for her was far more than mere lust. He was already starting to miss her animated face and her teasing voice, both of which made her unique among women.

A friend had once said to him, 'We cheat ourselves where women are concerned, by thinking that, like men, they differ from one another. They are all the same and made for one purpose only—and that bed.'

Even then, and it was before he had met Mary, he had refused to believe such a judgement could possibly be true. Women, like men, each had their own different set of qualities, and to demean them by believing otherwise was to demean one's self.

If Martin was thinking about Kate, she was also thinking about him. Before he had left Bretford House she could not have dreamed that she would miss him so much when his departing cavalcade had finally disappeared from sight.

She had nicknamed him the Bear, but the more she had grown to know him, the less he seemed to resemble that ursine animal. He had brought light and amusement into her life, and when—occasionally— he had behaved to his subordinates like a bear, he had allowed her to tease him until he was tame again.

Would he still be so gentle with her after they were married? Would the cheerful friendship which she had come to share with him disappear? She had known a number of women who had gone happily into marriage only to find that their husbands had shut them out of their lives, treating them as mere bed companions, leaving them to fall back on a drab and lonely existence.

And then there were the few whose husbands mistreated them brutally. One of her friends, driven to tell the truth to someone whom she could trust, had told her of the constant beatings to which she was being subjected. Worse than that, when she had complained to her husband that she did not deserve them, always having been a faithful wife, he had told her that she was rightly suffering for the sins of Eve and Delilah and must therefore accept her punishment cheerfully.

No! She could not believe that Martin would behave like that, but what she believed and what might be true could be different things. Something else, however, troubled her: now that Martin had left Bretford House, would he arrive at St Paul's cathedral on her wedding day?

It was at this point in her musings that Jennie came in and told her that Lord Clifton's brother-in-law,

Lord Padworth, and his family had just arrived at
Bretford House in order to be present at her marriage
and the celebrations afterwards.

'Alison? Is my cousin Alison with them?' Kate
asked joyfully, her recent worries forgotten.

'Indeed, she is, m'lady, which I made haste to tell
you, knowing what friends you are. She is in the withdrawing-room with her mother. Lord Padworth is
with the lords Clifton and Bretford in m'lord
Bretford's room.'

Alison was here! Alison, her very best friend, had
come to celebrate her marriage—if marriage there
were to be. No, forget that—and Kate ran downstairs
as fast as her stiff clothing would allow her, to find
Alison and her mother waiting to greet her.

All ceremony forgotten, Kate and Alison threw
themselves into one another's arms, until Alison held
her off to inspect her closely.

'Dearest Kate, is it not strange that you are the first
of our cousins to marry when you had so often vowed
that you had no wish to be a wife! And what is this
we hear?—that your future husband has disappeared
to somewhere unknown just before the wedding! We
had so hoped to meet him. Such a fairy-tale, is it not,
that he came from nowhere, not only to be Lord
Hadleigh, but also to marry his brother's betrothed.
Is he like his twin, John?'

'No, indeed,' replied Kate, while Alison's mother
begged her daughter in plaintive tones not to talk and

behave like a tomboy: 'for no one will wish to marry you, if you do!'

'Oh, pooh to that, Mama. As you are well aware, I have no want of suitors, since you and father are busily trying to decide which of them is the most worthy of me. Now, Kate, my love, to resume—if he does not resemble John, what is he like?'

Kate could not stop herself telling the truth. 'A bear,' she informed Alison, laughing as she spoke. 'He is very large, not smooth at all, and has lots of hair—but I like him.'

'Resembles a bear, and you like him! How very strange. Does he growl like one—or try to eat you?'

'He growls sometimes, but never at me, and when I tell him not to, he does as I ask, so the question of eating me has never arisen!'

'What a very odd bear he must be,' said Lady Padworth faintly. 'Are you sure that you wish to marry him, my dear? I know that he will be Lord Bretford and thus a great man one day, but nevertheless... Gossip also says that no one knows where he has been, or what he has been doing, since he left his home all those years ago. Has he said aught of that? It seems to me that you will be marrying a complete stranger.'

'He has said nothing of his past to me—and as for marrying a complete stranger, most women of our station marry them every day, so that is no matter. Besides, I have spent some time with him before marriage, which is more than many poor brides have done.'

There was no denying that, and the arrival of the three lords, all looking grim, served, in Lord Padworth's words, to cut womanly chatter short. By Alison's expression it seemed to be a favourite phrase of his. Kate reminded herself, with some pleasure, that one of Martin Chancellor's virtues was that he never talked down to her after the fashion of most men with their women.

She had little time for further thought, or speech, except to ask where Alison's brother Stephen was, to be told that he would arrive shortly before the wedding, since he was currently staying with the family of an old college friend. He, too, was longing to meet the mysterious heir to Bretford, as Martin had apparently been nicknamed.

In all this fuss Kate's questing mind was silenced, until she found herself alone in bed when, of course, misgivings and doubts, coupled with a few hopes, started plaguing her again.

Just before she finally fell asleep she wondered where Martin was, and what he was doing.

Martin was busy trying to forget that he was the heir to Bretford and the puzzle which Lady Kate Wyville presented to him. Back in his own home, and restored to the usual appearance of Captain Andrew Martin, he decided to visit the Friday Club in the hope that some of its livelier spirits would be there.

He was in luck. Raleigh was present, and in his usual corner, watching and observing, was silent Will Shakespeare. Martin occasionally wondered if he would ever turn up on stage one day under some betraying name. More than one noble or gentleman who belonged to the club had recognised himself on the boards, either to his amusement or his annoyance.

Raleigh, as usual far from silent, called him over. 'Well met. I have a letter for you from our mutual friend, who was apparently been writing to you at Saxon Hall but complains that he has never received a reply.'

'Oh, God, not Essex again,' Martin groaned. 'I thought that I had heard the last of him.'

'Indeed, not—or not until we have *all* heard the last of him, which, if his present mode of conduct is any guide, will not be long. Pray relieve me of it. I would not play at postman for anyone but you.'

Martin took the letter from him, and thrust it into the pocket of his capacious breeches. He was so finely groomed and dressed that Kate would not have recognised him—other than by his size, that is.

'What is the latest gossip about court, then?' Ben Jonson asked.

'Now why should you ask that?' queried Raleigh. 'Seeing that all your plays are about City merchants and the like?'

'Who knows?' Jonson grinned back at him, nothing daunted. 'I might decide to follow friend Will here and write about lords and ladies, Kings and Queens.'

For once Shakespeare took part in the conversation. 'I thought that your latest piece was to be a comedy.'

Jonson nodded. 'True,' he agreed. '*Cynthia's Revels* being its new title. But that does not mean that I don't enjoy court gossip with the rest of you.'

'There is none at present,' Raleigh declared. 'Save that Her Grace is old and ill.'

'Which is not news,' Shakespeare said, and fell silent again.

More drink was called for, which loosened people's tongues a little, but at the end of the evening Martin thought that he, too, must be growing old, since the club seemed to have lost a great deal of its sparkle lately. What might provoke liveliness would be a new scandal, of which there had recently been a dearth, or of Essex doing something terminally stupid.

Raleigh caught at his cloak when he left. 'Pray, old friend, go and see his would-be Highness in his den and persuade him that you are not to be wheedled into being fool enough to support him.'

Martin grinned at him. 'I promise, though I have no wish to, but in return I have one more thing I want you to do for me.'

'Which is?'

'This,' and Martin leaned over to whisper in Raleigh's ear.

His friend nodded. 'Agreed—I need something to liven my days. I will not ask why you are interested in Frampton, although I might guess.'

'My hearty thanks,' Martin said, and left.

The following morning he took himself to Essex House, but not before both Rafe and Webster had separately doomed at him.

'Is this errand wise?' Webster said. 'The man is a nodcock. You should have nothing to do with him lest you share his fate.'

'Prettily put,' smiled Martin. 'But listen carefully to me and learn that I trust him even less than you do. I go as a favour to a friend. To say good day—and little more. I have no wish to become one of his dupes.'

Rafe was even shorter and coarser in his advice than Webster. His reward was to be told that he, with Jacko, would accompany Martin on his visit to the deposed favourite.

He was still grumbling when they arrived at Essex House, where he and Jacko were told to wait in an anteroom while their master paid his respects to Robert Devereux, Earl of Essex.

Martin was led by yet another self-important steward—he had long observed that they thought themselves to be the equals of their masters—into a long room which had a dais at one end on which was a chair of state in which m'lord of Essex sat. He was the only person in the crowded hall who was not standing.

On the dais, a few paces behind him, were the most important of his followers. Among them was a little grey man whose fine clothing only seemed to diminish him. His presence distracted Martin a little from giving his full attention to the wayward Earl, who was splendidly decked out in scarlet and gold with a giant ruff circling a handsome, if rather weak, face. Fortunately the steward, once he was before Essex, made such a great meal of announcing him as Captain Andrew Martin that it gave Martin time to decide on what to say to his master.

Essex nodded his head thoughtfully and then said in a light and pleasant voice, 'You may advance, Captain Martin.'

Martin walked forward to the very edge of the dais, where he had a splendid view not only of m'lord, but of the grey man. He had seen him once before, and was suddenly sure that he was looking at, if rumour were true, Lord Essex's chief adviser, Bevis Frampton. It also struck him that Frampton might not only be his brother's mysterious B but also the little man who had paid the first assassin to murder him— if the rogue was telling him the truth; which was why he had asked Raleigh to find out as much as he could of any untoward rumours about Frampton's life.

He reminded himself of the reason for his visit and listened carefully to what m'lord Essex was saying.

'I am pleased to see that, at last, Captain Martin, you have chosen to do my bidding and wait on me, here at Essex House. Since Her Grace sees fit to imprison me here, I may not visit others, although they may visit me. Such, alas, are the rewards of one who has served his country on the battlefield and in the Privy Council Chamber.'

Not knowing quite what to say to this, Martin merely bowed his head in apparent agreement.

The Earl continued. 'I understand that you have served your country both on the sea, and in the City of London. It is such new young men as yourself whom I choose to welcome. For too long England has been ruled by old men and old women. The time is ripe for change. You understand me, sir?'

Only too well, Martin thought, but he did not say so. On the contrary, he honoured and respected the Queen, whose courage had defeated all her enemies and the great Spanish Armada itself.

'You are quiet, sir,' remarked Essex when Martin did not immediately reply.

'Such is my nature,' lied Martin and was happy that Rafe and Webster were not present to hear such a patent untruth.

'What say you then? I give you leave to speak your mind.'

Which he had much better not do! Nevertheless he would have to say something, even if what he might offer the man before him might not please.

'It is my belief, m'lord, that change is sometimes necessary. I would also trust and pray that such change might be peaceful in nature. It is not so many years since this country was torn apart by war and I would not wish to see that happen again. Thus I would seek to influence Her Grace and Her Grace's Parliament by words and advice—which, m'lord, I am sure is your wish also.'

Martin was not sure of this at all. Not with Bevis Frampton glowering at him, and his memory of what had been written in his brother's sad outpourings.

Essex leaned forward. 'Sometimes violence is necessary to cleanse a misruled state.'

Martin could not help himself. He said, in as detached a voice as possible. 'I have never thought blood to be a good cleanser of anything, m'lord. I trust to your good judgement in the matter, and would like to believe that you will only do what is best to maintain the peace and prosperity of this kingdom.'

He saw Essex's face darken. He heard mutterings among the courtiers standing behind him. Essex rose and turned his back on Martin, in order to leave the dais by the door behind him, but not before he had given a curt order to his steward, 'You may show this fellow out straightway with as little ceremony as possible.'

He could not have said anything more calculated to please Martin. He followed Essex's flunky into the anteroom where Rafe and Webster waited for him. Before they could leave, however, the little grey man entered the room, saying brusquely to the steward, 'You may show Captain Martin's servants out. I, however, wish to have a private word with him before he leaves.'

What was this, then? What could Frampton have to say to him?

Martin's response was brief. 'Why are you detaining me, sir?'

'Because I need to speak to the brother of my late friend, John, Lord Hadleigh, in order to advise him that it would be in his own best interests to agree to support m'lord Essex in his most reasonable wishes regarding the future of this realm. My name, in case you do not know it, is Bevis Frampton and I am always at your service.'

Martin's voice was ice. 'So, Master Frampton, did you always advise my brother what to do in *his* own best interests?'

Frampton's smile was as oily as his cold face could make it. 'Indeed I did, Lord Hadleigh, but he often chose not to follow it—to his own detriment. I would have thought that you might be wiser than he was.'

'And so I am, which is why I wish to have nothing to do with Lord Essex or your good self. What he was proposing, and you are apparently supporting, is little short of treason, and I, sir, will never betray my country. I give you good day.'

Frampton's pale eyes managed to glitter.

'Be sure that you will come to regret your refusal of m'lord Essex and of me.'

'Oh, I think not, Master Frampton. My regrets would be if I became one of his—and your—followers. Again, I bid you good day. I have much to do and may not waste further time here.'

It was plain to Martin that Frampton was boiling with rage at his cold rejection of him and all his works, and if provoking him to that degree was unwise, then so be it.

He turned on his heel and left the room.

Bevis Frampton was, indeed, boiling with rage. John Chancellor had been an easy target for him, but his brother was of a totally different temper. The sooner Martin Chancellor lay dead in the gutter from which he had risen to success and wealth, the sooner his murderer could rejoice in having finally punished Lord Bretford for the slights he had put upon him.

Martin Chancellor would do well to watch his back. No man had ever insulted Bevis Frampton without being severely punished for it.

## Chapter Six

For the future bride and groom a week had never passed so slowly, giving them both time to ponder on their possible future together.

One morning, shortly before the wedding, Kate was busy trying on her wedding gown, which was being made at top speed since her marriage was taking place at such short notice. Alison and another cousin, Avis, a quiet girl, whose gentry family had also arrived to take part in the wedding, and who was to be Kate's second bridesmaid, watched her turn and twist before a long mirror brought from Venice. When the fitting was over they remained in Kate's bedroom to talk of this and that.

That turned out to be more interesting than this, when Alison, whose curiosity about everything was famous, began to tell them of her latest exploit.

'Wonder of wonders,' she exclaimed, 'I have discovered a portrait of Lord Hadleigh done when he was fourteen. He was painted standing beside his brother. He didn't look a bit like John, nor did he resemble a bear. In fact, I thought he was rather handsome.'

Intrigued, Kate asked, 'Where did you find it? I was told by Lord Bretford that no portraits of him existed.'

For once quiet Avis began to giggle. 'So he told Alison, but that didn't stop her from looking for one. You'll never believe where it was hidden. Tell her what you told me, Alison.'

'Well, I was talking to the housekeeper, Mistress Cray. I said that it was strange that in a house full of paintings of the Chancellor family, including no less than four of John, there was not one of the new Lord Hadleigh as a boy. She gave me an odd look, and said, "Soon after Master Martin ran away Lord Bretford ordered that all the paintings and drawings in which he appeared were to be destroyed." Something in the way in which she spoke intrigued me, so I said, "Oh, dear, what a pity. I am sure that not only Lady Kate, but Avis and I would dearly love to have seen what he looked like when he was young."

'I seemed so sad, that she said to me, rather impudently I thought, "You are a talkative young lady—but can you keep a secret?"

'"I've kept many," I told her, which you both know to be the truth.

'She looked hard at me before remarking, "I hope that you mean what you say. Follow me—if you don't mind visiting the servants' quarters and the kitchen, that is.''

'Of course, I told her that I didn't, so she took me through a door covered in green baize. From thence she led me across the kitchen into a larder which had a little closet at its far end. You may judge of my surprise when she unlocked the closet door and opened it, to reveal hanging on its wall a dear little painting of two boys. One of them I immediately recognised as Cousin John. The other was obviously Martin. He wasn't handsome like John, but he was comely in his own right and was much bigger than John. You would never have thought that they were twins. I can assure you that he wasn't hairy then. Mother always told me that Martin had been ugly, but he wasn't in the painting. It is perverse of me, I know, but I preferred him to John. John was too smooth.'

Alison fell silent.

Kate said, 'Martin must have been beardless because he was still a boy, and you thought him comely. I wonder what he looks like now beneath all that hair.'

She began to laugh. 'And Lord Bretford does not know that this portrait was saved?'

'No, indeed. Mistress Cray told me that all the servants liked Martin and did not care for John. It would not be untrue to say that they hated him. They believed that his father treated Martin most unfairly and they were sorry when he disappeared.'

Avis spoke at last. 'We can't tell anyone of this,

Alison, since the promise you made to the house-keeper must bind all of us, too.'

'Yes, we must all agree on that,' Kate said. 'But only consider it strikes at everything we know about the brothers and their father. I was always told that Martin was the wicked, violent and ugly one who ran away—which frightened me before I met him. When I finally did, that story scarcely seemed to fit the man I came to know.'

Avis spoke again. 'This is all so strange that I have a strong desire not only to see the portrait but also to meet Martin. John I saw little of, so I couldn't judge him.'

'I, on the other hand, saw him often,' Alison said, 'but I cannot say that I liked him very much. What about you, Kate, what did you think of him?'

'I only saw John for a short time on the day we were betrothed, so I cannot pass judgement on him—except that I thought that he looked rather ill.'

'I know that he was unkind to animals,' offered Alison. 'I saw him beat one of his dogs cruelly be-cause it did not obey him immediately. I could never be fond of a man who mistreated animals.'

'Nor I,' said Kate and Avis together.

Once she was alone Kate began to wonder why the kitchen staff were so determined to keep at least one painting of Martin, despite Lord Bretford's orders that all of them were to be destroyed.

Well, if Alison had seen the portrait, so might she. She slipped into the easy unceremonial clothing which she wore around Bretford House when no visitors were expected, and ran down the backstairs to the green baize door of which Alison had spoken. She knew that the housekeeper's room lay on the other side. With the help of a startled kitchen maid she found it. Mistress Cray was inside, eating a late nuncheon, a tankard of ale before her.

She rose to her feet, surprise etched on her face. 'What may I do for you. m'lady?'

'You may show me the painting of the Chancellor brothers which you allowed my cousin Alison to see.'

'I told her not to tell anyone,' said Mistress Cray reproachfully.

'She has only informed me, and Mistress Avis Gantry, because we share all our secrets and have learned, quite painfully, never to tell anyone else of them. Besides, I think that I have the right to see a painting of my bridegroom as a very young man.'

'You will not betray me to Lord Bretford?'

'No, certainly not. I promise to keep your secret. It is becoming plain to me that Bretford House holds many secrets.'

The housekeeper nodded. 'That is true,' she said, but she did not tell Kate of the others to which she was privy. One of them being that she knew where Martin had gone when he had fled the house, what he had done after that, and that if he were not deceiving her, he was deceiving everyone else in Bretford House, including his future wife. Given all that he had suffered, she could not reproach him for that.

'Come with me.' And she rose, to take Kate to the locked closet where the little portrait hung.

Alison had been right. Martin had been comely, not handsome like his brother, but there was an air about him which Kate recognised because he still possessed it. She could not describe what the air was, only that it gave him, even at that young age, a look of power.

Mistress Cray then informed Kate of something which she had not told Alison. 'The painting is unfinished. If you look carefully at it, there is no signature on it, and some of the colour is not complete. M'lord disliked it because it made Master Martin, as he then was, look more...' she searched for a word and found one '...imposing than his brother. He ordered the artist to alter it, but he would not. He said that he had vowed only to paint the truth and not lies. M'lord refused to pay him and sent him away. The painting was hung in a dark corner until it was handed over to the gardener to be burnt. It was then that we saved it—in Master Martin's memory—for we believed that he would never return to this place where he had been so unhappy.'

'And have you seen him since he returned here as Lord Hadleigh?'

'Oh, yes, while he was staying here recently—although his father does not know.'

She was still keeping Martin's secrets for him. Had

he wanted his future bride to know of them he would have told her.

Kate looked carefully at the little painting, trying to imprint it on her memory. Martin looked happy in it. What intrigued her was that the more closely she examined it she could see in the youth he had once been the large and impressive man which he would become. A wave of love for him passed over her. Love for the mistreated boy who had inspired it in the servants of the house, so that in the truest sense there had been a place for him in the kitchens even if he were unwanted elsewhere.

As though she had read her mind, Mistress Cray said, still a little hesitant, 'I do not know whether I should tell you this, but Martin loved to come to the kitchens when he was left alone in the house, as he often was. Many is the time he ate with us at table— until m'lord found out and he was forbidden to visit us again.'

Another wave of love engulfed Kate, mixed with anger at the loneliness which Martin had suffered. However badly he had behaved, he had not deserved to be so unkindly treated. She leaned forward and took the housekeeper's hand in hers. 'Thank you for loving him,' she said. 'He must have been leading a most unhappy life.'

'Indeed, he was. May I say something to you, m'lady, which might sound impertinent? I think that he has been lucky in gaining you for his future wife, and you, too, are lucky. You would not have been happy with his brother, John.'

'You are not being impertinent if you are telling me the truth. Now I must leave you. Given every-thing, we must not be seen as conspirators.'

'Thank you, m'lady. My blessing goes with you.'

Kate's journey upstairs was a thoughtful one. She felt that, for the moment, she could not rejoin the rest of the company, knowing what she did. For the first time she was beginning to understand what had been the cause of the oddities of Martin's behaviour.

His father's behaviour was even odder. Whatever could have possessed him that he should have treated the lively boy whom she had seen in the painting so cruelly? What could Martin have done to deserve it?

Only when Jennie arrived to tell her that her two aunts and her cousins would welcome her company in the withdrawing-room did she allow her maid to dress her a little more finely before she joined them. Even then she was strangely quiet, as Aunt Padworth confided later to Aunt Gantry. Only Alison and Avis guessed at what might be troubling her.

Before she went to bed she told them that she had been to see Martin's portrait, but she said nothing of her conversation with Mistress Cray, for that had been a confidence freely given to Martin's future wife and to no one else.

* * *

Martin, unaware that Kate had discovered some of his secrets, had called Webster, Rafe and Jacko to a meeting which was as confidential as the one between the three girl cousins.

'I wish to consult with you,' he told them, 'about the mysterious fellow Bevis Frampton, who, I am now almost certain, has been trying to have me slain—for what reason I am still not sure. He is a follower of the Earl of Essex, indeed there is reason to believe that he is rather more than that, since he is one of those who are most busily engaged in encouraging Essex to plan an open rebellion against the Queen. Certainly I gained from Essex's conversation with me that he is seriously contemplating such a move.'

'The man's mad,' said Rafe.

'I agree with you. Now although it is certain that Frampton is behind the attacks on me, I have no real evidence which would allow me to move against him. What I would like from the three of you is that you will use your different talents to find out as much about him as you can. You, Webster, know the world of the court, you, Rafe, the middling part of life, and you, Jacko all the rogues and villains who infest London and those who use them for their own wicked ends. All three worlds intermingle, so to some extent you must also work with one another. I also have good friends whom I shall sound out. I want to know about his past as well as his present.'

'Good friends like Raleigh,' grinned Rafe.

'True, and he has already been very helpful to me. You must all be as hard-working and ruthless as the late Sir Francis Walsingham's agents were—and as careful too. You must bring to me at once anything you find which might prove useful.'

'And all this while you are getting married,' murmured Webster ruefully.

'Oh, life is not divided into convenient segments like an Act of Parliament, as you are beginning to find out,' was Martin's cheerful reply to that. 'I want you all at my wedding, and in your best clothes, and you, Jacko, must enlist Webster's help in that. He may hand me the bills for anything which might assist you to look a little more respectable.'

Webster closed his eyes, and opened them to see that Jacko was looking as mournful as he felt at the mere idea that he could ever look respectable. But orders were orders, and working for Martin Chancellor was, in many respects, the most rewarding task which he had ever engaged in.

'So noted,' he said, at last.

Martin ended the meeting and went to his own room to plan exactly what he intended to do on his wedding day. As usual, he was discovering that the most exciting and arousing thing about it was that he would be getting Kate into his bed when all the ceremonies were over.

Only two days to go now.

'Do you think that Lord Hadleigh will keep his word and be at St Paul's today for your wedding?'

Jennie was engaged in the daily ritual of dressing Kate—except that on this particular morning she was preparing her for her wedding. It was greatly daring of her to raise this matter with Kate so bluntly, but everyone in Bretford House—except some of the older servants—had been voicing their worries over the possibility of m'lord disappearing again as he had done once before.

'My answer must be yes,' Kate said, trying not to sound worried. 'He assured me most solemnly that he would be present and that he had no intention of betraying me in such a brutal fashion.'

'But he did run away once before.'

'He was only a boy then, and no one seems to know, or rather no one will tell me, why he was driven to such lengths as to leave his home and family and disappear for so many years. It is not a thing about which I can question him, either.'

Ever since she had first met him Kate had wondered why Martin had run away from his home and his life as Bretford's younger son. Rough and ready he might be, but he had never said or done anything which might lead her to believe that he would play such a scurvy trick on her—or on anyone else. Nevertheless, even after Mistress Cray's revelations, she could not help but feel anxious.

Perhaps everyone was right, everyone being the Lords Bretford, Clifton and Padworth, and apparently some in the servants' hall, too—except for Mistress Cray and those few who remembered him as a boy—

in believing that he would behave towards her as he had done towards his father and family in the past.

She recalled that in their short meeting John had never spoken of him to her, which was, perhaps, not surprising. Over the years since he had disappeared every reference to him—and there had not been many—had been of someone so unsatisfactory as a person that it must have been a relief to his father and his family that he had run away. There must have been a great deal of gossip about his disappearance at the time, but that had died down and over the years he had been forgotten until Lord Bretford became in desperate need of an heir.

What gave her hope that he would behave honourably was not only Martin himself, but also the boy in the portrait and Mistress Cray's belief in him. As well as that, there was the evidence of the respect the three men who were his constant companions had for their master. Their devotion to him was plain. Even Thomas Webster, who had joined him only recently, obviously admired him, and Webster was a young man of good family who possessed a great deal of common sense. His and their loyalty to, and open affection for, him could only be given to a good man.

At this point in her musings there was a knock on the door. Aunt Jocasta had arrived to give her approval of her niece's gown and of her general appearance. Her response at the sight of Kate's green and silver farthingale, her elegant bodice, her small, cream-coloured ruff and the care with which Jennie had dressed her chestnut tresses, which hung loose in token of her virginity, their only ornament being a circlet of small pearls, was a delighted one.

'You look as fine in that as I had hoped and expected. Lord Hadleigh will certainly be proud to acquire such a nonpareil for a wife.'

The way in which her aunt had come to accept Martin, after first criticising him every time she met him, was almost comical. Ever since the trip on the river, when Jacko had flattered her so outrageously, she had become the most devoted admirer of the new Lord Hadleigh and his retinue. She would not have a word said against any of them. On several occasions the three lords loudly dooming about him and his followers had evoked from her the most passionate defence.

Grateful for her support—which was such a change from the criticism which her aunt had always ladled over her—even though it made her laugh a little, Kate kissed her impulsively on her faded cheek.

'So you are not going to croak at me, like everyone else, about the possibility that Lord Hadleigh will not turn up to claim me.'

'No, indeed. I could see by the look in his eye when he was with you that he could scarce wait for the wedding to take place.'

Kate, for all her brave words to Jennie and her own belief in Martin's honour, still wished that she was as certain as Aunt Jocasta that he would not fail her. Preceded downstairs by the steward, she found the three Lords, also dressed in their grandest clothing, waiting for her in the entrance hall, together with Alison and Avis, her bridesmaids. They, too, were grandly dressed.

Avis, indeed, had complained that her heavy clothing quite diminished her, but for all that she would not have missed assisting Kate to the altar—the first of the three of them to marry. They both kissed and giggled at her and told her how splendid she looked in her wedding finery.

'But we shall not be known as the Three Graces from now on,' lamented Alison.

'We can be original and call ourselves the Two Graces,' offered Avis.

'It will not be the same, though.'

No, thought Kate, and even the Two Graces as a nickname would not have a long life, for both Alison and Avis were sure to marry soon and they would all go their separate ways.

Alison kissed her, and whispered in her ear, 'You are not to worry. I agree with your Aunt Jocasta that Lord Hadleigh will be there to marry you when you reach St Paul's. The boy in the portrait will not let you down.'

Kate was not surprised, however, when having approved of her appearance, the three Lords, like Jennie, privately complained to her that Hadleigh had not seen fit to remain at Bretford House, and expressed, yet once more, their doubts that he would have the goodness to turn up at St Paul's to celebrate his own marriage.

After the wedding party had assembled, they were led out in state to where several coaches and a number of outriders on horses waited to take them, and their attendants, to St Paul's. They had to make their way through crowded streets, constantly being held up by other coaches, as well as sheep, cows, horses, and carts laden with produce.

Kate could not help remarking, 'At our present rate of progress I think it most likely that my future husband is wondering whether *I* shall have the goodness to turn up to be married to him.'

Lord Clifton's frozen face—he was the only great man to travel on Kate's coach—told her how little he appreciated her mild attempt at wit.

'This is not a jesting matter,' he said reprovingly.

'Marriage rarely is,' was Kate's answer to that. She could not but remember how carelessly he had compelled her to accept Martin as her husband after his brother's death. Only the knowledge that she and Martin had reached some sort of understanding had enabled her to approach the coming ceremony without too many regrets to trouble her.

Finally St Paul's, that medieval monstrosity of a cathedral—no one could call it beautiful—came into view. There were no coaches or outriders waiting outside, so it seemed likely that Martin had not yet arrived. Passers-by stared curiously at them when they were assisted by footmen out of the coaches. They were ushered into the cathedral by one of the Canons: Martin and Kate were to be married by the Bishop. A few people sat in the pews at the back. Kate and Lord Clifton were asked to stand and wait some way away from the altar until the bridegroom should arrive.

'If he arrives,' was Lord Bretford's final comment before he took his seat, Lord Clifton nodding his head in agreement.

Time slowly passed. Kate's agitation grew—until through the open doors came the sound of commotion outside. A churchwarden ran up to the Bishop who walked slowly towards the door.

Martin Chancellor, Lord Hadleigh, had arrived to claim his bride.

To her surprise Kate's heart gave a great leap of pleasure—not just because she had been right to trust him and others had been wrong—but because for the first time she knew that she really wished to marry him.

The Bishop processed up the aisle, followed by two men who walked just behind him. In their rear were not only Martin's immediate retinue but a large number of other well-dressed personages, so that Martin's party greatly outnumbered that of Kate's entourage, large though it was. They seated themselves in the pews at the left of the altar.

The Bishop stepped forward. The three Lords stood up, and Kate turned to greet the newcomers.

But greet whom?

She, as well as some of the others, knew one of the men by sight. He was Sir Walter Raleigh, whom she had met on several occasions—but who was the man with him—and where was Martin?

The stranger was as tall as Martin, beautifully dressed in scarlet and gold, a costume which showed his powerful body and his long and shapely legs to the greatest advantage. His waving black hair, carefully trimmed, topped the clean-shaven face of the most handsome man Kate had ever seen. Only his bright blue eyes and his strong nose, almost that of an eagle, suddenly told her that it *was* Martin, divested of most of his hair and his careless seaman's loose and baggy clothing which had hidden his athletic body!

The Lords Bretford, Clifton and Padworth were equally confounded. They stared at this masculine vision of looks and fashion as though they had never seen such a splendid creature before. Kate's bridesmaids, standing just behind her gaped at this paragon of male beauty in wonder.

Lord Bretford quavered, 'Martin?'

At which his son bowed and said, 'Yes, sir?'

'Is it indeed you?'

'Who else? Since I am here to marry the Honourable Lady Katherine Wyville, to whom I am contracted.' And this time he bowed to Kate. 'Although I am sure that you are all aware of who my companion is, I must still have the honour to present to you my friend, Sir Walter Raleigh, who will assist me as groomsman in this morning's enterprise.'

Stunned though they were, everyone bowed and tried to pretend that matters were going according to their preconceived notions of Martin Chancellor's possible behaviour—to say nothing of his appearance. The bridesmaids, remembering the boy in the portrait, were not so greatly surprised. They curtsied to him, their admiration of him written plain on their faces.

Oh, yes, if this were the bridegroom then Cousin Kate was a very lucky woman!

Suddenly Kate wanted to laugh. She caught an answering gleam in Walter Raleigh's eye, and knew that he was amused too. Everyone in and around the court knew of Sir Walter's pranks and jests, and here he was involved in yet another of them.

Lord Bretford quavered again, 'Sir Walter is your friend?'

It was Sir Walter who answered him, not Martin. 'For these many years. I first met Lord Hadleigh not long after he sailed against the Armada, and since he chose to mention the word honour in my connection, I must inform you that I am honoured to have him for my friend.'

The Bishop, who had been trying not to stare too hard while he witnessed the confusion which Martin's arrival—and his unexpected appearance—had caused in the bride's party, said, 'You are here to be married.'

It was almost a question.

Kate and Martin said 'Yes' together.

'Excellent,' said the Bishop, motioning to the organist to start playing again. He had stopped on hearing the commotion created by Martin's arrival.

After that the service proceeded in the usual orderly fashion. Lord Clifton escorted Kate towards the altar, her bridesmaids behind her: Martin waited some way away down the aisle, an amused Sir Walter by his side, until he strode up the aisle to stand beside her.

Aunt Jocasta, who had been the recipient of a low bow from Jacko before he took his seat, thought that her niece had never looked so beautiful. It was Martin, though, on whom she gazed the most.

She could see some slight resemblance in him to his elder brother, but who would have thought, knowing his previous uncouth appearance, that he could possibly look like the impressively handsome man who now stood by her niece's side—and to have Sir Walter Raleigh as a friend? Not that Aunt Jocasta altogether approved of Sir Walter. Whatever had possessed Martin Chancellor that he should have dressed and behaved in such a fashion as to make his father believe that he had become a common seaman—and had remained one—after he had fled his home?

That he was rich was plain. The pearl in his ear—which rivalled that of Sir Walter—the gold chain around his neck, and all his apparel served to reveal his wealth, something which Kate, standing by him, had also grasped.

Kate was so consumed by her unsatisfied curiosity

on seeing Martin in his new incarnation that the marriage service of which she was a central part passed her by in a highly coloured blur. She scarcely heard her uncle give her away, and only some faint remnant of her usual calm control of life remained to help her to make the right responses at the right time.

A thousand questions were running through her mind—matched only by those which were troubling the three Lords—particularly Martin's father. He knew now that his son had consistently lied to him ever since he had walked through the doors of Bretford House for the first time in fourteen years.

To what end?

Realisation dawned even as the wedding ceremony reached its conclusion.

To punish him, of course, to trick him and to ensure that he looked a fool. He had even suborned Webster away from his service to make his masquerade complete. What puzzled him, and the other two Lords, was that they had never heard of anyone called Martin Chancellor being wealthy enough to provide the kind of consequence with which his son was surrounded.

Unless, of course, the whole thing was a jest organised by Sir Walter. But that cock would not fight, for even Sir Walter would not have pledged his own honour as to his friendship with Martin. Like Kate, the wedding ceremony passed him by until the ring was on Kate's finger, she was securely Lady Hadleigh, and the future of the Chancellor name, God willing and Martin permitting, was now secure.

Martin, who had caused the whirling emotions with which he was surrounded, was the only calm person in the cathedral. He had been enjoying himself mightily ever since Kate and the three Lords had clapped eyes on him, and was also happily participating in his second wedding ceremony in the secret knowledge that no one present knew of the first.

He had thought to feel sad, to remember Mary and her eager little face when he had kissed her afterwards, but it was as though, once his decision to marry Kate had taken place, she had begun to sail away from him, across the blue sea on which she had sailed towards him eight years ago.

Even so, Martin was sure that he could never feel for Kate the abiding love which he had felt for his first wife. He told himself that it was only his body which was reacting to her so strongly, not his heart and mind. He had given them away once and for all. He would try to be a good and kind husband, to do his duty by her, but he could never surrender himself to her as he had once done to Mary. He could only hope that Kate would feel the same towards him: that love, the dream of which the poets and playwrights sang, was not, and never would be, part of their life together.

The service over, he gave her his strong arm and escorted her to his coach. Immediately after he had helped her into it, he was approached by his agitated father.

'Hadleigh, I was not expecting that such a crowd

as you have brought along would attend the wedding breakfast and consequently there will not be enough to feed them. What…'

He got no further. Martin put a hand on his father's shoulder. 'Do not trouble yourself. I have already arranged that a large supply of food and drink would arrive at Bretford House shortly after you had left for St Paul's. My butler and some of my servants accompanied it in order to help your staff have the feast ready for the guests by the time that we reached home after the service had ended. I have also invited the Bishop and the two Canons to accompany us.'

This answer only served to agitate his father the more. 'Hadleigh,' he said, 'I do not understand you. How can you pay for this? How in the world did Sir Walter Raleigh become your friend?'

Martin's smile was not kind, even though his action in ensuring that his father had not been shamed by being unable to provide a feast large enough for all his guests had been a generous and thoughtful one.

'Everything will be revealed,' he replied, 'when the guests have gone. Until then you must exercise the kind of patience which I have had to live with for so long. Allow me to leave you now, to rejoin my bride.'

Lord Clifton, who had been listening, asked Lord Bretford anxiously, 'He did not reveal the truth of his changed appearance to you?'

'No, indeed. Merely told me to be patient.'

For Lord Bretford the tables had been turned, or,

to put it another way, he was now dancing to his younger son's tune as that son had once been compelled to dance to his.

Kate, seated by Martin, was longing to ask him all the questions which would solve the mystery of how and why he had changed from the man she thought that she had known to the one whom she knew no longer. Delicacy, and a certain measure of fear, kept her quiet. She fiddled with her hair, twisted the ring on her finger, and tried to stop herself from wriggling, for the new Martin was having an even stronger and more disturbing effect on her than the old one had done.

Martin was well aware of what was distracting his bride, and, for once, was not sure what to say to her. He put his large hand over her small, restless one.

'What is it, wife? I am sure that you are as puzzled as my father and his friends by what has happened here today. I am sorry that I could not tell you of my coming transformation, but I am sure that you will come to understand why I kept quiet.'

For some reason this calm answer infuriated Kate. 'No, I don't. I don't understand why couldn't tell me what you were about to do, and I don't understand why you felt it necessary to behave like a character in a bad play—by pretending to be what you are not.'

This outburst surprised no one more than Kate herself. At first she had been amused by Martin's sudden reappearance, but, now that the wedding ceremony was over, amusement had been followed by curiosity and by anger.

How—and why—could he have deceived them all so greatly? Did he not owe her, the woman who was to be his wife, more than that—in short, the truth? Would she never be able to detect when he was lying to her, as he had done so often in the past, sometimes implicitly, if not explicitly? Had he not deceived her by taking her to the alley off Forge Street and allowing her to assume that the house there was his only home when it so obviously was not?

Now she could quite believe in his bad behaviour, the behaviour which had led him to desert his proper place in life, where, before the present morning's revelations, she had come to question it because of his kindness to her and even more, the manifest loyalty of his attendants.

Their loyalty was now explained. It was that of dependants towards their rich master. But how had he become so rich? Sir Walter had spoken of him as sailing against the Armada, but that did not reveal how he had acquired his undoubted wealth.

Martin was dismayed by Kate's change of mood. Later he was to acknowledge how betrayed she must have felt when she recalled his many deceptions, but sitting in the coach, after being so roundly reproached, he could only feel that, once more, he had been rejected, and this time by his new wife.

When they alighted before Bretford House he offered her his arm but, although Kate accepted it, she kept her face resolutely turned away from him. He could almost feel her distress. Her rigid body, her pallor, told him of her disillusionment, of her loss of faith in him.

Over the last fourteen years he thought that he had become so hardened by the harsh treatment which he had suffered in his early life that he no longer cared for the opinion of others. Whether they judged him rightly or wrongly had been nothing to him, but Kate's turning away from him after their recent happy rapport told him that the hard shell he had created round his heart had been breached by her.

The pain which this was causing him was all the greater because he had the memory of Mary's unquestioning trust in him—but then he had never deceived her. To her he had always been the simple sailor whom she had met and married before success had transformed him and his life.

What a fool he had been! In his pursuit of some sort of revenge over his unloving father he had sacrificed more than he had intended. Love her or not, he had come to value Kate, to look forward to their married life, and now he had lost her.

No! He would not lose her. One way or another he would regain her confidence, if not her love and if that took time, then he had learned patience in a hard school.

The wedding breakfast was even more splendid than Lord Bretford had intended. Martin's butler had taken charge: like his master he had overridden all objections. The tables really groaned under the weight of the food and drink on them. The bride and groom sat at the middle of the long one, in the only arm-chairs in the room. Both of them were careful to hide their true feelings by giving the appearance of a happiness which they did not feel because they knew that they owed a duty to their guests and were determined to fulfil it.

Lord Bretford had wanted the marriage feast to be a rich yet subdued occasion. He had little enthusiasm for parading his unkempt and worthless second son before his family and friends. But Martin's intervention had turned it into a grand and jolly one.

The bridesmaids, giggling and wriggling harder than ever, found themselves sitting beside Martin's friends, many of them young, some with wives and some of them members, like Sir Walter, of the Friday Club. Others present included those important folk whom Martin had met in his life as a wealthy captain and merchant—the details of which he had not yet had the opportunity to reveal to his father or his bride.

The three Lords, also sitting in some state, gazed in wonder at the scene around them. Sir Walter, who was nearby, toasted them before saying, 'M'lord Bretford, your son may always be trusted to ensure that any ceremony for which he is responsible is a happy and successful one.' It was not an observation which Martin's father wished to hear!

Lord Bretford therefore found himself unable to

speak: he merely nodded his head in apparent agreement. When Sir Walter had subsided and had started to pay attention to Aunt Jocasta, who sat on his left, Lord Clifton leaned over and hissed at his fellow Lord, 'Are you aware that that uncouth servant of Hadleigh's has been invited to the feast? Of all things, he is sitting over there beside one of my Clifton nephews!'

'Jacko! You mean that Jacko is one of the guests?'

'Aye, and his other servant, too. Rafe something— but at least he looks as though he might be one of the regular guests—while the Jacko fellow looks like what he is.'

Lord Bretford closed his eyes. 'Is there no end to his deceit and folly?'

Lord Clifton muttered enviously, 'But, at the least, he seems to have made himself a rich man, if what I have already overheard is true. The future of the Bretford estates is more than ensured even without the addition of my niece's wealth.'

Lord Bretford grunted. It was beyond him to praise his younger son in any way. He looked across at Martin where he sat in all his splendour, smiling a little each time someone rose to toast the bride and groom. His one regret was that it was not John whom the day was celebrating. The food he tried to eat nearly choked him, and although he raised his goblet every now and then to yet another cry of 'All happiness to the bride and groom', the liquid in it did not diminish.

Lord Clifton, on the other hand, was in the process of drinking himself stupid. And no wonder, for had he not married his niece to a man who was already rich, whose wealth was in the here and now, who without it would have needed to wait until his father's death gave him the Bretford lands. For the moment he would enjoy the almost royal feast which lay before him. In token of his acceptance of him, he toasted Martin with the words, 'All honour to my niece and her husband.'

Martin and Kate responded immediately. Kate, like Lord Bretford, was finding it difficult to eat, but, unlike him, was finding it easy to drink. Each drop she drank made her feel more and more light-hearted, so much so that she was beginning to forgive Martin for his deceits. Owlishly, she tried to tell him so. Her manner was such that he took the goblet from her.

'How many of those have you drunk, while not eating anything?'

She blinked at him. 'I can't remember.'

Martin snorted and then began to laugh. 'So that is why you are forgiving me, then. It is but the drink talking. If you wish to walk to our bed, as a bride should, instead of being carried there, you must drink no more, but eat a little instead.' And he took a piece of pie from his platter and laid it on hers.

'Come, madam wife, begin to please your husband by obeying his first command to you.'

'And if I do not—for I think that food would choke, not sustain, me—what then?'

'Then I shall sue for divorce on the instant, you naughty creature. I did not think that I had taken a toper for a wife.'

Kate thought a moment. There was something which she ought to say to that, but what could it be? Ah, she had it—or had she?

'Since I have never before drunk more than a gobletful I cannot be called a toper; therefore your action would fail.'

To her surprise she had begun to find talking lucidly very difficult, something which Martin thought ought to be rectified immediately. He picked up the piece of pie from her platter, held it to her mouth and commanded sternly, 'Eat!' but his eyes were twinkling.

He looked so handsome, so different from the bear he had been, that she ought to be pleased by his transformation yet, astonishingly, Kate found that she was missing the bear. It had been easy to talk to him, to bait him a little—as one ought to bait a bear—but this sparkling gallant, whom reason said that she ought to admire the more, almost frightened her with his perfection. Nor could she refuse him, for in some indefinable way she found him forbidding.

So much so that, obeying him, she accepted the titbit which—yet another surprise—tasted like manna and revived her appetite immediately.

Perhaps it was time that she gave *him* an order. 'More, please,' she managed, sounding quite haughty, almost like the Queen, whom she had once seen send-

ing her courtiers to and fro, here and there, each word
from her a command which they dared not disobey.
Despite the haughtiness, she could not prevent herself
from smiling at him—it must be the hippocras which
was confusing, as well as fuddling her!

Now this was more like the Kate whom Martin had
come to know! He picked up her platter and heaped
it with slices of beef, of pie, of buttered eggs and of
the large cheese from the feast which covered the table, and topped the whole thing off with bread before
he laid it before her.

'Will that do, Lady Hadleigh—or do you wish for
more?'

More! Despite her reviving appetite, Kate stared at
this mountain of plenty with horror. He had, however,
been so obliging, and the smile he was offering her
with the food was the one which she had come to
know so well, being a marriage between teasing and
affection, that she thanked him profusely, saying, 'I
think so, but should I need more, you may provide
it.'

It was true, she found, that after she had eaten a
large part of it the drink she had taken ceased to confound her—as he had promised. To her surprise she
managed to empty the platter completely and when
Martin offered her a sugared cake, she discovered that
she was able to eat that too.

Time passed all too quickly, though, and the moment which Kate had been dreading, the ceremonial
procession of the whole company which would escort

them both to the bridal bed, grew nearer and nearer. The bride cake had been brought in, together with baskets of oats with which the guests would shower the newly-weds on their way to bed. Slices of the cake were handed around, particularly large pieces being reverently laid before the newly married pair, after the Bishop had blessed them with a rather lengthy prayer.

Kate thought that she was not the only one who had had too much to drink, for his prayer grew rather muddled towards its end, although the company, all of whom were now extremely merry themselves, did not seem to notice that he had lost his way.

She did notice, however, that Martin drank sparingly, and when she put out a hand to help herself to some more hippocras, he gently lifted it away from its pitcher, and said, 'I have cured you once, lady wife, I do not wish to have to do so again.'

His voice was kind, though, and looking around the table, where even Aunt Jocasta was behaving in a manner most unlike herself, and which she would deeply regret on the morrow, Kate decided that perhaps sobriety *was* the best bet. Martin whispered to her when she had reluctantly let go of the pitcher, 'Now that you have made our guests happy by showing how much you enjoyed the food, you must eat your bride cake, and be ready to demonstrate your pleasure with the rest of the ceremony before we are left alone together.'

Now that was going to be harder, much harder.

Aunt Jocasta had told her what would be expected of her, and from the few marriages which Kate had attended, she knew that she had been telling the truth.

'I wish,' she began, and then stopped. 'I wish that we could have been married privately and been spared the bridal feast and the bedding. I do not like public consequence.'

'I agree with you,' he told her, suddenly quiet, 'and I even asked my father and your uncle to allow us to be married quietly at Bretford House—or your country home—with a feast for close members of the family only, but they were adamant that the ceremony should be as public as possible. To celebrate it hugger-mugger, they said, might look as though they were ashamed of the marriage.'

'No one asked *me* what I wanted,' returned Kate mournfully.

'We are the prisoners of our families,' Martin said, 'when it comes to marriage and giving in marriage. What can't be cured must be endured, I'm afraid. Our only weapon is to look happy and not give them cause to reproach us.'

To Martin's surprise, Kate began to laugh.

'What amuses you, wife?'

'Is that why you arrived this morning looking quite unlike the self which you have shown to us all since you returned to your father's home? Did you think it would please him, or annoy him, to see such a change in you?'

'You know full well that I hoped to annoy him.'

'Because your father prefers to think of you as a poverty-stricken vagabond, it would not make him happy to see you dressed like a fit friend for Sir Walter Raleigh?'

'Exactly.'

'Even if he would be likely to reproach you for springing such a surprise on him?'

'It makes him happy to reproach me. He does not wish to praise me—he never did.'

From all Kate had seen and heard during her stay at Bretford House, that statement was sadly true.

'Do you not wish to forget the past and be reconciled with him?'

Martin's smile was a painful one. To reinforce it he shook his head. 'Alas, so long as he continues to think of me as his worthless son there is no chance of that.'

Kate dare not pursue the matter further, since for all his outward bravado it was plain that Martin was deeply hurt by his father's behaviour towards him. Nor was a wedding feast the proper place to discuss such unhappy matters. Impulsively she put out her right hand to grasp his left in an attempt to comfort him. He responded by squeezing it gently before releasing it so that she might reply to yet another toast, this time from Jacko, something which displeased Lord Bretford mightily.

Even her worries over what would happen when they were finally alone together in bed could not prevent her from giving a little shiver of pleasure at his touch, something which had been unaccountably absent since he had walked into the cathedral and she had first seen him in his splendid clothes.

'Thank you, madam wife,' Martin whispered to her once the toasting was over.

The feast finally reached its end. The boar's head had almost disappeared under the attentions of the carver, the cold meat pies had disappeared with the rest of the food which had been eagerly snatched up by the guests, the bride cake had been eaten.

The musicians, who were stationed in a corner of the Great Hall, now stopped playing merry songs and began to play a march—the signal that the feasting was over for the time being, plenty of food having been kept in reserve—and that the preliminaries to the bedding of the happy pair were due to start.

Lord Bretford's chief steward led Martin and Kate forward, the bridesmaids and Aunt Jocasta following, while the entire company, flown with wine and ale, clapped and cheered them. Lord Bretford's vision of a quiet and decorous ceremony was dead and gone. On the way Kate's gown was robbed of many of its bows by the guests, taking them both for luck and for souvenirs.

Aunt Jocasta and the bridesmaids led Kate upstairs to the bedroom which had been decorated in readiness for the happy pair and where the covers had been stripped from the bridal bed—a great four-poster which had gilt Viscount's coronets on top of each of its corners. There they helped her to undress. Her stockings and garters they kept to throw to the guests later.

Once she was in her elaborate nightgown, word was sent to Martin, who had been led by his friends to another bedroom where he, too, was undressed and helped into a linen nightgown with a pie frill around its neck. Kate could hear the cheering and the noise of the jests, many of them explicit, which accompanied this ritual, but fortunately for her she could not distinguish the words.

Next came the part which she had been dreading the most. Martin was brought in, followed first by the Bishop, who intoned yet another prayer, and then by the rest of the guests, who shouted encouragement to them both when Martin at last climbed on to the bed. It was at this point that Kate's garters, stockings and any remaining bows were thrown to the multitude to scramble for.

Martin's expression when he looked at his bride's white face was a rueful one. 'Courage,' he whispered to her, 'it will soon be over.'

'Kiss her, kiss the bride,' many of their audience bellowed at him, while others gave him even plainer instructions as to what was expected of him—and of Kate—once they were alone.

He duly did as he was bid. He felt Kate shiver beneath his kiss and did not know whether it was passion or fear which moved her—perhaps it was a mixture of the two. The merriment continued. Someone brought them a posset to drink. Martin handed the cup to Kate, who took a sip or two from it and then handed it back to him. He made sure that he drank the honey-sweet liquid at the place where her lips had touched it—which brought another cheer from the increasingly rowdy assembly.

Rafe came over to collect the cup and to slip a sheet over them. Now that he was near to her he could see that Kate was suffering the attentions of the guests rather than enjoying them. He took the empty cup from Martin, who had valiantly drunk all of its contents, and turning towards the crowd behind him bellowed, 'It is time to leave our friends to enjoy the marriage bed on their own.'

At which Aunt Jocasta clapped, Lord Bretford nodded a dour agreement, and the whole company streamed downstairs to finish off the remaining food and drink before reeling out into the cold evening.

# Chapter Seven

It was over.

Kate leaned back against her pillows and murmured, 'Thanks be to God,' although she knew that, for her, the most difficult part of this long day was still to come.

'Amen,' said Martin. 'I must confess that I have enjoyed being one of the guests at a wedding in the past, and it never occurred to me how upsetting it must have been for the bride and groom.'

'Particularly the bride,' Kate said with feeling.

'And for the groom, too. I believe that our forefathers often insisted on waiting until the groom had performed his husbandly duties before they left, something which would have made it hard for me to perform at all!'

'Well, I'm happy to learn that that particular custom has disappeared,' Kate told him. 'What remains was bad enough.'

'But not what we are about to do,' said Martin.

'That, I hope, will not be bad at all. I shall try to make it a pleasure for you, as well as for me.'

It was his often unexpected kindnesses which undid Kate and made her think that he might truly come to love her, as she was beginning to love him, whichever face he showed her—that of the bear or of the courtly gallant. Even so, she shivered a little.

Martin leaned over her. 'You must not be afraid of me, Kate. I shall try not to hurt you.'

'I know,' she faltered, trying to avoid his steady gaze, 'but there is something I must tell you.'

'Which is?'

'That I have no notion of what being a true wife for my husband will mean—other than that you will do more than kiss me. Aunt Jocasta has told me nothing, except that to be married and in bed with a man is a woman's painful cross which she must bear without complaining.'

Martin snorted. 'Much she knows about it—but are you telling me the truth, Kate? Are you really so ignorant?'

Miserably, she nodded. 'Yes. It is stupid, I know. But my mother died long ago. I have had few women friends and no one has seen fit to tell me anything about married life—other than that I must do as my husband bids me.'

Martin stifled an oath addressed at Aunt Jocasta and all those women in poor Kate's life who had left her unaware of those things which lie between a man and his wife. This was the second unknowing virgin whom he had married, and he would need to be as patient with Kate as he had been with Mary.

He had constantly told himself that he did not love Kate, but he knew that he lusted after her and wished to initiate her into the pleasures of marriage—which, of course, he would enjoy all the more if she were his willing partner.

'Look at me, wife,' he said, 'I shall go as slowly as I am able, which will be difficult for me since I have been longing to make you my true wife ever since our marriage was decided on. I shall have to hurt you somewhat when we, at last, become one, but I hope that the hurt will be a slight one. After it, I trust, we shall enjoy ourselves as man and wife were meant to.'

'Are you saying,' Kate asked him gravely, a twinkle in her eye for the first time since they had left the Great Hall, 'that you are going to be my tutor?'

'Yes, but if we continue to talk, and not to act, my patience will be sorely tried.'

'Then, m'lord Hadleigh, you must begin my first lesson at once. I will try to be an apt pupil, but you must forgive me if I make a few mistakes.'

Martin began to laugh. He could tell that Kate was a little fearful of what the next few minutes might bring, but that was the true virgin's prerogative. 'Oh,' he exclaimed, 'you have made my task the easier. Come nearer to me, sweeting,' for she had edged away from him once the last guest had reeled from the bedroom.

Kate was suddenly all obedience. She did as she was bid, so he kissed her on the cheek.

'Is that the beginning?' she asked. 'If so, it seems easy enough.'

'True. Now you must allow me to kiss and stroke you a little, and if you are so inclined you may kiss and stroke me, too.'

So saying he kissed her, not on the lips, but on the cheek, and then the neck, before finding her lips and kissing her there, gently at first and then more passionately. At the same time he stroked her neck above her nightgown. Kate gasped her pleasure. If to touch his hand had been so exciting in its effect on her, his kisses, particularly the last ones on her lips, pleasured her much the more—to say nothing of that which his stroking hands had given her. Her body rose to meet his, for he had manoeuvred her slowly on to her back, and when he pulled away she found herself stroking and kissing him, as he had asked of her.

Martin, his whole body thrumming with desire, to the degree that he was almost in pain, said hoarsely, 'You liked that—shall we move on to the next lesson?'

Kate managed, 'Please.'

'The next one might be a little more difficult for you. If we are to truly enjoy ourselves, we must be transformed as the first man and woman were, naked and unashamed, even if they were thrown out of Eden for their behaviour. If all goes well, I hope that we shall find ourselves in that happy place before we sleep—so allow me to relieve you of your nightgown and then you must help me to remove mine.'

Kate realised that Martin was talking to her at such length and so gently in order to dispel her natural fear. She smiled shyly at him when they were finally naked. It was not so much that she was troubled by him seeing her unclothed, but that the sight of a superb and roused male body was such an unexpected one.

Words burst from her. 'Does that hurt you?'

Martin knew exactly what she meant. 'Yes, but not as you might think, my wife. It is you, and you alone, who can now give me relief from pain there.'

'I can?'

'Yes, and now we must continue with your lesson, for hard though it might be for me to delay the final act, unless I make you ready to take pleasure in it, then I shall have failed you as a husband.'

He kissed her and stroked her again, touching this time parts of her body which Kate had always thought of as private to her alone. The pleasure which he had promised her was already with her. Her body was an instrument on which he played, and the music which he was creating was her moans and sighs of delight.

Was it possible that her pleasure could be even greater? Indeed, it could, for his right hand had reached her very core, was stroking it, oh, so gently, even though the ecstasy it finally produced was so overwhelming that she cried out at the moment of climax, losing herself in a great wave of pleasure, until she fell, shuddering, back on the bed.

Martin, having given his bride pleasure at the expense of his own, was shuddering himself. When she looked up at him, her eyes wild, he asked her, 'You liked that?'

'You know I did. I had not expected—I did not know... But you, is that your only part in this?'

'No, indeed, for in a moment we shall reach the end of the lesson when we shall try to enjoy our pleasure together. As you accepted my hand, you must now accept me.' And he began the final stage of Kate's initiation.

To Martin's young bride what happened next was so all-consuming and so unexpected that even the pain of his entry could not overcome her willingness to please him as he had pleased her.

At her cry of pain he paused, only to have her exclaim, 'Oh, do not stop. I wish to share everything with you.'

And so she did, for after pain came pleasure, not quite so great as the first, but since she shared it with him it meant more, so very much more, to her. It was as though they had climbed a steep hill together and at the top had been briefly translated into another world where instead of two they had become truly one.

Martin was the first to awake in the early hours of the following morning. He propped himself on his elbow and looked down at his sleeping wife. He remembered that Mary had been frightened that first night, and that it had taken a little time for him to give her pleasure because her fear of the act of love remained so powerful. It had also taken him some time to enable Mary to experience with him the pleasure which he had enjoyed from the first night he had bedded her.

It had been so very different with Kate. Her frank, if artless, response to his caresses had been manifest as soon as she had understood that she had nothing to fear from him. It had not taken long for her to be ready to accept him and to revel in their joint ecstasy.

He had refused to make love to her again before they slept, lest he cause her further pain. She had demurred a little at that, but he had reassured her with, 'Let us wait until tomorrow morning. By then you may have healed a little and will be the more ready for me.'

'I had not thought that you would be so kind,' she had told him.

'It is not kind, but right and proper that you should enjoy yourself as much as I do when we make love.' And then he lowered his head and kissed her tenderly. She gave a little moan and rolled over on to the haven of his broad breast. They were still naked, and the thought of that, and the promise he had given her, caused him to kiss her again, not quite so gently, so that she opened her eyes and asked, 'Is it morning?'

'Not yet, and when morning comes and we do awake we must pleasure ourselves immediately, since Aunt Jocasta, your bridesmaids and all who care to accompany them will arrive as early as possible to inspect the bed sheets in order to discover whether you were truly virgin.'

Kate sat up sharply.

'I had forgotten that. At the only weddings which I have ever attended I was not allowed to take part in the rituals of the bedchamber.'

'Well, you may be sure that we shall not be spared them. We must remember to put on our nightgowns so that we may appear to be seemly.'

'What a lot of things we have to remember,' said Kate sleepily.

'True.' And then, holding her gently in his arms they slept the sleep of the truly satisfied until morning at last arrived.

Nor were they, as he had prophesied, spared anything. Before Martin had time to celebrate the new day with her, there came a knock on the door and Aunt Jocasta and a train of eager spectators entered.

Kate was rousted out of bed and wrapped in a long brocaded coat, as was Martin. The covers were thrown back to reveal the stained bottom sheet, which one of Aunt Jocasta's acolytes seized and held up so that all might witness that Kate had indeed gone virgin to the marriage bed.

A servant came in carrying a tray with mead on it for the bride and groom. Other servants carried in ale for the spectators. More toasts were drunk, so much so that Kate feared that Aunt Jocasta's acolytes would not be able to walk safely down the stairs to where more food had been prepared so that they might all be able to break their fast.

At last Aunt Jocasta shooed everyone out, excepting Jacko, who insisted on giving her his arm so that she might go downstairs in safety— 'As though,' she later said to Kate with a laugh, 'I had been drinking hard with the rest of them. But it was kind of him, all the same.'

Once they were alone, Martin sank back on the bed, and catching Kate to him, announced firmly, 'Now we may enjoy ourselves again.'

And so they did.

Later Martin walked downstairs to break his fast. He had arranged that Kate should enjoy her first meal as a married woman in their room, so that she would be spared inquisitive eyes and double-edged conversation over her food.

He had barely had time to sit down before his father's steward entered. 'M'lord, my master has asked that you attend upon him, and Lord Clifton, in his study so soon as you have finished eating.'

'So noted,' Martin said, beginning to devour several slices of cold roast beef. The night's exertions, followed by the morning's, had left him hungry, particularly since he had eaten little at the wedding feast. He knew why his father wished to see him and deliberately took his time over his meal. Most of yesterday's guests had left the night before and only a yawning Rafe sat opposite to him.

'When do we go home?' he asked.

'As soon as possible,' said Martin briefly. 'I have no wish to remain here any longer than I need,' something which he intended to tell his father shortly.

The face his father offered him when he entered his study was a choleric one.

'So, here you are at last, Hadleigh. I trust that you will be good enough to explain to me—and to Lords Clifton and Padworth—from whence came this sudden affluence which you chose to demonstrate yesterday after presenting me with the aspect of a beggar since you returned home.'

'This place, whatever else it is, is not my home. That is elsewhere,' said Martin, his voice as low and deadly as he could make it. 'For your own ends you strove to find me, and when you did you found me using my birth name, Martin Chancellor, as a jest when I wished to enjoy myself away from the wealth and consequence which I had created for myself by my own exertions.

'It was not the name which I took when I left home. To avoid being found by you—and punished yet again—I called myself Andrew Martin and went to sea, at first against the Armada. By great good fortune I early found a patron, who admired my seaman's abilities and my devotion to duty as I endeavoured to better myself in the harsh world in which I had chosen to live when I fled from what was called my home.'

It was Lord Clifton who interrupted him. 'Andrew Martin, you say? Can it be that you are the Captain

Andrew Martin who made himself a fortune by his successful attacks on the galleons carrying treasure back to Spain from the New World, and who then became a merchant? The man who refused a knight-hood?'

Martin bowed his head. 'It is as you say. I am that man. My home is Saxon Hall in Bishopsgate. And yes, I refused a knighthood. I wish to be my own man and not the servant of anyone powerful, even if that person were my Queen. I have seen what hardships befell my friend, Sir Walter, when he failed to please his monarch. I do not wish to share them.'

His father who had been staring at him, speechless, spoke at last.

'Can this be true?'

'I do not lie, sir, and never did—whatever you may once have thought of me.'

'You lied when you came here in the guise of a vagabond.'

'Nay, I called myself Martin Chancellor, which was no lie, and you never once cared to ask me what I had been doing in the years since you last saw me. Had you done so, I would have told you the truth. You deceived yourself. You saw what you wished to see—and were happy in the seeing.'

It was the other two Lords who nodded at this, not his father, who said, 'Nevertheless you lied by infer-ence when you chose to confound us by arriving dressed and behaving as one of Captain Andrew Martin's seamen might have done—without telling us what you had become. You did not tell the truth until the morning of your wedding.'

Martin said coldly, 'I owed it to my future wife to be married in the appearance of my true self. I regret that I felt unable to tell her the full truth before I had informed you of it.'

Now Martin knew that he *was* lying. He had kept quiet because he had wished to savour to the full his father's surprise when he had turned up in the full might of his wealth, and yes, his power, with his friend, Sir Walter Raleigh, by his side. He knew that Raleigh's nickname—given to him by those who feared him—was Lucifer, but Raleigh had always played fair with him as he, in return, had tried to play fair with all those he had met in his life as Andrew Martin. If he had not played fair with his father, it was because his father did not deserve that honour.

He said, bowing to the three Lords, 'I shall straightway inform my wife of all that you have learned this morning—and before we leave for her new home, I assure you all that, whatever you might believe of me, I shall treat her kindly and be as good a husband to her as a man may be.'

It was Lord Clifton who answered him. 'I think, Lord Hadleigh, for that is your title by right, that my niece is a lucky young woman, since you bring to her as much, if not more, than she brings to you.'

Lord Bretford said sourly, 'I shall let time decide that for me. Leopards do not change their spots.'

'What a very true remark, sir,' said Martin sweetly,

'seeing that I have not changed my spots. I am still the same man that I was when your mistreatment of me caused me to flee Bretford House. And now I must leave to inform my wife that we shall be returning to Saxon Hall, which will become her home as well as mine.'

With that he bowed low, and left them. From what had been said Lords Clifton and Padworth—although the latter had said little—were prepared to accept him for what he now was. His father, though, remained implacable.

Kate, fully dressed after a hearty breakfast, was pondering on the married state. What surprised her was how much she had enjoyed herself in Martin's arms. True, she was a little sore, but she could not regret the pleasure which had brought that about.

One thing puzzled her a little, and that was the state of Martin's back, which was covered in long-healed scars, as well as what was evidently a branded T on his left shoulder. Elsewhere his body was flawless. She knew little of life, but she was fully aware that at some time he had been cruelly beaten, perhaps more than once—she could not imagine why he had been branded.

Curious though she was, Kate had said nothing about any of this to him, for she knew, without being told, that he would not wish her to question him about it. Especially when some instinct which she had not known that she possessed, informed her that the beatings had almost certainly been inflicted on him during his early life at Bretford House. It could not have been at sea, for he must have behaved well enough there for him to have risen so rapidly towards fame and fortune. No sailor who deserved a flogging would ever have been allowed advancement. It was yet another of the mysteries which surrounded him—and not a pleasant one.

Jennie had just finished fastening her sleeves to her dress when Martin came in. She knew at once, before he spoke, that something had troubled him, had made him angry, even though he was perfectly polite to her. Perhaps it was his very studied politeness which gave him away.

Another instinct told her not to press him on what had disturbed him.

'M'lord,' she said, somewhat tentatively.

'Husband,' he said, a brief smile appearing as he spoke, 'not m'lord—or Martin, if you would prefer that. I think of Lord Hadleigh as my brother.'

Kate smiled, 'But I think of him as my husband.'

That brought her another smile. They had been standing while they spoke, and Jennie had slipped discreetly out of the room.

'Pray sit, my logic-chopping wife. I shall have to set Webster on to you. He has a talent for it, too,' he told her, and added, when the smile had faded, 'I have something to tell you.'

Kate did as she was bid, spreading her ample skirts around her. She had wished to wear something simple, but Jennie had said, 'Lord, no, m'lady, your dress must be fine now in order to do honour to your husband,' and had immediately fetched out one of the more splendid gowns in her trousseau.

Kate thought, naughtily, that Martin probably preferred her with nothing on at all, but she did not tell Jennie so, nor did she now tell Martin.

Once they were comfortably settled, he at last told her the truth of his past, but gently, and not after the manner in which he had spoken to his father and the two lords.

'I am sorry to have deceived you, but you must understand that I do not regret that I deceived him. If you feel that you wish to reproach me, then do so— it is no more than I deserve from you.'

What Kate understood was that he had run away from home with nothing more than the clothes he was wearing, and that, by dint of hard work and his own enterprise, he had made himself a rich man, respected by those who knew him only as Captain Andrew Martin, and not as Lord Bretford's black sheep of a son.

'Any desire which I may have had to reprove you for deceiving me flies away in the face of what you achieved after you left Bretford House. Of your behaviour to your father I cannot speak, since I do not know why he treated you in such a fashion that you fled the comfortable home into which you were born to make your own way in the world.

'I can only speak of the man I know and whom I

have come to respect. I trust in your judgement, husband, as I hope that you will trust in mine now that we are married.'

The expression which Martin offered her was one of relief. He had been prepared for anything except the measured words which Kate had just used to him. His wife was a woman of many surprises and he could only hope they would always be pleasant ones.

'That being so,' he said, 'I hope you will not oppose my decision to leave Bretford House at once. The sooner we are in our own home the happier we shall both be.'

'Rafe, Webster and Jacko will be pleased, too,' returned Kate, teasing him a little to make his smile return.

It did.

'And will you be pleased, wife?'

'Of course, Bretford House is a most unhappy place. I trust that Saxon Hall will be different.'

'You think that, you truly believe that?'

His urgency surprised her. 'Yes. You see, I believe that houses have their own characters as we do. My home was a happy one until first my mother and then my father died. Clifton Hall, my uncle's place, was not unhappy, but it was cold and severe. Bretford House...' and Kate shuddered before saying, 'Bretford House almost frightens me. Jennie does not like it, either, but cannot tell me why.'

Kate thought that she knew one of the reasons for its scent of unhappiness. She believed that an unloved and ill-treated boy still haunted its rooms and corridors, even though he was now a grown man and his youthful pain was long over—or was it? She feared that Martin might dismiss her explanation as feminine nonsense, but he did not.

Instead he nodded his head slowly, saying, 'You must tell me if Saxon Hall seems to be an unhappy house, and, if so, we must all try to make it happier.'

'You do not think me fanciful then?'

'No, for I have never felt happy here—and sometimes I have wondered whether it was my fault.'

Impulsively Kate rose and walked over to kiss him on his warm shaven cheek. 'I think not.'

His answer was to pull her on to his knee and begin to kiss her passionately, so passionately that for a moment Kate thought that she was about to faint with divine pleasure. She was restored to earth again by Martin saying crossly, 'Why do women have to wear such damned elaborate clothing? It will take forever to undress you and by then Webster is sure to come in to bother me about some detail connected with our move.'

Kate leaned away from him and murmured wickedly, 'You would prefer me in a peasant woman's smock perhaps?'

'Well, at least I could get at the woman underneath it more easily. Does it hurt to wear all that whalebone and canvas?'

'Not exactly hurt, but I admit that it's most uncomfortable. Does it trouble you to wear those padded breeches?'

'Yes,' said Martin irately, 'and particularly at the present moment when my body has such a strong desire to pleasure my wife, and can't, because of all that brocade and embroidery wrapped around you.'

In her wildest imagination Kate could never have foreseen that she would be having such an improper conversation with her husband. She wanted to tell him that she felt as frustrated as he was by their fashionable clothing, but thought that it might be a mistake.

She was just about to change her mind and tell him exactly that, when there came a knock at the door.

'Webster,' Martin groaned. 'I knew it. Come in,' he bawled, pushing Kate off his knee and towards her vacant chair.

Yes, it was Webster, looking smug.

'I have informed the driver and the footmen that we shall be leaving for Saxon Hall as soon as m'lady's luggage is ready to be packed on to the coach. I trust that that is satisfactory?'

Martin was about to howl at him, in his best quarter-deck voice, something to the effect that, of course, it's satisfactory, you nodcock, so why trouble me with it? But the sight of Kate's amused face told him it might not be wise, for if he did she would be sure to lecture him in the appropriate fashion in which to speak to a person of Webster's standing.

'Yes,' he ground out at last.

Webster still did not move away. 'Have you any further instructions for me, m'lord, before we leave?'

'Martin!' This time, and never mind what Kate thought, he bellowed the word at Webster. 'For sweet pity's sake, you are not to call me m'lord. How many times do I have to tell you that?'

'Begging your pardon, Martin, most people hearing me speak to you in such a disrespectful fashion would think me grossly impertinent.'

'Then let them. Their thoughts are of no consequence to me, nor should they be to you. I lost all respect for titles and ceremonial when I was virtually a beggar. That I am styled Lord Hadleigh grieves me. I was once Captain Martin and that was a title I earned and did not hesitate to use. Lord Hadleigh had merely to be born in the right bedroom.'

'Perhaps,' said Webster, greatly daring after his employer had come out with this astonishing tirade, 'I could call you Captain Martin.'

Martin closed his eyes. 'Since I no longer ply the trade of seaman, no.'

'Begging your pardon, Martin, if all men thought as you did and there was neither station nor degree, then anarchy would be sure to follow.'

'You hear him,' said Martin turning to the still amused Kate. 'Now you have discovered why I told you he was a logic-chopper. God knows why I should have two of you inflicted on me. Note that I have said nothing about abolishing station and degree. If I were to pursue this with you, Webster—which damme, for my sins I seem to be doing—then I would tell you that I have no objection to those titles and orders which are earned by merit. Now go away and practise your wit on others. Try Jacko for a change—he probably wouldn't understand you, but he'd look properly respectful.'

'Oh, I doubt that, Martin,' said Webster with a grin, bowing his way out of the room, 'since, so far as I can judge, Jacko respects nobody.'

'Which is as it should be,' said Martin to the closed door. 'What are you laughing at, wife?'

'You, him,' choked Kate. 'And Jacko, for some odd reason, does respect Aunt Jocasta, so Webster was a little awry there.'

Martin put his head in his hands before lifting it again and kissing her fiercely on the lips. 'Go to, wife, this is a fine start to our married life. Be off with you and see that your chests and bags are ready to be transported to Saxon Hall as soon as possible. The day wears on and I am minded to be away from this place as soon as may be—or sooner if it comes to that.'

He strode to the door, where he turned and blew her a kiss. 'I will see you downstairs anon. Pay your adieux to your assembled kinfolk and then we must be away. The air of this place stifles me.'

Now that was a gross exaggeration, thought Kate. There was not much evidence of Martin being stifled when he dealt with both Webster and her, but wisely, she did not tell him so.

* * *

Kate had no notion of what she would find at Saxon Hall. She was well aware that Martin had not gone to Forge Street when he had left the Strand a week ago. In any case, common sense told her that there was no room in that small cottage for the butler and all the servants who had visited Bretford House to provide the amazing feast which had greeted the wedding guests when they had arrived there after the ceremony.

What she found when the coach came to a stop on a gravel sweep was an imposing mansion built of mellow red brick with many windows. A low flight of steps led up to a large oak door. It reminded her a little of Hampton Court, which she had once seen as a child.

As was usual, there were a number of servants waiting to greet them, as well as several footmen and the inevitable steward, who showed them in with somewhat less fuss than that which was common at Bretford House.

Martin's dislike of ceremonial was shown the moment he walked into his home. Regardless of the convention and ritual which demanded that the great men of Her Grace's world would always retain their hats indoors and take them off rarely, he threw his at one of the footmen, as did Rafe and Webster. Jacko had already exiled himself to the kitchens, entering the Hall by its back door. He hadn't been wearing a hat, but a kind of turban fashioned from a piece of coloured cloth.

By the standards of Bretford House and the other places in which Kate had lived, Saxon Hall was sparsely furnished, but what there was, was beautiful. The largest room—after the Great Hall—on the ground floor was a library cum study, but she was not to discover that until later.

Although their journey had been short, Kate, after being introduced to the housekeeper, was taken upstairs by her to her private sitting-room, which was reached through the bedroom which she was to share with Martin. Both of them had little in the way of furniture, but once her own luggage had been unpacked and the splendid Italian chest which held her clothes had been brought upstairs, it would, she hoped, look more homely.

Martin's room, when she inspected it, was furnished with only three chests, a mirror, an armchair and a four-poster bed which Kate thought was large enough to allow at least four persons to sleep in it in comfort. Beside the bed was a closet with a key in the door, but when Kate, curious, pushed at it, it proved to be unlocked. Inside a small table stood before its back wall; on it lay a locket containing a curl of blonde hair. Above the table hung a small wood panel on which had been painted the face of a very young woman. The artist had plainly been, unlike the one who had painted John and Martin as boys, a novice, but he had somehow managed to give her pretty face a wistful and longing look.

Kate wondered who she could be, and why her portrait was hidden away. Some feeling that she had been prying into Martin's private affairs made her lock the closet door: she was sure that it was meant to be kept locked, and only by mischance had it been left open.

What she had just discovered, and Saxon Hall itself, were proof that Martin had led a life the details of which she knew nothing, other than the bare bones of what he had earlier told her. She had hidden nothing from him, for there was nothing to hide. Her own past was that of a sheltered young girl: there was neither scandal nor untoward incident in it—but that was almost certainly not true of her husband's.

When she finally went downstairs she found that there were no portraits on any of the walls, but some fine Flemish tapestries showing imaginary landscapes where nymphs, shepherds and satyrs were enjoying themselves. The withdrawing-room off the Great Hall possessed a singularly beautiful one depicting Hercules' first labour, in which he was killing the lion.

Kate found it strange to be alone. Always before she had been surrounded by attendants, with her Aunt Jocasta nearby. But her aunt would not be arriving at Saxon Hall until the newlyweds' honeymoon was considered to be over—perhaps in a sennight.

To pass the time until he reappeared, she wandered round the room, inspecting its contents. Among them were relics of Martin's life as a seaman, including many objects which she later learned had come from the Americas. She was particularly fascinated by a collection of tiny wooden statues of strange animals and men. Martin was later to tell her that they had been part of the cargo of a Spanish treasure ship which he had captured. Most of the gold in it had, of course, gone to the Queen.

In the middle of her examination of a cross-legged little man who appeared to be wearing a bucket on his head, the door opened and Martin came in.

'You must forgive me for leaving you alone,' he said, after kissing her on the cheek, 'although I thought that, after yesterday's excitements, you might prefer to rest once we had arrived here—but I had urgent business to attend to in the stables. If you would like to inspect them yourself, I would be only too happy to escort you there. By the by, I have never asked you whether you can ride—I have rather taken it for granted that you do.'

'Only a little,' Kate confessed. 'My father's first wife died from a fall from her horse not long after they were married. The consequence of that was that I was not allowed to mount a horse at all. I escaped once to the stables and persuaded one of the lads to let me ride on a tame and elderly mare. After that I rode in secret for a time until my father, by chance, saw me one day. I thought him to be away from home, but he had returned early—and that was the end of that. He dismissed the poor stable boy and I only escaped a thrashing for disobeying him because my mother interceded for me—and since she was then slowly dying of a wasting illness, he could deny her nothing. My father died not long after she did—of grief, everyone said.'

'What a sad life you must have had,' Martin said, once Kate's story was over.

She shook her head. 'At first, perhaps, but when my uncle became my guardian I met Alison for the first time, and Avis. Avis came to live with us when her Papa became part of the embassy in Paris. He didn't want her learning bad ways there, he said.'

'I can't imagine Avis learning bad ways anywhere,' Martin offered. 'I have never met a quieter and more well-behaved young woman.'

'Unlike me?' quipped Kate.

'Oh, you are quite different. I think that you will always be true to yourself and will travel along your own road—and now that you are married to me I will have to try to persuade you that it must be the same road as mine.'

For some reason his reply surprised Kate. Looking at him, at his size and his brute strength, she would have thought that he would have no hesitation in insisting that his wife would always do what he demanded and commanded of her. But he was speaking of persuasion, not of force.

'If we continue our debate much longer,' she told him merrily, 'then night will have come before we visit the stables. I am longing to see them.'

'Now that I truly doubt,' he said, 'but no matter. Take my arm, wife, and let us make our first promenade in our own home.'

Kate immediately did as she was bid, thinking that she had never had a real home of her own before: she had always lived in someone else's. First it was her father's and then Lord Clifton's and, for a few weeks, it had been Bretford House.

My home, she thought, and my husband. How strange it seems. I had dreamed once of having my own home as a spinster, without a man to control me, and now that I have my own home, it is because I have a husband whom custom tells me is my master in all things. I never wanted that, but here I am, and I must make the best of it—and him.

I never thought that I would marry a bear, either, except that now Martin is clean-shaven and wearing courtiers' clothing he does not look very much like a bear, nor does he speak to me as a bully might...yet.

Kate added this proviso because she had little knowledge of what the future might bring. In the meantime she walked along beside him, out of the Hall and into the stable-yard where a groom was exercising a pretty, cream-coloured mare.

'Oh, how beautiful!' she exclaimed.

Martin's face glowed. 'You like her?'

'Who could not?'

'Bravo. Sim, put the mare through her paces so that my lady may see what a talented and obedient creature she is.'

'At once, master.' Sim eased himself into the saddle and trotted the mare around the yard.

'Her name is Swallow,' Martin told Kate, watching his bride's entranced face. 'She is yours—I bought her for you and she is my wedding gift to you. Sim will teach you how to control her if you need some help after being so many years out of the saddle.'

'Oh!' Impulsively Kate threw her arms around Martin and kissed him on the cheek. 'Thank you, thank you, you could not have given me anything better. Once I can manage her properly we may ride together, may we not?'

'Certainly, which is why I bought her for you— and then when you told me your sad story I knew that, quite by chance, I had hit upon the one thing most sure to please you.'

He had wanted to please her! Not only that, he had arranged for the mare to be present on the day on which he took her to her new home—which was surely a good start to their married life. When Sim, on his master's orders, dismounted, Martin introduced the mare to Kate. Or should it more properly have been phrased that he introduced her to the mare? Kate thought with some amusement. He encouraged her to stroke and pet her present, although she really needed no encouraging: she was only too delighted to show her pleasure in being able to do what she had long wanted, but had so long been denied.

Martin, watching her pleasure, found it difficult not to take her in his arms, to make love to her there, in the stable yard, but with some difficulty, he controlled himself. Later, when he was dressing before retiring to bed, he was to remember that Mary had been a timid little thing, who had been so frightened of horses that she would never go near them, let alone ride one. Candid and lively Kate, on the contrary, told him when they finally left the yard that she could not wait to be properly dressed so that she could take Swallow for her first ride.

The other thing which surprised Martin, although it shouldn't have done, was that the more he was with Kate, the more his memories of Mary began to fade. For years he had been able to imagine the pretty little woman Mary had been before she began to carry his child. Once she had begun to breed, however, she had changed. She grew ill, found eating difficult, and lost her zest for life—which was one of the reasons, the physician had told her distraught husband, why she and her child had died during its birth.

Pray God Kate will not be afflicted so, was Martin's sudden thought, and then: but she is not a delicate thing like Mary—and it was that delicacy which attracted me to her. How strange that my second wife should be the exact opposite of my first one—but then I did not choose her, she was chosen for me—which makes it all the more strange that I am coming to lust after her so greatly.

Before that, however, they had arrived back in the Hall, a happy Kate clinging to his arm, to find

Webster waiting for him with the news that he had a visitor.

'A surprising one,' Webster said, 'in view of everything. It is Master Bevis Frampton.'

'Frampton!' exclaimed Martin. 'I thought that I had seen the last of him at Essex House.'

'Apparently not. I had him escorted to the withdrawing-room and was about to send a footman to inform you of his arrival when you and your lady returned.'

'I don't suppose that my lady will wish to meet Master Frampton, eh, Kate?'

Kate shook her head. 'Lord Clifton thought little of Frampton. I only met him once, and I could see why. I will retire to the library, if I may, until he leaves.'

'Well said.'

'Do you wish the steward to escort you to the withdrawing-room, Martin?' Webster asked.

'Certainly not! I'm sure that I can manage the few yards from here to there on my own.'

'Protocol might demand that the steward escorts you to a visitor of Master Frampton's station,' Webster offered with a grin.

'So it might, but I shall not heed any of its demands,' said Martin, before striding off to the withdrawing-room, thinking: now why do I think that Webster is baiting me? He knows my wishes about informality—but I suppose he is playing a game in which he scores points with his nonsense and I score mine with my sense.

He pushed open the door to find Frampton busy examining the tapestry of Hercules. If he was surprised that Lord Hadleigh did not enter the room after a bellowing steward, he did not show it.

'A very fine piece,' he said, waving a hand at the tapestry.

'Indeed it is, which is why I bought it,' Martin replied, without any polite overtures such as, I trust that you have not being waiting long, or, what important errand brings you to my home, Master Frampton? Instead he waited for Frampton to speak again, which he did when he realised that Martin had finished without indulging in any of the flowery rhetoric usual on such occasions as these.

'I have come, m'lord, to try to persuade you to change your mind over the matter of Lord Essex and his quarrel with the fashion in which our beloved country is run.'

'Then I fear that you have wasted your time, Master Frampton. My mind is quite made up. It has not changed since I last spoke with you.'

'That is a great pity, m'lord. I hope you will not think me impertinent if I suggest that you ought to give more consideration to the powerful arguments which Lord Essex and I employed on that occasion.'

'Oh, but I do think you impertinent. To arrive here without an invitation and suggest that I have made an important decision without due and proper thought *is* impertinent.'

If he had thought to silence Frampton with that

brusque answer then he had been mistaken. Frampton gave him a slightly pitying smile, before saying, 'But then, m'lord, think. You must have been somewhat distracted by your sudden rise in rank, due to the unfortunate death of your brother, and then of course, to your marriage with the beauteous Lady Kate, and therefore unable to give your full attention to those matters occurring in the great wide world outside.'

Martin stared at him.

'Your impudence, Master Frampton, is unparalleled. I am now prepared to give my full attention to your presence here and to the arguments you have been presenting to me. I shall immediately act on it.'

He walked to the door, looking out to where Webster sat, working at a table in the Great Hall, doubtless waiting to be sent for in the unlikely event of Martin needing his advice during his interview with Frampton.

'Webster!' Martin bellowed in his best ship's captain's voice.

'Coming,' exclaimed Webster jumping up.

'Excellent,' said Martin when Webster stood before him. 'You have been reproaching me for the lack of protocol in the affairs of Saxon Hall. I will remedy that immediately. Pray send for the steward and ask him, with all due ceremony, to escort Master Frampton from the premises with instructions that he is not to trouble me here again.'

'Is this wise?' asked Webster, trying to stifle a grin.

'Wise? You ask me that after your constant complaints to me that matters at Saxon Hall are too informal, and then, when I am trying to comply with your wishes you question me? Pray do as I ask, at once.'

'Yes, m'lord, certainly, m'lord,' bowed Webster thinking, here is a fine tale to amuse Rafe and Jacko. Something told him that this was all a pantomime, that Martin Chancellor was a great deal more cunning than men thought him to be. What game was he playing now?

He carried out his instructions. The steward did as he was bid, his master having disappeared upstairs to visit his bride of a day. Master Frampton did not protest and left as quietly as he could, vowing, once again, even more vengeance on Lord Hadleigh—and, if possible, soon.

His master was—as Webster suspected—playing a deep and dangerous game. He was deliberately provoking Frampton so that if he truly were the unknown assassin he might, in his anger, act so unwisely that Martin could trap either him, or his agent.

# Chapter Eight

**K**ate spent her day wondering what the second night of her marriage might be like, the first having been so unexpectedly rewarding. She was also haunted a little by the young beauty whose portrait she had seen in the closet in Martin's room. She was tempted to ask Martin who she might be when he came upstairs after dismissing Frampton, but remembering what a private man he was, she decided not to. After all, she thought, it might not be wise to confess that she had been secretly prowling around his bedroom.

He found her in her sitting-room, stitching away at her canvas work. Jennie was busy lifting her clothes out of one of the chests, refolding them and carefully laying some of them away in the other. She looked up when Martin strode in, and immediately left them together.

Martin laughed. 'You have a well-trained maid there,' he said, leaning forward and kissing Kate on the cheek. 'She probably knows why I have come upstairs.'

'Oh, why?' asked Kate, apparently artlessly.

'For this,' Martin told her, scooping her up into his arms, and once she was safely there, tossing her canvas work on to the bench on which she had been sitting.

'Oh, whatever are you doing?' squeaked Kate, who knew perfectly well what her husband's intention was, particularly when he threw her on to the giant four-poster, and after kissing her until her senses reeled, began to undress her.

'Something you will enjoy,' he promised her. Which she did, crying out his name when they had scaled their mountain of delight together, to lie quiet in his arms.

'Oh, you were right,' she panted at him when she could speak again.

'About what?' asked Martin, who was also having trouble with his breathing.

'I enjoyed it,' she managed.

Martin, who had sunk back on the bed to lie by her side, raised himself to lean over her.

'So, you would not be troubled if I pleasured you again? When I have recovered a little myself, that is.'

Kate decided that he needed to be teased.

'I'll think about it,' she said.

'Minx!' he exclaimed, the mere sight of her naughty mocking face arousing him all over again. 'You deserve to be punished for that.'

His punishment of her was all and more than Kate could have desired. When it was over she whispered in his ear, 'Now I know what the poets mean when they write of love. I love you, Martin.'

His reply was not what she had expected. He pulled himself away from her, to sit up. 'No, Kate, I would have you my satisfied and happy wife, but you are not to love me.'

'Why?' It was Kate who was sitting up now, and challenging him. 'Why should I not? It is the truth. From the moment I first saw you at Bretford House when I thought you were a servant, you have never been far from my thoughts. At first, I did not know that it was love, but now I do. Can you not love me, too?'

'No!' The cry was wrenched from him. 'I must not. I do not wish to lose you, which I might if I am tempted to love you. I will make you happy, if I can, but do not ask for love—nor speak of your love for me.'

The bright day dimmed a little for Kate, who was seeing her dream of love shattered. 'I cannot deny what I truly feel,' she said quietly, turning away from him.

'Because I cannot love you does not mean that I cannot honour and treasure you, Lady Hadleigh. No man could value you more.'

'Truly?' she whispered, turning towards him again.

'Truly. I will never lie to you, Kate, however many

lies I have told to others. You do not deserve to be lied to, and they did.'

Kate was on the verge of asking him who the young woman whose lock of hair and portrait he so obviously treasured was. She desisted. She must not demand too much of him.

I will make him love me, whether he wishes to or not, was her last thought, after he had pleasured her again and she was sinking into the deep sleep which comes to some fulfilled lovers, if not to all, quite unaware of the treacherous tear which was sliding down her face.

Her sleep was another blessing for her—one which was not given to Martin, who raised himself on his elbow in order to look down on to her tranquil face, his busy mind whirling.

I have vowed to treasure her, and that I will do to the utmost of my ability, but, alas, time and chance may thwart me as they did with Mary. Pray God it may be otherwise with Kate.

Webster and Rafe were with Jacko in his room. It was a small, if comfortable, one over the stables. He had refused better quarters in the house, saying that he would be happy to make his home with the servants, but Martin had insisted that one of his oldest friends was worthy of something more than that. The room over the stables was large and comfortable and well furnished.

The three of them retired there when they wished

to be private. 'No one in a big house is private,' Rafe
said, and Jacko was happy to have his friends with
him occasionally.

'So, how goes the hunt for Martin's assassin?'
Webster was asking him.

Jacko shrugged. 'He thinks that Frampton is trying
to top him and I agree with him. Proof is difficult.
Frampton is a fool who thinks he is cleverer than he
is, but gossip says that he has sent more than one man
to his doom, either directly or indirectly.'

Rafe said, 'But why? Does he work for others who
need such offices done for them?'

'No proof of that, either. He works alone—or so
all I have questioned say.'

'He came here today,' said Webster.

His hearers stared at him.

'For what?' Rafe asked.

'I know not. He did not stay long. Martin threw
him out in a mockery of politeness.'

Rafe began to laugh. 'He is a master at that, is
Martin.'

Webster unbent enough to offer Rafe a small grin.
'So I am beginning to find out. Tell me, has he been
married before?'

Jacko fixed Webster with a truculent stare. 'Why
do you wish to know?'

'Curiosity—something he said once, which made
me think.'

'You think too much,' grunted Jacko.

'Probably,' Webster offered him.

'It cannot hurt to tell you the truth,' Rafe said. 'Better that I should, rather than that someone who hates him should tell you lies.'

'And the truth is?'

'Years ago, when he was on his way to becoming the magnate he was before ever his father sent for him, he married the daughter of his benefactor, Mary Williams. It was a true love match. Her father, James Williams, having no son, had already become Martin's patron and encouraged rather than opposed the match. They were a pair of lovebirds if ever man and woman were. She was expecting his child, but before she reached her term and while he was at sea, the child arrived early. She was a little thing and both she and the child died. He arrived back in England to find her three weeks buried.

'I have never seen anyone so stricken. Before that he had always been a hard man, but jolly. Afterwards he was quite different. Now that I know a little of his past, I believe he must have thought that the gods were determined to punish him.'

Webster thought for a long moment, before saying, 'She was small and delicate—not like Lady Kate then.'

'Quite unlike.'

'And this James Williams, what of him?'

'You might almost say he adopted Martin after his daughter's death. He died early, too, of a wasting illness—leaving a small fortune to Martin, who was a rich man himself by then.'

'Tell me, Rafe, if you will, how it is that you know all this?'

'I was James Williams's distant cousin, and had worked for him since I was a child. When Martin married my cousin Mary, Master Williams suggested that I became his lieutenant. I went to sea with him and I was at his side when he landed in England to learn that his wife was dead. I have been with him ever since; Jacko, too.'

This explained many things which had puzzled Webster. 'It did not distress you that James Williams left Martin his fortune?'

Rafe smiled. 'Not all his fortune—half of it came to me. No, I could not grudge Martin his share; he had made both Mary and her father happy until Mary's sudden death.'

'Yet you still work for him even though you could have become your own master.'

Rafe shrugged. 'We have become brothers—he being the elder. I have learned so much from him, and he saved my life once, nearly at the expense of his own. I owe him that. I know that if I wished to leave him he would release me on the instant. I am not like Martin, I am too easy. I never suffered hardship in my early youth and prefer to follow orders rather than give them.'

Jacko had been nodding his head during this recital. Now he said in his downright way, 'If Mistress Mary had lived until my master died, Martin would have inherited everything—as her husband. It was Martin

who persuaded the old man to leave Rafe something
for his faithful service. He is a good man, is my master. His damned father neither knows the true man,
nor wants to.'

Webster could not prevent himself from asking yet
another question. 'This is my last,' he promised. 'Do
either of you know how, and why, he came to leave
his home?'

They shook their heads at him. 'Something to do
with the elder brother perhaps,' Rafe offered, 'but that
is mere assumption.'

Nevertheless, these revelations had provided
Webster with an explanation for some, though not all,
of the puzzles surrounding Martin Chancellor's life
after he had fled Bretford House.

'I'll say one thing,' Jacko muttered. 'Mary
Williams was a sweet young thing, but Lady Kate will
be a better wife for him. Mary was as gentle as an
angel, but, myself I don't think angels fit for this
world.'

This astonishing piece of insight nearly confounded
Webster, who had been thinking the same thing. He
looked at Jacko with renewed respect. There were
those who thought that only the educated, the nobility
and the gentry were able to make accurate judgements
about life, but Webster was rapidly beginning to learn
otherwise.

'I ought to go and find him,' he announced, rising.
'He said that he needed me to write some letters
for him.'

Jacko put a hand on his shoulder.

'Best you wait,' he advised. 'He went upstairs to Lady Kate some time ago, and I doubt me whether he'd be very pleased if you interrupted him while he was alone with her on the day after they were wed.'

Webster sat down again. 'I defer to your wisdom,' he announced—and he was not mocking Jacko.

It was evening before Martin reappeared, and by then Webster decided that it would not be tactful to badger him over the letters. There was a glow about him, rather like the one a starving person possesses when he has eaten a good meal after many days' short commons.

Kate did not come down. Jennie took her supper up to her, found her dozing in the big four-poster and, smiling knowingly, had to prod her gently to awaken her.

'Is it morning already?' Kate quavered, still lost in a dream in which she and Martin had been walking in a beautiful garden. He had just turned to kiss her when Jennie's hand on her shoulder snatched her from her dream of bliss.

'Lord, no, m'lady. It is but early evening. M'lord ordered me to bring you some supper. No need to rise until tomorrow, he said.'

'Oh!' Kate sat up. Now everyone would know how she and Martin had spent their afternoon. 'That was very good of him. Put the tray on the table over there and I will get up to eat it. What is it?'

'Broth, m'lady, and good wheaten bread and butter with a deal of cheese, some sliced beef, a couple of sweet biscuits with apples for a dessert, and a tankard of good hippocras to wash it all down when you've supped the broth.'

Kate had not realised how hungry she was until she began to drink the broth. Later, she was to tell Martin how surprised that made her. 'After all,' she said, 'I hadn't done anything but sleep this afternoon.'

'No?' Martin's eyebrows rose in amusement. 'It's hard work pleasuring ourselves—think how heavily we panted afterwards.'

'As though we had run a race,' said Kate, remembering how, when she had been a young tomboy, she had huffed and puffed when she had joined the stable lads' vigorous games when they were off duty.

'Exactly.'

'Are you still hungry?' he asked her, throwing off his clothes—she was later to discover that, unlike most gentlemen, he had no body servant to help him in and out of them.

'Yes, but not for food.'

This was the answer he wanted, and in a trice he was in the bed with her and the whole delightful business started all over again, to end in deep sleep and dreams of power for them both, for to please the loved one is to exercise a form of power over them. True, Martin denied that he loved her, but he behaved as though he did and surely that was all that mattered.

This time they fell asleep together, hand in hand,

and it was morning before Kate woke to the gentle sound of a lute and a man singing in a low voice.

She sat up, wondering who the musician could be—to discover that it was Martin. He was seated where he could see her and she could hear him. He was wearing an elaborate full-length night robe.

He stopped playing to smile at her. 'I thought that you might like to wake up to music, so I have been tuning my lute so that I could sing you a song which you may not know, although, during our frustrated transports yesterday, you said something which reminded me of it.'

'I had not thought that you could play and sing so well,' was all Kate felt able to say, so surprised was she.

'No?' He raised an eyebrow at her. 'I learned before I left home, but did not find time to play again until after I left the sea. Oh, I sang shanties and bawdry with the best, but nothing like this. To sing this I must keep my voice low, or I lose the tune—which did not matter when I was on board ship.'

He winked suggestively at her before beginning to sing a popular song called 'Beauty's Self', which Kate had never heard before.

> My love in her attire doth show her wit,
> It doth so well become her;
> For every season she hath dressings fit.
> For winter, spring and summer
> No beauty she doth miss

When all her robes are on;
But Beauty's self she is
When all her robes are gone.

'And since we were married,' he said, watching her
blush when he sang the last line, 'you have been
Beauty's self for me many times.'

He had surprised her yet again. She said, 'Are there
no end to your talents, husband?'

'Do not flatter me, wife—even though it pleases
me when you do—since you are showing me proper
respect. I am a very humble troubadour; my true talents lie elsewhere.'

'Nevertheless,' said Kate earnestly, although she
knew that she was treading on forbidden ground,
'since you come from a family which denies that you
possess any talents at all, you must allow me to ap-
plaud you each time you show me a new one.'

'Which was not why I sang you that song,' he told
her, rising and putting the lute down. 'You must be
feeling hungry again after all the exercise we took
last night, so you must allow me the honour of going
down to the kitchens and bringing up a small feast so
that we may break our fast.'

'Oh, I do so allow,' remarked Kate grandly, as
though she were the Queen herself. 'But I demand a
kiss from you before you go.'

Martin shook his head. 'Alas, I must deny you such
a favour. If I were to kiss you, I fear that I should
leap into the bed in an instant, with the result that we

should not eat our breakfast until the time for supper arrives.'

He was not lying. To his own profound astonishment, the mere sight of her still had the power to rouse him. He felt like a boy again, enjoying the first delights of lust and love, call it what you will.

'In that case, I bid you go, but only on condition that you will return before supper arrives!'

'Now *there* is a condition with which I shall have no difficulty in complying,' he said, giving her yet another meaningful wink before he left.

So far married life was proving quite different from what Kate had expected—but how long would this carefree, idyllic existence last? She had already gathered, from what she had overheard of Webster and Rafe's conversation, that Martin led a busy life as some sort of merchant. The world in which Kate had lived until she had married him had had little to do with merchants. Well, one way or another, she would try to find out exactly what it was that merchants did.

At the moment this particular merchant appeared to have but one idea in his head, and that was to pleasure her as often as he could. She lay back in the bed, and easily drifted into sleep again.

Martin's arrival with a footman and two trays of food did not disturb her. It took a kiss from him to rouse her—in more ways than one! She was rapidly learning the verbal tricks and ploys which went with love and would shortly be as dexterous as he in using them.

The food was simple—Kate was beginning to find that she liked simplicity. The drink he brought her was mead, which he discovered that she preferred to hippocras when she seized it avidly and began to enjoy it before starting to devour what he had brought her.

Kate could not remember ever having felt so hungry before, not even on the previous evening. Martin, too, was tearing at his bread and cheese as though he had not eaten for weeks. He looked at her, mischief written on his face.

'One hunger begets another,' he said cryptically.

At first Kate did not take his meaning. When she did she blushed again. He laughed, winked at her once more and added, 'I like a woman with a good appetite.'

It was only when he had said it that he remembered that Mary had never been a great eater. At the time he had liked her for that: it seemed to show a pleasing delicacy. Now he suddenly wondered whether her poor appetite had been partly the cause of her death, since she had lost weight while carrying their baby, not gained it. Her father had always been urging her to eat: he had been a great trencherman himself. Now, Martin found himself relishing Kate's obvious love of food.

He looked out of the window. The late September morning was fine and sunny, if cold. He resisted the temptation to leap into bed with Kate because he also wanted her to take her first ride on Swallow and didn't wish her to suffer too much discomfort in the saddle through over-vigorous love-making, particularly since he had only just found out that she had not ridden for years.

He said, apparently casually, 'I thought that you might like to have your first outing with Swallow in the forenoon.'

'Oh, yes,' breathed Kate. 'But only if you will go with me.'

She could not have said anything to please Martin more.

'Of course, it will be the first of such journeys together, I trust.' He rose. 'That being so, we must make ready for the day immediately.'

Kate leaped out of bed. 'I shall ring for Jennie straightway. I have several dresses which might be suitable for me to wear on horseback. I think that I may still own the boots which I wore when I first tried to ride.'

'If not,' Martin said, 'you may borrow a pair from one of the younger stable-boys.'

Impulsively Kate kissed him, then blushed again. Perhaps he might think her forward. But he seemed to like her being forward, for he kissed her back, and then had to school himself strictly not to leap back into bed with her again.

'I will see you in the stables later,' he told her when she retired to her sitting-room to wait for Jennie to be sent for to help her to dress.

\* \* \*

Martin, successfully dodging Webster, who he was sure would be waiting for him with some duty or other to perform, arrived in the stable-yard, booted and spurred. There he found Sim being talked to earnestly by Gabriel Watts, his head groom.

Gabriel saluted Martin when he entered, saying, 'I was about to ask an audience of you, m'lord, but now that you are here I will tell you my sad story.'

'There's nothing amiss with Swallow, I trust.'

'Fortunately not, but last night someone broke into the yard and killed two of the dogs, we think by feeding them poisoned meat. They also laid waste to the tack room, stealing much and smashing what was left. Fortunately they made rather more noise than was wise, and Sim, who is a light sleeper, heard them, got up, and taking a lantern with him, went to find out what was wrong. They had just tried to enter Darius's stall when they heard him coming and ran off. Sim chased after them, but he was too far behind them to catch them up, so they escaped.'

He paused, then added, 'This is not the first time lately we have found damage done in the yard and in the little park at the back of the Hall. Some of the wooden benches were smashed and quite a number of plants and shrubs were uprooted and the pretty little statue of Cupid destroyed—and now this. I have not troubled you before, m'lord, but this latest piece of wickedness, added to what has gone before, makes me wonder if someone is deliberately trying to harm you. Imagine what might have happened if they had got at Darius.'

Martin grinned at him. 'Say rather what that lively stallion might have done to them. But you are right. I shall immediately arrange for guards to patrol the Hall and park at night. And thank you, Sim,' he said, turning to the lad who had been standing by while Gabriel told his sad tale, 'for acting so promptly.'

Sim shook his head. 'I'm only sorry, m'lord, that I didn't catch one of them.'

'Never mind that, you tried. Now you must ready Darius and Swallow for me. I shall be accompanying m'lady on her first ride.'

While he was waiting for Kate, Martin exercised Darius, whom he had not ridden for some time. He was also trying to decide whether this was yet another piece of nastiness organised by Frampton—if in truth he was his unknown enemy—designed to unsettle him. He would send Jacko and Webster out again to try to discover some hard evidence on which he could act.

Kate's arrival drove these musings out of his head. He dismounted in order to make sure that she was properly equipped. She smiled at him. 'I found my boots,' she told him proudly, 'and they still fit me, see. And this old dress will serve to ride in.'

Martin thought that anything she wore would be suitable for her to go anywhere, either on horseback or not. He was, he admitted, falling so far under her spell that he would shortly be witless if matters continued in this fashion this much longer! He was beginning to admit that he had never reacted like this to Mary. She had affected him in quite a different way: his feelings for her had always been protective. She had offered him silent worship, whereas Kate cheerfully teased and tempted him with every word she uttered.

He was not surprised to discover that she had a natural talent for controlling a horse and enjoying herself at the same time. Side by side they rode through the park at the back of the Hall and then on to a lane, or byway.

'We are making for Moorgate and the Moore fields,' he told her, 'from whence you may see the Finsbury windmills and the open spaces where the citizens of London meet to enjoy themselves. On the way we shall pass the house where Sir Francis Walsingham, the Queen's spymaster, lived. Like ours it has a small park at its back. I have no notion who bought it after his death.'

Kate was constantly being surprised by how much Martin knew. He kept a firm eye on her to ensure that she was never in any danger, but at the same time he told her about the people who lived in the fine houses off the narrow lanes through which they rode.

'I shall not always be able to escort you,' he said when they finally returned to Saxon Hall, 'and you must promise me that you will never on any account go out without a suitable escort.'

Kate had already noticed that two of the grooms

had followed them, but that apparently was not enough to protect her if she were not with him, for he went on to say that if Jacko were not free then Rafe, or another of the two other attendant gentlemen in his service, either Robert Field or James Riley, must always accompany her. He did not add that they would be armed, but he would notify them of that before they rode with her for the first time.

It had already occurred to him that, now that he was married, his enemy might strike at him through Kate, but he told her nothing of that. She would doubtless put his insistence on her being surrounded by protectors to an excess of caution. After all, they were not living near to the parishes where those criminals, who preyed on the incautious, lived.

Her smile for him when he handed her down from Swallow, was a brilliant one. 'Oh, I really enjoyed that,' she exclaimed. 'May we do it again, some time soon?'

'Yes, while we are still on our honeymoon. After that, my duties may call me away, but provided that you always take someone to guard you, there is no reason why you should not ride as often as you like.'

For Kate, that ride seemed to set the pattern of their life together. Of course, once the honeymoon was over the mad whirl of excitement in which they had enjoyed one another to the full by day and by night had to yield to the demands of ordinary living—at least in the day. One thing, however, remained constant. Martin always rose before her and woke her up each morning by singing and playing gently to her. He seemed to know a remarkable number of songs, some of them tender, some funny and some which were so earthy that, at first, they made her blush.

She found that time had never passed so quickly when they were pleasuring each another, nor so slowly, when, after the honeymoon, she waited for him to return home. He was away one afternoon, when she had an unexpected visitor. It was her former guardian, Lord Clifton, who was bringing Aunt Jocasta with him to be her companion now that the honeymoon was over.

Kate was in the library, inspecting an old map which Martin had told her was an imaginary picture of the New World which was very far from the truth. 'Quite useless if you wished to explore it without becoming lost,' he had told her.

In one corner strange men, with their faces between their shoulders and wearing weird clothes made of leaves so that they looked like fledgling trees, were parading in single file. In another a little motto proclaimed Here be Dragons, which was a piece of nonsense, Martin had told her, because he had spoken to many men who had travelled in the Americas and none of them had ever seen a dragon, nor for that matter had they met people with their faces in the wrong place.

She was interrupted by the majestic entry of the

steward. He had come to inform her that she had visitors.

'It is m'lord Clifton and Mistress Jocasta. I have shown them to the withdrawing-room to await your arrival.'

Kate put the map down immediately. 'I shall go there at once.'

The steward coughed, and looking down, said, 'Your pardon, m'lady, but I would be greatly pleased if you would allow me to escort you to them and introduce you in due form.'

He was so apologetically wistful when he came out with this that Kate suddenly realised that Martin's refusal to allow him to practise his trade properly, was making him profoundly unhappy.

'Of course,' she said. 'Pray lead on.'

Proudly he raised his staff, and walking a few paces before her he led her to the withdrawing-room, where Lord Clifton and Aunt Jocasta rose on his entrance, bowing to Kate as his announcement of Lady Hadleigh's arrival rang out with the pomp and ceremony which he was rarely allowed to muster.

Kate, repressing a tendency to giggle at his grandeur which, by its manner, undoubtedly impressed her visitors, welcomed them warmly.

'I understand,' Lord Clifton began, 'that Lord Hadleigh is visiting the City today.'

'Indeed, but I am only too delighted to entertain you both. I thank you for having had the goodness to accompany Aunt Jocasta on her journey here rather than leaving her to make it alone.'

'Yes, your aunt thought that it was time that she took up her duties with you, and as I am leaving for the country in a few days I decided that I would wish to see you both before I did. I am sorry to have missed your husband.'

This was all so different from his behaviour when he had first met Martin that Kate had to repress another giggle, particularly when he added, 'I am pleased to see you looking so well, niece. I must admit that your air of good health pleases me greatly, because when the new Lord Hadleigh arrived at Bretford House I began to worry somewhat about the wisdom of a match between you. Now, however, that I have come to know the details of his life during his exile, I do not regret allowing you to marry him. At the time, however, I considered whether, despite your—and my—legal obligations I ought to withdraw my consent to it. Fortunately, I allowed the marriage to continue.'

Not knowing quite what to say to this confession, Kate nodded at him, which was not very polite of her, but was better than saying something tactless.

His answer to that was, 'I must, however, ask you this question. Are you happy with him, my dear?'

Kate could not truly offer him an unqualified yes. She was still aware that, for all his kindness and care for her, Martin was still withholding something of himself from her, so she said, quite simply, 'We deal well together.'

This seemed to satisfy m'lord and Aunt Jocasta as well, if their smiles were to be believed. Indeed, Lord Clifton beamed at her. 'Excellent, my dear, excellent. I must admit that since your wedding day I have been a little troubled about your welfare but, by your appearance, I see that I was wrong to worry.'

His care for her future welfare surprised Kate a little, and if she had ever believed that her uncle had never had any true feelings of affection for her, she now knew that behind his stiff and reserved manner he had always loved her and wished her well. Impulsively, and to his surprise, she kissed him on the cheek.

The rest of the visit passed happily except when her uncle said, with regret, that he had asked Martin's father to accompany them, but he had refused, pleading old age. This was not the truth. He had snorted at Lord Clifton, 'Visit Martin! Never! I hope never to have to see him again.' He could, however, hardly tell Martin's wife that.

Aunt Jocasta's first remark when m'lord had gone was to ask Kate, in an apparently idle way, whether Jacko was still with them.

'Indeed, he is,' was Kate's reply. 'He has accompanied Martin to the Royal Exchange in Southwark this morning. Martin has promised to take me with him one day. He says that the shops there are even more splendid than those in Cheapside. You must come with me, Aunt. It seems that there are stalls where one may eat and drink.'

Her aunt sighed. 'How strange it is that Martin continues his trade as a merchant, particularly since he has no need to work for a living now. He has inherited his late mother's large dower, and I understand that he is already rich.'

'He says that he likes working and that the Chancellors were not always grand people. His great-grandfather was a sheep farmer who made his money by trading with the Low Countries. When he grew rich enough to buy an estate and be granted a title, his first coat of arms had three sheep on it to remind everyone where the family's wealth sprang from.'

'There are no sheep on it now,' was Aunt Jocasta's reply to that.

'True, that was because Martin's grandfather was ashamed of his father's origin and changed the sheep for an animal which looks like a cross between a cow and a griffin.'

Martin had told her that it was the usual thing for newly-made aristocrats to alter not only their arms, but also their names. 'For example, the real name of the very rich Willoughbys of Wollaton in Nottinghamshire, was Bugge—which then meant bucket and signified that they were originally humble servants of a great man.'

The look of distress on Aunt Jocasta's face when Kate informed her of this was a profound one because, like many, she believed that the gentry and aristocracy were the chosen of God who were thus different from all other men and women.

'Even if what you say is true,' she finally murmured, 'it is best that it is not widely known, lest we lose the respect of our inferiors.'

Kate decided not to take Aunt Jocasta's education in the realities of life any further. Instead, she accompanied her to her room, which her lady's maid was making ready for her. She could not prevent herself from hoping that Aunt Jocasta's presence would not interfere with the happy life which she was beginning to enjoy with Martin, but her aunt had nowhere else to go but the poorhouse, being the daughter of a gentleman of the Saville family who had gambled his property away and had then died, leaving her penniless. It was Kate's Christian duty to look after her, since she had no other relations to turn to.

Her aunt happily settled, she returned to the library and, having looked her fill at the map, began to explore its shelves further. On one of them a commonplace book rested on top of a great pile of paper. She pulled it down and opened it to find that she was looking at the text of a play. What was most intriguing was that it was written in Martin's careful and legible handwriting, which was greatly like that of a trained clerk. It was a talent of his which she found surprising, since it clashed with the notion that he was principally a man of action.

Kate was particularly intrigued when, on reading it, she discovered that the first scene took place on board ship in a storm—something which Martin must have experienced. When she turned the pages, however, and reached the second scene, she found that corrections and emendations had been made in another, less clerkly, hand.

Obviously someone else had read Martin's play and had also slipped in a page of dialogue, with at the end of it, after the words 'Note well': 'The action must continue at speed, not dally and delay.'

So Martin not only played the guitar and sang. He also wrote poetry, for she was sure that he had composed one of the bawdier songs which he had sung to her in the morning. Like many of those around the court he was engaged in letters and humane learning as well as in seamanship, and now, as she had lately discovered, in earning a living as a successful merchant. Raleigh, his friend, was yet another whose interests were wide.

And all this from a man whom his father despised.

Kate put the commonplace book down. She had learned many things from it, one, in particular. Her husband was an even more remarkable man than she had first thought him. So much so that his breach with his father and his family seemed more inexplicable than ever.

# Chapter Nine

**B**evis Frampton had had little time or opportunity lately to arrange any further attempts on Martin Chancellor's life. M'lord Essex had fallen ill, seriously this time—he had pleaded ill-health every time he had been ordered to appear before various meetings designed to make him give evidence as to his behaviour, not only when he had been in Ireland, but also when he had been placed under house arrest.

It was announced that he was suffering yet another attack of unidentified malaise. Some weeks later, when it was identified as an ailment known as the Irish flux, many Londoners assembled in the streets to demonstrate their displeasure at his persecution by the Queen. In this they differed from many around the court who knew only too well of his lack of common sense and of the maladministration and poor generalship which had led to his failure in Ireland.

Many, like Sir Francis Bacon and Walter Raleigh, who had been his fervent supporters, had been alienated by his behaviour after he had arrived back in England. On the other hand, a large number of disaffected, poverty-stricken noblemen and gentry had flocked to join him, hoping that if he were successful they would gain power and wealth. The most prominent among them were the Lords Rutland and Southampton.

Bevis, like them, believed that the common people had the right of it and, more to the point, that if Essex were to succeed in mounting a successful rebellion against the Queen, using their support, he would be one of those who would finally achieve the public office which he thought that his talents deserved.

To ensure by his daily encouragement that Essex persisted in trying to bring about such a coup was taking up much of the time which he needed to bring about Hadleigh's downfall. Nevertheless, once Essex's sickroom was forbidden to him and to Essex's other supporters, he was able to seek out and order several bully boys to keep watch on Hadleigh, who daily went into central London, and to try to find an occasion to dispatch him—preferably in the capital's crowded streets where his attackers might easily evade capture.

Martin, who had noted that the efforts to assassinate him seemed to have ceased, was, like his wife and Bevis, also having a busy day—and not only in that part of London where the merchants congregated. He had arrived at his Counting House to discover that there was a letter waiting for him from none other than Sir Robert Cecil, that devious son of a devious father, the late Lord Burghley. On Sir Francis Walsingham's death he had succeeded him as the Queen's Secretary of State.

The letter was brusque and to the point. It asked Lord Hadleigh to report to him at once at Greenwich Palace, where he was at present in attendance on the Queen in order to discuss a matter of some urgency. No explanation was given as to what the 'matter of some urgency' might be, but Martin could only conclude that Cecil was aware that he had been visiting Lord Essex. He had never met Sir Robert, but he knew of his reputation as a cold and merciless man, even harder than his father, and he did not particularly relish this sudden summons.

He left matters in the charge of Webster, before calling on Jacko and Rafe to accompany him. The court was at Greenwich, which would involve him in a journey down river on a bitterly cold day in early November, since Cecil, like all the Queen's senior advisers, had no office of his own, other than some rooms in Whitehall. He often travelled with Her Grace as she moved from palace to palace.

'It's Essex, isn't it?' Rafe exclaimed suddenly. 'That's why he has sent for you. To find out if you're committed to him.'

Martin said, 'Perhaps. Nothing is ever certain where these great people are concerned.'

He wondered if Raleigh had reported to Cecil of

Essex's wish to enlist him as an ally—particularly since many of the Earl's old friends had recently deserted him. More than that, the latest news about the fallen favourite was that he had been taken ill, although how seriously, no one quite knew. Martin had no intention of joining Essex, a man who could rely on such poor creatures as Bevis Frampton, but he might have some difficulty in convincing Cecil of that.

The palace, when he reached it, seemed to be in a state of great excitement—something on which he later commented to Raleigh, who told him with a grin that it did not signify. Palaces were always in a state of great excitement. Even so, Martin discovered, they were not places of great urgency. He was kept waiting in an antechamber by a harassed-looking young man who told him that Sir Robert would see him shortly.

Shortly turned into over two hours, and just as Martin was on the verge of consigning Sir Robert and all his works to the devil by leaving the palace without further ado, the young man returned and told him that Sir Robert would see him now.

He left Rafe and Jacko behind, staring at the wall, and was led to a small room where Sir Robert sat writing at a desk. A black-robed clerk stood before another, tall one, at some distance from his master. He was copying something into a ledger. Sir Robert was not quite what Martin had expected. Unlike his father, who was reported to have possessed an imposing presence, Sir Robert was a white-faced cripple with no presence at all who might have passed for one of his own clerks. Except that, as Martin soon discovered, he had a mind like a knife, and a sharp manner to match.

'You may leave us, Skelton,' he ordered, without looking at Martin, even though he had been announced by the young man with a great deal of formality. Skelton turned out to be the man already in the room—he departed through a door behind Sir Robert's desk. The young man left the room by the one through which he had entered, without needing orders to do so.

Fortunately, after a chilly river journey and the equally draughty and cold ante-chamber, Sir Robert's office was warmed by a great fire in an ornate hearth.

There was a spare chair and a bench in the room but Sir Robert went on writing without informing Martin that he might sit. He was just about to commit a form of *lèse-majesté* by walking out when Sir Robert looked up at him and said, 'Lord Hadleigh, I believe.'

'You believe rightly, unless, of course, your lackey made a mistake.'

If he had thought to rile Sir Robert by this riposte, he was the one who was mistaken.

Sir Robert inclined his head and said, 'I met your father once. You do not greatly resemble him.'

Now how should he answer that? To say nothing might be best.

Sir Robert ignored his silence too, and drove on, to the point, Martin hoped.

'I have been informed that you recently visited m'lord of Essex. I should be interested to know what the purpose of your visit was.'

'A simple one, sir. I had a letter from him—as I did from you—asking me to call on him at Essex House. As a matter of courtesy I did as I was bid, but only to inform him that I had no interest in becoming part of the group who have gathered around him in order to support him in his differences with Her Grace.'

'And that was all?'

Martin restrained himself from saying, 'Quite enough, I should think,' and came out instead, with, 'Yes, apart from m'lord asking me to think again and change my mind.'

'And your reply was?'

'That I had considered the matter carefully, and my mind was quite made up. I had no intention of supporting him.'

'Was m'lord alone?'

'No, Lord Southampton was present with a number of other gentlemen, none of whom I knew—other than Master Bevis Frampton.'

'Oh, Frampton,' said Sir Robert dismissively, tossing his quill pen down. 'And that was all,' he repeated.

'Yes. Lord Essex dismissed me after that. He was not best pleased with me.'

'I know the feeling, m'lord. I suspect you have caused it in more than one of those whom you have met in your encounters with the great of this world.'

His grin when he said this, while picking up his pen and pointing it at Martin, made him seem almost human.

'I always try to speak to the point, Sir Robert.'

'You are adamant, then, that you will not change your mind about supporting him?'

'I am.'

'Excellent—and very wise of you, I am sure.'

Sir Robert sat silent for a moment before picking up a small bell which stood on the desk before him and ringing it sharply, whereupon Skelton reappeared.

'Skelton, please note that I am about to take Lord Hadleigh to be introduced to Her Grace, who has expressed a wish to meet him, but before we leave, I trust that Lord Hadleigh will grant me the favour of drinking some rather good sack with me after taking the chair which stands across from my desk.'

'If that is your wish, Sir Robert, I will comply with it.'

'To adopt your own mode of speech, Lord Hadleigh, if it were not my wish, I would not have made the offer. Quick march, Skelton, we must not keep Her Grace waiting too long.'

Martin sat down. He was to meet the Queen, the monarch who had confiscated most of the treasure which he and the other sea-captains had captured during their raids on the Spanish galleon run.

'You were married recently, I believe, Lord Hadleigh—to Clifton's niece,' was Sir Robert's opening gambit when they began to drink their wine.

'Yes.'

'Correct me if I am wrong, but was she not pledged to your brother John shortly before he died?'

'That is true, Sir Robert.'

Sir Robert nodded thoughtfully. 'I must inform you, Lord Hadleigh, that you are quite different from the man I expected you to be. From your career as a captain who attacked the Spanish galleon run I would have thought you reckless. The man I have just interviewed is far from that. By the by,' he added, apparently as an afterthought, 'you said that when you visited Lord Essex you met Master Bevis Frampton. I would be interested in your opinion of him.'

What to say? On the face of it this was almost an idle question. But did Sir Robert Cecil ever ask an idle question? Martin very much doubted it. He must go as warily as he could for, who knew, it was just possible that Frampton might be one of Cecil's spies.

'My talk with him was of the briefest. He did not seem to be other than one of m'lord's hangers-on.'

Sir Robert smiled. 'Of whom he has many,' he finally said. He looked across to check that Martin had drunk his sack. 'Now we must go to have audience with Her Grace. We must not keep her waiting. When she was told that Captain Andrew Martin, who had refused a knighthood, was Bretford's long-lost son, she was most intrigued.'

'I gather, from all that I have heard, that she was not the only one.'

Sir Robert laughed out loud this time. 'She will be even more so when she finally meets you.'

He rang the bell again, twice. This time the first young man reappeared.

He bowed. 'I am at your service, Sir Robert.'

'You will escort and announce us to Her Grace, who is waiting to grant us an audience in the Long Gallery.'

The young man said nothing, merely bowed his head again and led them along two corridors to a huge room at the far end of which the Queen sat on a dais. A few gentlemen stood around her, and an even larger number filled the floor of the Gallery.

Upon their being announced after they had followed him to the steps which led up to the dais, the Queen, who had been leaning sideways and talking to a portly gentleman, looked in their direction and motioned them up on to the dais.

'Sir Robert, you are welcome, and you, too, m'lord Hadleigh—or should I call you Captain Martin?'

'Whichever most pleases you, Your Grace,' Martin said smoothly, after taking off his hat and bowing to her.

She laughed. 'I see that you have a diplomatic way with you, sir. Is not that true, Sir Robert?'

'Up to a point, Your Grace,' returned Sir Robert, as smooth as Martin, and equally adept at two-edged conversation.

Now that he was near to her, Martin could see what the ravages of great age had done to his monarch. All the paintings of her, even recent ones, showed her to be a red-haired beauty with a porcelain complexion and fine blue eyes. Alas, her wrinkled face was so powdered and painted, and her blue eyes were so faded and rheumy, that only the caricature of what had once been a pretty young woman was left.

Oh, her clothes and her jewels were as beautiful as ever, but their very elegance merely served to emphasise the change from what she had been to what she had become. Her manner and her voice were still queenly, and as she spoke to them it was plain that her intellect had not been impaired. Martin could only wish that he had met her when she was in the pride of her youth and he could understand a little the resentment which some of her courtiers, particularly Essex, felt at being the servant of a fading old maid.

Not that he condoned it, for she still remained the woman who had defeated the pride of Spain and turned Britain from a country despised by the great European rulers into one which they now feared.

She began to question him shrewdly about his past. 'They tell me that you ran away from home, m'lord. Why was that?'

'I was unhappy, Your Grace. I wished to live my own life.'

'What was the cause of your unhappiness?'

He could not answer her truthfully, but his evasion

must be carefully made so that she might not interrogate him further on the matter.

'That of many young men, Your Grace. I wanted my freedom.'

She laughed a little at that. 'But I understand that you began your new life as a common seaman. There must have been very little freedom for you on board ship.'

'But it was my choice, Your Grace, no one else's.'

'And you were present at the action in which the Armada was defeated?'

'Which I survived, to my great good luck—and to my future fortune.'

Beside him he heard Sir Robert give a dry cough. Doubtless he was appreciating the manner in which Martin verbally fenced with his Queen as he had earlier fenced with him.

The Queen now turned her attention to Sir Robert. 'I understand that my lord of Essex was foolish enough to try to persuade Lord Hadleigh to join him as one of his supporters. I cannot believe that the man whom I have just met would have had so little judgement as to agree to any such thing.'

'He has assured me that he gave m'lord short shrift in the matter, Your Grace.'

'Which, having met him, does not surprise me.'

Sir Robert nodded his head at this, at which the Queen resumed her questioning of Martin. 'I understand that you have just married Lord Clifton's niece. I wish you joy of her, and will add that if at any time you expressed a wish to enter my service in any capacity I would be most pleased to employ you.'

Again, Martin did not know quite what to say. This time he simply bowed his head and said, 'I appreciate the honour you have just done me, Your Grace, and if my duties as a merchant would be of use to the Crown then I shall remember what you have just said.'

The Queen laughed, Sir Robert smiled.

'Go to, young man, your wit equals Sir Robert's best. Has my Secretary of State been tutoring you?'

Sir Robert intervened with, 'He needs no tutoring, Your Grace, I do assure you. I, too, will bear Lord Hadleigh in mind should I need the kind of assistance he might be able to give me in future.'

'Well said,' pronounced the Queen, and then waved her hand to dismiss them. The audience was over. They might leave or stay in the Gallery, but were not to converse with her further.

Martin breathed a sigh of relief. Whatever else she was, his Queen was also uncommonly shrewd. She and Sir Robert were a good pair—as she and his father, Lord Burghley, had been. Lord Essex was a child beside them.

Sir Robert obviously thought that Lord Hadleigh was no child. 'You are exactly the kind of new man, if you will allow me to say so,' he told Martin when they had returned to his office, 'who ought to be serving the Queen—and, when she is called to her last rest, her successor.'

Martin shook his head. 'I was not formed to be a courtier, and I believe that all who serve her at court in any capacity, must inevitably, after a short time, become a courtier. My talents, such as they are, lie elsewhere.'

'Nevertheless,' said Sir Robert, 'should you change your mind, you know where I may be found. Oh, and as a last piece of advice, I think that you would be wise to have as little to do with Master Frampton as possible.'

Martin knew that that was the paraph which ended his interview with Sir Robert Cecil. Now he must leave. He found that the effort of being cautious, of not saying what he truly thought, had made him sweat, something which physical danger had never managed to achieve. Not only that, he wondered why Sir Robert, who was reputed to know everything about everyone of importance in London, should warn him against Frampton.

Not of course that he needed warning—but was Sir Robert aware of that, too?

He was strangely quiet on the way home. So quiet that when they were on their way upriver Rafe asked anxiously, 'What did you tell Sir Robert?'

'As little as possible,' was Martin's dry reply. 'Which was also the nature of my answers to Her Grace.'

Rafe looked baffled at this, but that sharp cove, Jacko, began to laugh. 'Aye, that's the way to avoid the headsman. There's many a talkative fool who's underground because he couldn't keep his gob shut.'

Rafe said, 'Her Grace? Never say that you had an audience with the Queen?'

'Yes, and she offered me a post at court—which I refused as politely as I could. Sir Robert assures me that the offer remains permanently open.'

'You refused?' gasped Rafe. 'Most men would have fallen over their feet to accept it.'

'I am not most men, and, as Jacko has just hinted, I have a mind to keep my head upon my shoulders.'

'What did you say to her which caused her to make you such an offer?'

'As I told you, very little—which I think pleased her.'

Jacko began to laugh. 'I know your very little, Master, as I know your quite a lot.'

Rafe was bewildered. 'Ever since I have known you, you have striven for advancement. Now the greatest offer of all has been made to you, and you have refused it.'

Martin sighed. 'I value my freedom. I am a merchant, as I was once a sea captain, with no one above me to tell me how to think and what I ought to do. To bow and scrape and lie for others, not myself— for that is what being one of Sir Robert's agents would make me—is not my understanding of what my future ought to be. If my country were in direct danger, I would fight for it, but this underhand plotting and scheming is not for me. One day I would forget myself, speak the truth and likely end up on Tower Hill, as Jacko has suggested. Now let the matter lie. I would prefer that you say nothing of this to Webster until I have had a chance to speak to him.

'And that is an order. Now let us be quiet.'

He so rarely gave a brusque command to any of those who served him that the effect was always the same: complete obedience. The rest of their journey passed in silence.

Kate had begun to worry, although she gave no sign to Aunt Jocasta that she thought something might be wrong. Night was starting to fall and Martin had not yet come home. Always before he had returned by mid-afternoon, and she found this departure from his usual custom more than a little disturbing.

She ordered dinner to be delayed, but when more time passed she rang for Webster, who was also a little worried that Martin and his attendants were so very late, particularly in view of the attempts on his life.

'Did m'lord say that he might delayed at the Royal Exchange today?' she asked him anxiously.

'On the contrary, he told me that he expected to be back early, but it is possible that some problem arose which demanded his immediate attention.'

Kate thought for a moment. 'Have you eaten since breakfast?' she asked him, knowing that he usually dined with her, Martin and Rafe.

As she had expected his answer was No.

'That being so, I think that, bearing in mind that Mistress Saville has not enjoyed a meal since she broke her fast early this morning, it would behove me to order supper to be served for the three of us straightway. M'lord and the others could then, when they arrive, determine what they might wish to eat.'

Webster bowed his head. 'I think that might be wise.' He did not say kind, but he thought it, having experienced the callousness of other great ladies where their servants and dependants were concerned.

'Very well. I shall ring for the butler to prepare a meal with all haste.'

It turned out that her decision was a wise one. Martin did not return until several hours after they had eaten their fill. Aunt Jocasta had already gone to her room to retire for the night, after explaining that the day had been a long one for her. He was looking tired, Kate thought, which was a new expression for him to wear. His first words, though, were of concern for her.

'I hope that you have broken your fast, my dear. I did not mean to be so late, but first I was required to attend Sir Robert Cecil at Greenwich Palace, which also entailed me in taking part in an audience with the Queen. After that when I returned to the Counting House I discovered that one of my clerks had made a mistake which might have cost us dearly. To correct his folly took longer than I might have deemed possible beforehand.'

'You are not to excuse yourself,' Kate said swiftly,

'only tell me whether you have eaten recently as I have done. If not, I will ring for something for you and Rafe and Jacko to eat.'

'Rafe and Jacko have gone to the kitchen for a meal, so you may look after me at your leisure.' He sank into the nearest armchair. 'If it is possible I should like to eat here informally, rather than in the Hall with a great deal of ceremony.'

'And so you shall,' Kate told him before ringing the bell again and making all the necessary arrangements, 'and while we wait, I will tell you of my day. My uncle arrived here, bringing Aunt Jocasta with him, as we had previously arranged.'

Martin looked around him before saying, 'So you were not alone for too long—but where is the good woman?'

'Retired to her room. She said that she was weary and needed to rest, but I think that she was exercising a great deal of tact by leaving me to look after you on my own when you arrived.'

Martin extended his stockinged legs towards the fire, Jacko having helped him to pull off his boots before he joined Kate. 'It was kind of your uncle to accompany her here. Did he have aught of sense to say?'

'Only that he was pleased by our marriage, whereas before he had been worried about it and he also asked me to pay his respects to you. He was sorry to learn that you were absent today.'

Martin laughed. 'Oh, bravo—that I have made

someone happy, I mean. You will be interested to learn that both the Queen and Sir Robert wished to make me part of her retinue. I am not sure how pleased they were with me when I refused.'

'They did? Of what like was the Queen when you met her?'

Martin was brief. 'Very old, but exceedingly clever.'

Kate was silent before saying slowly, 'I am glad that you refused their offers. Had you accepted them, then we should have had to part, since the wives of her courtiers are not allowed to attend court with them—which would mean that we would be separated very soon after marriage.'

'I am not formed to be a courtier, but fortunately I am prepared to eat the good meal which I can hear coming. You will drink a bumper with me, I trust.'

'Indeed.' And then Kate could not help saying, quite simply, 'I not only missed you when you did not arrive home at your usual hour, but I was also worried that some harm might have befallen you.'

Martin looked at her over the bread which he was buttering. 'You were really and truly worried for me?'

'Yes.'

He popped the bread into his mouth and chewed vigorously before saying, 'However tired I am I shall reward you for that when we retire this night. No one has ever worried about me before.' And that was true, for it was he who had worried about Mary and not the other way round.

'Not Rafe and Jacko?'

'That's different.' Martin picked up his tankard. 'I wish to drink to my wife who does me the honour of caring for me.'

He did not say love, for the word seemed to be anathema to him, but it was perhaps a sign that he was not only on the way to accepting her love, but was also nearing the time when he might be able to admit his for her. Not that she would talk to him of that tonight. He was tired after a long and difficult day, and it was her duty to see that he was not further troubled.

She watched him eat his supper with relish and they drank together at the end of it, before retiring upstairs where, tired though he might be, he did his husbandly duties with all his usual enthusiasm.

Martin had not lied to his father when he said that he had a business to run, and even though, in Thomas Webster, he had acquired a most useful secretary, he enjoyed the business of being a merchant so much that he had no wish to surrender it to another.

Besides, he was of the opinion that Webster was that most valuable of men, an excellent lieutenant, who would carry out his orders to the letter when he thought them good and sufficient, but would not hesitate to query them if he thought that they weren't. In his experience such men were rare, and the pair of them were working successfully together in the city after the same fashion which he and Rafe had employed on his ship.

He also thought, correctly, that Webster had no mind to supersede him. What he did not know was that Webster had come to admire his new master greatly. So much so that what puzzled him the most was the mystery surrounding Martin's abandonment of his life as Lord Bretford's son. M'lord had spoken of him as having been unregenerate, wild and wicked, but nothing in Martin's career, first as a humble seaman, then as a successful sea-captain, and now as Lord Hadleigh, Bretford's heir, lent credence to such a description. On the contrary, in a deceitful world full of liars and tricksters, careless of other people's feelings, he stood out as a man of honour, considerate in his dealings with those who were thought to be his inferiors, unlike many great men who trampled on all those around them.

So what had he done, all those years ago, to merit such a vile reputation that it had earned him, according to those who had known him in early youth, the most savage of punishments? The last of which had been so severe that as soon as he had recovered from it, he had run away from home.

What was even more puzzling was that Lord Bretford had worshipped his elder son, John, whom he had considered to be a paragon, but when Webster had, apparently casually, enquired about the dead man, his hearers had shrugged their shoulders, and one had even gone so far as to say, 'I could tell you some odd tales but one must not speak ill of the dead.'

Webster decided that it was useless to waste his time worrying about a problem which appeared to be insoluble, and would concentrate instead on reducing the backlog of work which had accumulated while Martin had tried to deal with everything on his own before appointing him as his secretary.

As a consequence, early one morning he wandered into the office at Saxon Hall which opened off the library to discover his master there, busy at his desk. He needed to work with the inventory of Martin's property in order to bring it up to date, but he had not been able to find it.

He gave a small cough to attract m'lord's attention.

Martin looked up at him. 'Yes, Webster, what is it?'

'The inventory, m'lord. you asked me to add to it the details of all those new goods and chattels which were acquired when you took possession of Saxon Hall, but I cannot find it.'

Martin was silent for a moment before saying, 'I thought that it was strung on the file with the rest of my business documents.'

Webster shook his head. 'No, m'lord, I have looked through them all and it is not there.'

He was so scrupulous and careful in all his doings that Martin believed him. Suddenly he exclaimed, 'I am the world's clodpole. After we moved here last year I put it in a chest which contained my most per-

sonal papers of all so that it might not be mislaid. I
have probably forgotten to return it to its proper
home. It is in one of the three which are stored in my
room. One moment and I will find the key.'

He pulled a brass-bound box towards him, opened
it with a small key from a chain around his neck, and
took three larger ones from it. He stared at them before saying to Webster. 'I believe that one of these is
the correct one. You will, perhaps, have to try them
in the locks of all three chests: one contains clothes,
another valuables and the third my personal papers:
the inventory ought to be in the last one.'

Webster took them. 'I will return them to you later,
m'lord.'

Martin sighed. 'Could you bring yourself to forget
that I am m'lord?'

Webster smiled. 'I'm afraid not. And if, as you say,
you believe in a man's freedom to speak as he wishes,
you will allow me my little foibles—such as addressing you by your proper title.'

Martin made a noise between a groan and a laugh.
'Go to, you rogue, to bait me with my own beliefs!
Call me what you will—and be damned for it!'

All the way upstairs to Martin's bedroom, Webster
laughed to himself. As m'lord had said, there were
three chests there: two of them were of plain wood,
the third was a highly decorated Italian *cassone*.
Logic said that the papers would most likely be in
one of the wooden ones, so he tried them first, only

to find that the inventory must be stored in the *cassone*.

The key slid sweetly into the lock. He threw back the lid to discover that inside was a medley of things valuable, and things which were only kept because they were dear to their owner's heart. Webster took them out one by one, to find halfway down something which looked as though it might be the misplaced inventory.

It was a book bound in vellum.

Webster lifted it out and opened it. What was immediately plain was that it could not be the inventory, for written on the title-page in faded ink were the words *John Chancellor, his book*. He was about to replace it when his curiosity overcame his usual reticence.

Why was it there, carefully stored away and hidden from the world? He began to turn the pages, first quickly and then more slowly. He was a rapid reader, because he did not say aloud the words on the page before him, but sounded them in his head instead—a trick which few men had mastered. He would have bet good money from what he had seen of him at work that Martin Chancellor was one of them.

What he found there was the answer to everything which had puzzled him about his master—only for a further puzzle to be presented to him. M'lord Hadleigh had only to give this to his father to read and nearly every word would prove that his supposed wickedness had been the product of his brother's envy and jealousy. What sort of man could John Chancellor have been, who had so resented his younger brother, a man who had nothing while he, being the heir, had everything, that he felt the necessity to destroy his life?

There was no reasonable explanation which he could think of for such dreadful behaviour, and now that John Chancellor was dead it was unlikely that there ever would be. Was that why Martin had said nothing to his father once he had found the book—preferring to leave a dying man with his illusions? That was another question which could not be answered either.

He carefully put the book back exactly where he had found it, after also noting that John must have been in the toils of someone who was able to control him by eyes and voice together. It was something of which Webster had heard before and had sworn that if the trick were tried on him he would try to resist it most strongly. He thought no more of that, for it was the other revelations which shocked him the most.

All that he had read made him respect the man for whom he now worked, even more than he already did. It was wrong that he was so misunderstood, but so long as he refused to disclose his brother's villainy, the whispers about him and his integrity would never cease.

It was no use repining, and he still had to find the inventory, which was the very last thing which he pulled out of the *cassone*. Now what was he to do?

There was only one answer to that. He would lock the *cassone* again, return the keys and the inventory to Martin, and tell him which one had opened the chest with the inventory in it.

Which was exactly what happened next. Martin put the keys down, saying ruefully, 'It was very careless of me not to label them—I hope that it was not too much trouble for you to unearth it.'

'No trouble at all,' Webster said, shading the truth a little.

'Good. I will be more careful in future. In fact, you may have them when I have finished checking them—your records are a model of excellence.'

Later, alone in his room, Webster made a resolution which he was determined to keep. M'lord must never know what his secretary had found, nor that that same secretary was determined that by some means or another he would ensure that Lord Bretford would learn of the gross injustice which his younger son had suffered at his hands.

# *Chapter Ten*

Kate was a little disappointed. Martin had promised to take her to the Royal Exchange in the near future, but some time had passed and he had not yet kept his word—which was unlike him. He was so kind and attentive to her when he was at home, however, that she did not like to raise the matter with him. What pleased her the most was that every morning he made it his practice, however busy he had been on the previous day, to wake her with a song.

That particular morning—one she was always to remember—she rolled drowsily over to find him seated in his usual chair, offering her a quiet song, not a lively one. Before she had fallen asleep she had wondered whether he would be too tired to rise early enough to serenade her—he having arrived home very late on the previous evening. She had been foolish to think any such thing, because now that she lived with him she was discovering that he was never idle.

He stopped to murmur in her direction, 'Wake up,

wife. I have a mind to take you to the Royal Exchange this morning. From something you said the other day I gather that you have never visited that part of London.'

She sat up. 'No, indeed. Until I came to Bretford House to marry you, although I had visited London several times, I was only allowed to visit those parts of it where the nobility and gentry lived.'

'That being so, I must further your education. You must not dress too grandly. First we shall visit the shops in the square, after that my Counting House, and we shall conclude our excursion by dining at an ordinary.'

'Will Aunt Jocasta be accompanying us?'

'Not today. Another time. Today is to be my wife's day of glory, and we shall travel in my new coach. It was brought specially for me from Germany where they make the best and most comfortable ones. Jacko, Rafe and some grooms will accompany us on horseback. That great merchant Lord Hadleigh must be seen to be wealthy, and what better way than grandly squiring his wife in London town. Besides, I neglected you yesterday and I must make up for that today.'

He was laughing when he told her this—but behind his mirth was real pride. He would be showing the world what he had managed to do for himself, not because he was Bretford's son, nor because the Queen or Sir Robert Cecil had chosen to favour him. He was as much a self-made man as most of the merchants with whom he was dealing in this new world of bustling commerce.

English trade was beginning to span the globe itself.

Kate clapped her hands together in joy, 'Oh, thank you, Martin,' she exclaimed, springing out of the bed and running across to kiss him on the cheek.

Whereupon he put his lute down and hoisted her on to his knee, there to kiss her vigorously before striding over to the bed and dropping her on to it, whispering, 'For that, Lady Hadleigh, I must reward you on the instant.'

Which he did with such vigour and with such mutual enjoyment that it was only with great reluctance that he pulled away from her, saying, 'Enough, we must stop now, or we shall not reach the City this forenoon—which would be a pity.'

'So we're not taking Mistress Saville with us today,' was Jacko's grumbling remark when they were assembled on the sweep before Saxon Hall, ready to climb into the coach, or mount their horses to act as escort for the most noble Lord and Lady Hadleigh.

'Next time,' Martin said. They were all, including Kate, dressed very plainly so that they would not be remarked on when they left the coach and walked among the seething crowds of the City. Not only that, Martin would be meeting some of those who still thought of him as Captain Martin—Lord Hadleigh being a strange and curious bird of a kind not usually seen in Stock Exchanges and markets.

'There is one question I must ask you, Martin,' Kate said, once they were safely on their way and before they reached the crowded streets and squares of the City. 'I hope that you will not think me over-curious, but yesterday I found a most interesting commonplace book in the library.' She paused.

For one dreadful moment Martin thought that she might have discovered his brother's self-incriminating journal, but common sense told him that it was locked away in a chest to which only he had the key.

She continued. 'It seemed to be in your handwriting and when I read it I found that it was a play—all about the sea. I did not know that you wrote plays.'

'When I was a lad,' Martin told her, 'I thought that it might be clever to be like the late Sir Philip Sidney, who was not only a soldier but a poet and a teller of tales. Years later when I became friendly with Walter Raleigh and the members of the Friday Club, I decided to try to follow his, and their, example. I thought, seeing that I had been a sailor, that I would write a play about the sea.

'When I had finished it I gave it to Raleigh and asked him to tell me what he thought of it. He passed the manuscript on to one of the men who writes plays for the Globe and who reads the work of novices like myself who do not belong to a theatrical company. It seems that he sometimes asks if he might improve them if he thinks that they are almost good enough to be staged. He liked bits of mine and wrote notes to me suggesting changes which would make it possible for the players to perform. I have been so busy lately that I have had no time to revise it. I was flattered by his attention, for he is well-known as an actor and writer.

'You may not have heard of him but his name is Shakespeare. He is an odd fellow, for he comes from the country—but he is a businessman, too, and a shrewd one.'

Kate leaned forward, her eyes shining. She was trying not to let the rocking motion of the coach distress her. 'I think it would be a pity if you did not try to improve it yourself.'

Martin shook his head. 'It was a child's dream. The interesting thing is that he liked the beginning about the sea best—which is, of course, something I know of very well. I am thinking that I might hand it to him to do with it as he will.'

He laughed, 'And that's an unintended pun, for his name is Will, and he is a great punster.'

'I should like to meet him. Best of all would be to go to see one of his plays—or any play.'

'One day I will take you,' promised Martin. 'Now we are nearing Southwark and the Royal Exchange and it will grow more and more difficult for us to make our way through the crowd.'

He was right. Their progress grew slower and slower and finally the coach stopped for some time. People looked in at them, their eyes avid, and Kate began to understand why Martin had told her not to dress too richly. She was a little fearful that someone

might throw the door open and try to attack them—
which was why Rafe and Jacko had been brought
along.

After a long wait which seemed endless, they
started off again, and when they neared the great
square where the Royal Exchange stood the crowds
thinned a little. The coach stopped before Martin's
Counting House and warehouses which were situated
in a narrow street nearby.

'One of the shops in the square is mine,' he told
Kate when he had helped her down on to the muddy
lane which passed for a street. 'It is a draper's. I propose to take you there, for my boast is that I sell the
finest linen in London.'

'Oh, I would like that,' she exclaimed, and when
they all reached the shop, for Jacko and Rafe were
accompanying them to act as guards, Kate discovered
that the shop assistant was a pretty young girl with a
cheeky face who was shouting her wares in the street.
When she saw Martin she bawled at him, 'Ho, there,
master, have you brought your new wife to sample
our fine goods?'

'Indeed, Peg darling,' he said, and stood back,
smiling, while the girl, after ushering Kate into the
shop, immediately began to unroll linen and fine cambric, 'which is good for a nightgown,' she bellowed,
'that is, if you need one,' winking meaningfully at the
watching Martin who was enjoying himself mightily.

Kate, greatly taken by the beauty of the material,
asked to buy a length of the fine linen of which

Martin had earlier spoken. She enquired how much it cost, and immediately produced the correct coins from the small leather purse which she was carrying with her.

To her great surprise Peg refused to take her money, shaking her head and laughing again. 'If you weren't the master's wife I wouldn't be telling you this,' she roared, 'but I can see that you are an innocent so I shall have to show you how to cheapen me down. Take note that you must never accept the first price that I offer you, but instead you must begin to bargain with me. Not, mind, that I always bring the price down—because sometimes the goods are worth exactly what I ask for them—but you must at least try to make me accept less.'

'I can see that shopping is rather more difficult than I thought,' Kate told Martin, who had strolled over to stand by her. 'How much less shall I offer?'

'Whatever you think is fair and reasonable.'

'But I've no notion of what that might be.'

'Use your imagination—if she jumps at what you propose then cheapen it down again.'

Kate shook her head.

'Very well,' he said, 'now watch me. Fair maiden,' he whispered, leaning forward over the counter, and speaking in an admiring and confidential tone, 'if I were to offer you a groat less than you are asking, you might make an immediate sale. What say you to that?'

'That you drive a hard bargain, Master. Make it half a groat and I would agree to your terms.'

'Done,' Martin said, pulling out his own purse. 'Now wrap the material up for my lady.'

'That is all very well,' said Kate, 'but I am not a man to woo a shopgirl as easily as you did.'

'No, indeed, but the principle is the same, and you are also likely to have to trade with a man and you may smile at him, as I smiled at Peg. Always offer something less in tones of great good humour since the saying, ''More flies are caught by honey than by gall'' is a useful motto in dealing as well as in life.'

'Who are you calling a fly, Master?' Peg roared at him while she measured out the linen. Her voice seemed to possess no low notes after years of hawking Martin's wares.

'The fly was imaginary, like the gall,' he told her with a grin.

'Then why trouble me and your lady with them?' she cried triumphantly. 'Now, m'lady, is there aught else you need?'

Kate waved her hand at the cambric, asked its price by the ell, and immediately began bargaining over it after the manner which Martin had suggested. She succeeded in bringing the price down a little, although, as she had suspected, once they had left the shop, after also buying some cheapened-down silk, several ells of brocade from France and a length of gold cord, Martin told her that she had still paid over the odds for the goods which she had bought.

'But at least you have begun to learn how to bargain successfully,' he ended, giving her a surreptitious kiss.

Jacko grumbled at them when they were out in the crowded street again. 'You took a devilish long time in there, master. Did you buy all the goods in the shop?'

'For that,' Martin said, thrusting the heavy parcel into Jacko's arms, 'you may carry our purchases. I was busy showing m'lady how to shop, seeing that she has never done so before.'

'A lady who has never shopped,' teased Rafe. 'That's a rare bird indeed!'

'I was never allowed to. It was always done for me. M'lord made it seem easy just now, but...'

'But she learned quickly,' Martin told them. 'Now we must visit a jeweller's, for I have not yet bought my lady wife a proper wedding present. After that, we shall go on to one of the shops which sells food and drink, or perhaps an ordinary where they sell the ale which Jacko loves in return for making him a beast of burden. I don't suppose that you have eaten out before, my sweeting, have you?'

He had called her his sweeting before Jacko and Rafe: it was no longer a word reserved for the bedchamber. Kate saw Rafe's eyebrows rise, but the look on honest Jacko's face was one of approval—whether at the prospect of food and drink or because Martin had called her sweeting, she could not guess.

'No, everything we have done today has been a new thing for me—including being given a present.'

Kate was speaking the truth—and she was starting to understand why Martin had not wanted to bring Aunt Jocasta with them. This was her day and no one else's. They set off at once, walking round the square to where the best of the jewellers' shops stood. The man behind the counter knew Martin by his sailor's name, unaware that he had been translated into the nobility.

'What is it this time, Captain?' he said cheerfully. 'A gold chain, or fine spurs?'

'Neither. I wish to buy a present for my wife, something not too large and not too small.'

'A ring, perhaps?' suggested the jeweller, addressing Martin and not Kate.

'You must ask my wife what she would like, dear or cheap, she shall have it. I cannot say fairer than that.'

'Oh, very fair, Captain, is it not very fair, Mistress Martin?'

Kate noticed that Martin did not correct the jeweller over his use of his old name, since, like Peg, he did not know his new one. She guessed at once that Martin preferred to come back to his usual haunts and be addressed as Captain Martin rather than Lord Hadleigh, which he still thought of as the name belonging to his dead brother.

He watched while a series of trinkets were laid on the counter for Kate to examine. She hesitated over them. They all seemed to be rather large and gaudy, priceless though they were. Finally she looked at Martin and said, 'I know that it might be a strange thing to ask for, but London is such a smelly place that I would very much like to have another pomander with fine scent in it to hang on a chain round my neck so that when the reek becomes too strong, I may sniff at it. I would like it to be a small one—the one I already own is rather large and cumbersome.'

Before Martin could answer her the jeweller exclaimed, 'I have the very thing. One moment, while I fetch it from my strongroom.'

Martin said a trifle anxiously when the jeweller had disappeared, 'You are sure that you would not like a precious gem—a fine emerald from the Americas set in a ring?'

She shook her head. 'No, the pomander will be useful and I can wear it every day and remember your kindness in giving it to me—and letting me choose my present.'

Oh, he could have kissed her on the spot, there in the jeweller's shop, when he thought of some of the other women for whom he had bought presents who were dissatisfied when they thought that they did not suitably match his wealth. Not that there had been many of them, and Mary, he remembered, had never demanded presents from him—in which Kate was like her.

The jeweller returned with the pomander, a tiny thing on a fine chain, not a heavy one, which Martin placed round his wife's neck. She was then walked over to a large Venetian mirror on the far wall so that she might see how beautiful her new treasure was. Its scent was beautiful, too, delicate, but not too much so, that sniffing gently at it, Kate found that the foetid reek of central London was no longer in her nostrils, either in the shop, or later when they were in the crowded, muddy street again making their way to Martin's Counting House.

He advised her not to fetch it out from under her warm coat when she was in the open, since thieves were known to snatch such valuables from around ladies' necks. All in all London seemed to be a dangerous place, since Rafe and Jacko had already warned her that she must beware of pickpockets and those who might wrest a parcel from her hand and disappear with it among the milling crowd. Which, of course, was another reason why the grumbling Jacko had to carry the parcel. His very appearance was enough to put a would-be thief off, since many of them were little more than children.

He went ahead, pushing a passage for them through the chattering throng, but it was as they were turning the corner into the lane where the Counting House stood that all the many warnings Kate had been given came true. A pair of burly men, dressed mostly in leather, came towards them, shoving their way past Jacko, who shouted abuse in their direction.

Kate turned aside to avoid being knocked down, only to have one of the men grab her by the wrist in order to try to pull her away through the crowd. The other sprang on Martin, a dagger suddenly appearing in his hand. Kate screamed; Rafe, unaware of the attack on Martin, caught her by her other hand and tried to wrestle her free from the man who was bent on kidnapping her.

Martin meanwhile, narrowly avoiding a dagger thrust meant to kill him, tried to get at his sword, but in vain. Death suddenly seemed to be upon him, except that Jacko, seeing what was happening, threw the heavy parcel he was carrying at the back of Martin's assailant, striking him with such force that he lost his balance and fell forward. This gave Martin the opportunity to seize his dagger hand, while Jacko dealt him a death blow with the dagger he had drawn the moment after he had flung the parcel.

The crowd around them had retreated. Jacko picked up the parcel, and howling, 'Tally ho, tally ho, Master, let's rescue the mistress,' charged after Rafe and Kate and the first man, who were rapidly disappearing into the crowd. Martin followed him, a red mist before his eyes at the prospect of losing Kate.

He and Jacko soon caught up with Rafe, who had been knifed in the shoulder after being pulled away from Kate. Covered in blood, he was being helped by a bystander, who shouted at them, 'That way, he took her that way,' pointing to a narrow lane running at right angles to the one they were on.

At the far end they could see Kate being dragged along, only to disappear as her captor hauled her to the left down yet another of the maze of streets which made up this part of London. Martin and Jacko raced after them—to discover that Kate's captor had pulled her into a cul-de-sac, where he stood panting, still clutching her with his left hand, a dagger in his right.

'Stay where you are,' he shrieked, 'or I'll kill the doxy.'

'That you won't!' roared Jacko, and threw the parcel at the kidnapper, with as much success as he had done before. It struck the kidnapper such a blow in the face that it threw him back against the door of a small warehouse, causing him to involuntarily release Kate. She ran towards Jacko, while Martin seized the shocked bravo by the throat, and in his rage would have killed him. Except that Jacko roared ferociously, 'A dead man can't tell us anything, Master, let him live!'

His sanity returning, Martin took his hands from the fellow's throat and bellowed at him, 'Who paid you to do this?'

'No one,' panted the man, who was now the hunted, not the hunter, being held in Jacko's iron grip. 'A rich doxy is a good prize.'

'And the dead man who tried to kill me. Did he mistake me for a rich doxy, too?'

'Dead! Wilkins is dead?'

'As a doornail. Now tell me the truth, or you can join him in his slumbers.'

His prisoner shuddered.

'It were a man—in a tavern. A little grey man. He

made us watch you on the way to your Counting House for two days, then told us to do for you today, and so we would have, but we didn't bargain for the doxy being with you and that damned great brute as well.'

'Nor for being a pair of clodpoles, one of whom couldn't slaughter a helpless sheep, and the other being too eager to make off with a helpless woman to assist his fellow,' Martin raged at him, sure now that 'the little grey man' must be Bevis Frampton; it was such an accurate description of him. 'What do we do with him, Jacko?'

They looked at one another and then at Kate, who had sunk on to a low wall and was nursing her bruised wrist. They knew exactly what they would have done to the foul brute had Kate not been with them.

'Nowt, for the time being. You take the mistress back to try to find Rafe, and I'll see to him.'

'Done,' said Martin, and bent down to help Kate to her feet. Once up, she shuddered against him. 'Oh, Martin, I thought... I thought...'

'Hush,' he told her, as gentle now as he had been fierce a moment ago. 'It's all over, you're safe again. Let's find poor Rafe and an apothecary to treat him.'

Rafe was being tended by a large motherly woman and a little man—an apothecary who had been part of the crowd and had volunteered to help the poor young fellow who had been injured. A short distance away, the body of the dead would-be assassin had been dragged on to a cart: a constable, whose duty it was to keep the peace in the precincts of the Royal Exchange, stood by.

He was being assured by the bystanders that, no, they didn't know who had killed him, there'd been a scuffle and then the man was dead on the ground, and no, they hadn't seen anyone but a big fellow who'd thrown something at the dead man. No, they'd not seen the man who had killed him before, and had no notion who he was. Nor had they seen who had wounded the poor chap over there, either. Everything had happened at once.

It was plain that nobody wished to have anything to do with any enquiry which might be made, or bear any sort of witness as to what had actually happened.

No one mentioned Kate being dragged away, because they had been too busy watching the affray, and had only seen Rafe when all the excitement was over. Martin was relieved that he had not brought Jacko back with him, to be identified by some know-all in the crowd. He walked over to where Kate was helping the woman and the apothecary to care for Rafe. She also had the presence of mind to say nothing to the constable or even to Rafe's helpers, Rafe having said that he had no idea why he been attacked.

'Come,' said Martin, when Rafe had been bandaged and given a foul-tasting potion to drink. 'We'll return to the Counting House and take the coach back home.'

The apothecary, who was packing his bag, said,

'London's a dangerous place these days and no mistake.'

Kate remarked soberly to Martin while they walked to the coach, 'I see now why we were all dressed so plainly. Had we been in our usual fine clothing we would have stood out in the crowd and someone might have been able to identify us and set the constable on us. As it was, we looked just like everyone else—exceedingly commonplace.'

Martin remarked, 'Very true.' He was not surprised to find that Jacko had reached the coach before them. He was on his own, carrying the now somewhat battered parcel, a look of supreme self-satisfaction on his face. Kate was just about to open her mouth to ask him what he had done with his prisoner, but some instinct made her shut it again.

'Home now,' Martin ordered, 'your visit to an ordinary will have to wait until another time. I dare not risk yet another attack being made on us. Rafe,' he added, 'you must travel with m'lady in the coach. I will ride your horse home for you.'

Rafe began to protest, but was silenced with, 'No, you are in no condition to ride.'

'Isn't that just like him,' Rafe told Kate when he was seated opposite to her, grateful for the comparative comfort of the coach. 'To think of me before himself. How many grand gentlemen would have given a thought to my discomfort, let alone surrendered their own comfortable seat?'

'True,' murmured Kate. 'His compassion is one of his many virtues, even if he claims that he has none.'

'And how many grand ladies would treat their servant as kindly as you have been treating me—particularly when I failed to rescue you from that vile swine.'

'I don't think of you as my servant,' protested Kate. 'You are my friend, as you are Martin's. Try to rest now, and remember that you were only wounded because you tried to help me. No one man could have done more. It needed both Martin and Jacko acting together to save me.'

Rafe smiled in gratitude before closing his eyes and allowing the potion he had been given to lull him into sleep.


Martin, riding beside Jacko, who had been relieved at last of his useful parcel which had been stowed into the coach to be looked after by Kate, had much to occupy his mind. What was surprising him were the feelings which had overwhelmed him after Kate had been snatched away. He had been overcome by a sensation of absolute horror at the mere idea that she might have gone from him for ever.

It was as though he was being robbed of a part of himself, something which was so precious to him that the thought that he might lose it was beyond bearing.

No, it could not be, not Kate, he could not lose Kate. God could not be so cruel as to take away first Mary and now her. The red rage which had swept

over him and which, had it not been for the intervention of Jacko, would have made him kill her captor
on the spot, had shocked him by its violence. Like
many soldiers and sailors he had experienced battle-
rage, but even that had not been as strong, or as fierce,
as the sensations which had roared through his body
when they had found her.

How had she come to mean so much to him? Was
it love, that emotion which all the poets, whether
courtiers or commoners, celebrated? Had he, who had
sworn after Mary's death that he would never love
another woman, been stricken again by Cupid's arrow
to the degree that he believed that life without Kate
would be a barren desert?

But it was the fierceness of the whole business
which shocked him the most. His love for Mary had
been a gentle thing, not this strong, demanding passion. Why was he so surprised? For was not Kate a
quite different woman from Mary? Mary had been
gentle, and had aroused in him a desire to protect her
from harm. The transports of passion which he was
sharing with Kate would have frightened her.

How was it possible for a man to love two such
different beings? Perhaps it was because with Mary
he had still been, despite all his dreadful experiences,
an innocent boy, but with Kate he was a man who
had seen life in all its aspects, both good and bad,
and what he now wanted was a woman who could
meet and match him. He would never have wrangled
with Mary as he often did with Kate, because it would

have frightened her, whereas Kate took it as an opportunity to fight him at all points...

Even as he thought this he experienced yet another shock, for they had already reached Saxon Hall and in his musings no time at all seemed to have passed, nor had he been aware of the distance which they had travelled.

Martin dismounted, threw the reins of his horse to a groom and stalked into his home, a man who had just learned something about himself which he had never thought to know.

When they were alone again, after Rafe had been helped to bed and Jacko rewarded for his heroism by a purse full of gold, Kate said to Martin, 'Jacko killed that man, didn't he?'

'Perhaps,' was the only answer she got, and thinking about that and the day's events, she decided that the man had earned his fate the moment he had tried to kidnap her.

They were in the withdrawing-room. Kate had changed into a simple gown, Martin was still in his City clothes. They were waiting for dinner to be served. Webster, who was surprised to see them all back so early, had already informed Martin of the details of his day's work, and, having broken his fast earlier, had left them to have their meal alone.

Kate debated whether to ask Martin any further questions about the attack on them, but since she wished to know whether what had happened that morning had been a random, rather than a deliberate, act, decided that she ought to.

'Was the attack meant for us?' she said. 'Or was it that we were unlucky to be singled out by a pair of bravos?'

Martin decided not to lie, even if he did not tell Kate the truth, the whole truth and nothing but the truth.

'I think that it was meant for us. We were probably ambushed because I was recognised as a rich merchant, and you were taken because you were a pretty woman. I fear that they were hoping to enjoy you and the gold they hoped to find on us.'

Kate shuddered, remembering the man's hateful grasp of her, and feeling the pain of the bruises which that grasp had inflicted.

'Does it mean that I may not go to the City with you again? That would be a pity.'

'Indeed, but I think that for the moment we must go carefully—not only in the City, but elsewhere. There are many gangs of such brutes lurking around London, and any one of them might have thought that they would gain rich pickings if they attacked us. I have already ordered Webster to arrange for extra guards to be hired to protect Saxon Hall. It would usually be Rafe's job, but at the moment he is out of action.'

'I had not known that the world is so wicked.'

'We are rich and they are poor. They cannot hope to earn by working what they might gain by crime.'

'Are you trying to excuse them?' Kate asked.

'No, only explaining to you the true nature of the world in which we live.'

Martin was sorry that he could not tell Kate that the money the two bravos had hoped to earn by killing him and capturing her would have been paid to them by Bevis Frampton if they had been successful: but the less she knew the safer she would be.

'I was poor once,' he added, 'and it was a hard life. Fortunately for me, I found a way out of it.'

'And are now rich—by your own efforts,' said Kate.

'And by great good luck, too—never forget that, for I do not. And now, by chance again, I am married to you.'

He desperately wanted to make love to her at once, to prove that love does indeed conquer all, as the saying went, but the footmen would soon be arriving with their meal. After that, though...

Yes, after that, he would take her upstairs to comfort her, but in doing so he could not erase the new knowledge which his innocent—and hitherto protected—wife had gained: that the world was a cruel place and to survive in it demanded not only determination, but also luck—the workings of chance which no man could control.

Bevis Frampton's bravos had been told to report back to him when they had accomplished their mission. But the day wore on and they did not reappear.

Nor did they on the following day, nor the day after that.

He was so enraged at this latest failure to snare Lord Hadleigh that he decided that the only way to get rid of the swine would be to take a hand in the game himself. He would try, once more, to use the power of his eyes on either Hadleigh or one of his servants. It had been easy enough to snare his brother by using them—but he had been younger then. Unfortunately, he had discovered of late that the force of his glare and his voice working together was not as powerful as it had been in the past.

Or, better still, if Essex should decide to try to organise a major uprising against the Queen, then he might turn that to his own advantage by, under cover of it, planning a fatal attack on Hadleigh himself.

Whatever means he used the next time he must succeed—never mind the cost. Hadleigh's luck would surely run out some time and his own would prevail. By all the powers, let it be soon!

## Chapter Eleven

The year wore on. The Queen, who had hitherto left Essex to stew in his own juice, grew impatient with his intransigence and decided to move against him. She ordered that a speech reciting all his many offences should be read out before the Star Chamber by the Lord Keeper, and that Essex should then be summoned to appear before a special court. He declined to attend on the grounds of his illness, whereat the Queen took the unprecedented action of having herself rowed to Essex House to try to speak to him in person and persuade him to attend.

What exactly happened there was never to be known, other than that she never met him—or so it was reported. On the following day, November the 29th, the court was held in his absence, and it ended by listing again all his many misdemeanours, which, it was claimed, taken together, amounted to treason.

He was not, however, immediately arrested, but remained in confinement at Essex House, from where, shortly afterwards, the news filtered out that he was gravely ill, this time of a combination of a stone in the kidney and dysentery.

The citizenry of London buzzed and roared as each new act in the drama was played before them. They were largely on Essex's side, and decorated many of the City's walls with graffiti supporting him and attacking the Queen and Cecil, who were thought to be plotting his doom. A number of the nobility went so far as to write letters urging James VI of Scotland to invade England with their help and depose the Queen.

All his supporters, both gentle and simple, were aware that Essex, who had once been the Queen's favourite, was living in a world turned upside down, where it seemed more and more likely that he would shortly be ending his life on Tower Hill.

Martin's whole world had also been turned upside down. The self-sufficiency on which he had prided himself since Mary had died had disappeared. His life had been so easy, his goals so simple and direct. How was it, then, that Kate had come to twine herself around his heart so that the thought of losing her made him feel sick? He did not want this; no, not at all.

He had always told himself that if he married again his wife would mean no more to him than any other household chattel, there for him to use when he so willed, without it in any way engaging his feelings. Yet now, no matter how many times, in her absence, he told himself that he would not allow her to affect him so strongly, once she was in his presence he immediately fell under her spell.

He had never been able to understand how it was that some men saw women as witches, as sirens, luring them on to do what they would not, but now that mystery was solved. Yet Kate was no siren. Her innocence was so patent, her goodness so plain, that every time he witnessed it, as when she had comforted Rafe after he had been wounded while defending her, his heart felt nigh to bursting.

All those love songs he had performed half in jest, he now sang in earnest. More than that, to his utter surprise, the muse who had proved shy when he had tried to write a play now became bold, and the words flew from his pen. The many songs mocking love which he had written in the past were quite forgotten, for now he admitted his love for her in every word he wrote.

He did not yet dare to tell the secrets of his heart to Kate. He who had been so forthright all his life was now timid before her, lest, because he had refused to allow her to confess her love to him, she might be reluctant to believe that he had changed. So, slowly and subtly, he would woo her, and pray that his conversion had not come too late to save him.

In the meantime he would finish the song he was writing and, one day soon, he would sing it to her. The music for it was already running through his head

even as the words, almost as by magic, formed themselves on paper.

> Cupid shot me, this I know
> With just one arrow from his bow,
> I fell before my lady fair
> Enraptured by her face and hair
> Her eyes, her walk, hold me in thrall,
> Her voice is like a songbird's call.
> Sweet Jesu grant that she and I
> May live in Eden 'til we die.

It was so unlike anything which he had written before that he stared at his work in wonderment. So rapt
was he that it was only at the last minute that he
registered that there had been a knock on his door.

He shouted, 'Enter!' and hastily stuffed the paper
in a drawer, trying to look as though he had been
busily working at the large ledger which he pulled
before him.

It was Jacko, acting as a postboy. He handed
Martin a letter which had just arrived. 'The man who
delivered it said that it was urgent,' he announced,
'and he would like an immediate answer.'

Now who the devil could it be from? Sir Robert
Cecil? M'lord Essex? Master Bevis Frampton? Or
was it from some dealer who wished to ride on the
back of Andrew Martin's success? The size of the seal
which he began to break told him that this last guess
was unlikely.

It was from Lord Essex, and was half a plea and half a demand that Lord Hadleigh should visit him again.

Martin pulled a sheet of paper towards him and started to write at speed.

'Lord Hadleigh thanks M'lord Essex for his most gracious invitation, but regrets that, at present, he is so busily engaged on a new venture that he must ask him to be forgiven if he is unable to take advantage of it.

'He remains your most humble servant.'

He closed it with a seal nearly as elaborate as Lord Essex's had been, and handed it to Jacko, saying, 'Give that to M'lord Essex's messenger.'

'Essex!' exclaimed Jacko, making a rude noise with his lips. 'Him as thinks that poor folks like me are on his side. Does he want you to lend him money? Or raise an army for him? Best you do neither—the poor fellow's a clodpole.'

This earthy admonition set Martin laughing. Trust Jacko to get to the point straight away. There were even times when he thought that he might be the best man to ask for advice over the dilemma he was in with Kate.

Never mind that, he must attend to his work again—he mustn't be so moonstruck that he lost a useful deal because he was wool-gathering, as the saying had it. Nevertheless he wondered why Essex was so determined to have him on his side. He had told Kate he would be late home this evening because he had decided to visit the Friday Club, from which he had been absent since his marriage.

If Raleigh were there he would ask him why he thought that he was being pursued so determinedly by the Queen's fallen favourite.

'Money,' said Raleigh pithily. Although he was often a man of many words, there were times when he was a master of brevity. 'He has none, you have much—oh, and your wits, of course. Those around him are not blessed with many.'

Martin nodded. 'That's a reasonable explanation.'

Raleigh grinned. 'And your good lady—is she being reasonable now you are married?'

'Manifestly so. She gave her blessing for my visit to the club today. Some of her cousins are coming a-calling and they—and the old aunt—can have a fair old gossip in my absence.'

'Talking of gossip, I have heard that Southampton, through Sir Gelli Meyrick, has been badgering the players to put on *Richard II*, that old drama of Shakespeare's, to help Essex's cause along.'

'Why,' asked Martin, 'should the actors do anything so dangerous, since it might even be considered treasonable to stage it? Especially after the judgement the Star Chamber has recently handed down?'

'Money again. At the moment I believe that Southampton is not offering enough. Besides, the matter is not yet urgent. Essex is still ailing and is in no condition to lead a revolt. They are talking of delaying it until after Christmas.'

'Well, if he and Essex are short of money it does explain why they are trying so hard to enlist me on his side.'

'Exactly. Of course, if Southampton were to offer them enough money the players would do as he wished—however dangerous it might be. Shakespeare in particular is noted for driving hard bargains of a similar nature. He is that odd thing, a man who is a poet and a businessman, too.'

'If I wrote poetry would you call me odd?'

'Certainly, even odder than Shakespeare.'

By now the room was beginning to fill up as the club members arrived.

Martin decided not to show Raleigh his latest songs yet. They were too personal, too much a part of himself that he had never yet revealed to anyone. They were quite at odds with the man everyone, including his father, supposed him to be. Did Raleigh write poetry which he showed to no one?

Ben Jonson, who had just come up to beard Raleigh, was certainly odd, and Martin would bet that he showed everything he wrote to anyone who would read or listen to it. By his expression Raleigh was finding him tedious, and when the man had moved on he muttered at Martin, 'I wish someone would tell Jonson how to pronounce my name properly. It's Rawly, not Rally. It may be stupid of me, but I find it annoying to have a man who is so confident that everything he does is perfect misname me so consistently.'

Martin solemnly nodded agreement. His solemnity hid his amusement that Raleigh, who spelled his name a different way in every document he signed, should be so troubled about how it was pronounced.

Well, he thought, all men have their vanities, and although they recognise those of others, they are often unaware of their own.

Some days after Martin had refused again to support Lord Essex, Webster was working in the office when the steward came in to announce that he had a visitor.

'It is Master Bevis Frampton, sir, and when I informed him that Lord Hadleigh was out he asked if he might speak with you.'

Frampton! Who had he really come to see? Martin or himself? Logic said that he must be the fellow's target, since he must surely know that Martin visited the City every day. But what could Frampton want with Martin's secretary?

'Admit him,' he ordered.

'Here?' queried the steward.

'Of course, where else?'

Frampton walked into the room, bowing and fluttering in Webster's direction as though he were Lord Hadleigh himself.

'Most gracious of you to see me. I trust that I do not disturb your labours.'

Of course he was disturbing Webster's labours, but he did not say so.

'I always have time for visitors if they have something substantive to say to me.'

'Most wise of you, I am sure. It is about the matter of Lord Essex that I wished to speak to m'lord, and you will doubtless report to him anything which I have to say to you.'

'You may depend upon it.'

'It is the following.'

Bevis leaned forward and fixed Webster with a hard and unwavering stare, at the same time beginning to beat monotonously on the desk with his forefinger.

'You can hear me, I hope,' he said, not once, but twice and then again. 'And will at all times acknowledge me as your one and only master.'

He repeated this again and again, keeping his baleful eyes fixed on Webster's.

Webster recognised at once the true nature of Bevis's behaviour. Some called it the evil eye, others had more fanciful names for it. Whatever happened, he must not allow Frampton to take control of him in order to force him into doing something against his will.

The fellow must be allowed to believe that his tricks were working, and Webster prayed that he would be strong enough to overcome them.

'Repeat after me,' he was ordered, 'the following words, "I will always carry out your orders, Master."'

'I will always carry out your orders, Master.'

'Again.' And the tapping grew more and more relentless.

'I will always carry out your orders, Master.'

'Excellent. Listen carefully to me. On the first occasion on which you are alone with Lord Hadleigh in this room, you will take up the dagger I shall give you and thrust it into his breast with such force that he dies. Now repeat that after me.'

Webster did as he was bid in a monotone.

'And again.'

Bowing his head, the slave appeared to obey his master yet once more.

'Yes, you will always obey my orders in future. Take the dagger and hide it where you may easily find it when the time comes to use it. Say again that you will carry out my orders.'

'I will carry out your orders.'

'Good, now hide the dagger!'

Webster pulled open a drawer in his desk and placed the dagger in it.

'Excellent. Now, as proof that you have become my servant, who will obey me whenever I command you to do so, fall on to your hands and knees, crawl towards me and lick my boots until I tell you to stand again.'

Webster, swallowing his revulsion at this loathsome command, did as he was bid.

'Now stand up straight and look me in the eye.'

He was obeyed again.

Bevis, his eyes still hard on Webster's, intoned, 'When I snap my fingers together you will forget what I have just told you, but when the time is right you will remember my orders, and will act upon them.'

Webster blinked after seeing the snapping fingers, and then said, brightly, as though nothing untoward had happened since Bevis had spoken to him of his wish to leave a message for Martin, 'I understand that you require me to report to Lord Hadleigh on certain matters relating to Lord Essex. You may give me your message and I will inform Lord Hadleigh of it when he returns.'

'Well said: it is this. Lord Essex asks Lord Hadleigh to reconsider his refusal to join him in his enterprise. Once that enterprise is successful he may choose whichever post in government he wishes and in due course will receive a Marquessate. That is all. You will not forget?'

Webster shook his head. 'No, Master Frampton, I never forget anything. Ever. I do assure you of that.'

'Then I will bid you good day.'

After Bevis had taken his leave, Webster pulled his kerchief from his sleeve, poured water on it from a pitcher which always stood on his desk and scrubbed his mouth vigorously in order to take away the foul taste of the humiliation he had recently suffered, but which he felt sure had been necessary to convince Frampton that his vile trick had worked.

\* \* \*

Martin was early home that day. He immediately walked into the withdrawing-room, to find Kate and Aunt Jocasta there. They were busy making a purse to hang from Kate's waist—or rather Aunt Jocasta was. Kate was admiring her aunt's dexterity with the needle while she read to her.

'I hoped that you would not be late home today,' Kate told him when he walked forward to kiss her on the cheek—a simple act which set his passion for her boiling again. He wondered whether he had the same effect on her, but since he had told Kate not to talk of love to him, she had tried to obey him by not committing any act which could be construed as provocation.

Unknown to her, far from cooling him down, her reticence set him on fire. He wondered how he might get rid of the old aunt, but before he could frame some sort of excuse, Kate said, 'Master Webster asked me to tell you that he wishes to speak to you on a most urgent matter and begs that you will do him the honour of attending on him as soon as you arrive.'

'Oh, I am always ready to honour Webster, as he well knows, but today I prefer to honour my wife first.'

Aunt Jocasta, who was learning to recognise when her presence was not required, picked up her needlework and said, 'I wish to take a short walk in the park before night falls. I wonder if I could have Master Jackson with me to act as my guard.'

'Certainly,' both Kate and Martin replied together, and once she had gone they joined in laughing together at their eagerness to be alone.

'I don't think that I can wait to pleasure you until we retire upstairs,' Martin told her, seating himself on the long settle and pulling her on to his knee. 'I have noticed that you have taken to wearing much less in the way of stiff court clothing lately, and consequently it will be easier for me to undress you.'

Kate teased him with, 'Your clothing is as cumbersome as mine was, if not more so. What do you propose to do about that?'

'Take off my breeches, and since your skirts are so light today, you may keep them on and lift them for me so that we may enjoy ourselves without delay. The floor will give us more room than the settle and you may use one of the cushions from it to support your head once we descend there.'

And if, when they reached it, the floor was uncomfortable, neither of them, in their mutual joy, noticed it. Kate, her skirts above her head, felt like a parlourmaid accommodating her master, something which made Martin's lovemaking even more exciting—if that were possible.

That they might be interrupted at any moment was another thing which added to her pleasure. Never mind that they were man and wife, to enjoy themselves on the withdrawing-room floor, instead of respectably in bed, gave the whole glorious business an illicit air.

Both of them must have felt it, for they rapidly shuddered simultaneously into such a powerful climax that they lay there exhausted for several minutes without moving. Martin, who was usually the first to recover, suddenly sat up, kissed Kate on the cheek, and picked up his breeches which he had thrown on to the settle in his haste to get at her, saying, 'I know that we are husband and wife, but we do owe an example to our servants, and making love in the early afternoon is not one we ought to encourage.'

Kate sat up, too, rearranged her skirts, and picked up the cushion, remarking, 'It wasn't as comfortable as the bed, but that did not matter overmuch. Besides, the difference seemed to add a certain zest to the act.'

Martin pulled her to her feet, laughing again. 'Go to, wife. Next time we'll try the wall. Who knows, you might enjoy that even more.'

Soon the only evidence of their love-making was in their flushed faces. Martin had scarcely finished fastening his breeches when there came a knock on the door.

'Enter,' he called, trying to look as grave as though he had just been reading a book of sermons.

It was the steward.

'Master Webster asks, m'lord, if it would be convenient for you to attend him in the office as soon as possible. He begs pardon for troubling you so soon after you have returned home, but says that the matter he wishes to discuss is an urgent one.'

Well, Webster might really have had to beg pardon if he had sent the steward along a few moments earlier, was Martin's immediate reaction. He turned to Kate, who was contriving to look extremely demure for a woman who had just been enjoying herself so earthily only a few minutes earlier.

'You will excuse me, wife.'

She smiled coyly at him. 'Only if you will promise to engage me again in a similar project to the one which we have just enjoyed.'

'With pleasure,' he grinned back at her. 'And now to see what is engaging Webster so mightily.'

He found his secretary seated at his desk, an odd expression on his face.

'Come now,' asked Martin, who was all aglow after his recent bout with Kate. 'What is it that occupies your interest so strongly that you need my presence with such urgency?'

Webster rose, opened a drawer in the desk, pulled something from it and held it out towards Martin.

'This,' he said.

This, to Martin's surprise, was a dagger. He took it, for once bemused.

'Why is this urgent? Is there something remarkable about it?'

'Yes,' Webster told him and fell silent again.

Martin examined it carefully. 'It looks very ordinary to me,' he said at last. 'Cease to bait me before I attack you with it in order to gouge a proper explanation out of you.'

Webster's laughter was heartfelt. 'A very apt answer, m'lord, as you will see when I tell you how it came into my possession.'

'It's yours, then?'

'Not exactly, or perhaps, after a fashion, yes. This afternoon I had a visitor, our suspected assassin, Bevis Frampton. He said that he came to visit you, but, in truth, as I soon discovered, he had come to visit me. After we had exchanged a few polite words he turned an evil eye on me to bend me to his will—together with a drumming finger and a constant repetition of the same words.

'Briefly, when he thought he had conjured me into a state where he could control me with his voice, he gave me the dagger you hold and told me to kill you with it when we were next alone together. By great good fortune I had heard tell of this wicked trick and was able, by an act of will of my own, to behave as though he had genuinely overcome me. He then bade me to forget what he had ordered me to do, until you and I were alone together when I would instantly carry out his fell intent.

'For a moment I thought to kill him, or take him prisoner, but I dare not risk being unable to convince anyone that something so strange could be true. Better by far to present you with the dagger and hope that you would believe me.'

Martin put the dagger down carefully and stared at Webster.

He thought of what his brother had written in his Commonplace Book before he spoke.

'Yes, your story *is* a strange one, but recently I read an account written by someone who had suffered a like strange experience at the hands of a man who was almost certainly Bevis Frampton. I was inclined to believe this to be a fable from someone who was ill when he wrote of it, but you are not ill. Are you prepared to swear on the Bible that you are telling me the truth?'

'Willingly.'

'Then you need not swear—I believe you. What do you think that, knowing this, we ought to do about Frampton?'

'We can do nothing through the law,' Webster said slowly, 'for my story would sound like a fantasy which I had invented. We must go carefully, all of us, and try not to be alone with him.'

'That is not enough. He must be dealt with, but short of murder, how? There is a puzzle for us, and only for the two of us. Best you say nothing of this to anyone else.'

'The other and more important question is,' said Webster, 'what will Frampton do when he learns that I have not killed you, and that he has failed again?'

Martin said, slowly, 'I have found in the past that, in the end, time and chance often solve such puzzles for us. I would like to act against him immediately, but, as things are, it might not be wise.'

'So we do nothing?'

'For the moment, yes. What is of more immediate importance is that I must thank you for saving my life—for had you not tricked Frampton while he believed that he was tricking you, I would be lying here dead.'

'And I would be on my way to the gallows,' remarked Webster dryly.

'True, but it does not lessen the favour you have done me. One way or another I shall repay you.'

Webster shook his head, 'No need for payment of any kind. I was but doing my duty.'

'You must leave me to be the best judge of that,' was Martin's answer.

The matter was left there.

'Was Webster's business really very urgent?' Kate asked Martin over supper, to receive a light-hearted answer from him. 'Not really, secretaries tend to believe that all matters which they deal with are urgent. Suffice it that the problem was soon settled.'

Webster had asked to be excused from joining them in their meal that night. 'Safer so,' he had said privately to Martin, 'One or the other of us might say something which would enlighten your clever wife as to what happened here today. By tomorrow it will be a little behind us, and not the first and only thing on our minds.'

So only Rafe ate with them and Aunt Jocasta, and

he was full of the latest gossip which had run round the ordinary where he had taken his midday meal.

'It is said that the Queen has banished Bacon from the precincts of the court, and that she is considering taking similar action against Raleigh. There is talk that he belongs to a mystic circle which meets privately to discuss topics which are best left to those who rule England.'

'I know,' said Martin, ready to defend Raleigh, a man whom many, jealous of his varied accomplishments, lost no time in attacking, 'that he's a member of a group called the School of Night. He told me recently, however, that they discuss quite different matters—such as the nature of the world we live in and its true history, together with other theories which Dr Dee has propounded.'

'Which means,' Kate said shrewdly, 'that he—and they—might be questioning the truth of the Bible. Were Sir Walter to live under Catholic rule he would be in danger of death by burning rather than simply being banished from the court.'

'True,' said Martin slowly. 'Her Grace is not so harsh as most rulers, but you must understand that there are times when only the most condign punishment of those who are traitors will answer.'

'Such as the execution of the Queen of Scots,' Rafe said.

'True again, and it took Lord Burghley many days before Her Grace consented to sign the death warrant of a woman who had repeatedly encouraged those who had tried to murder her.'

'Perhaps,' said Kate, showing how quickly she was beginning to understand the devious nature of the great world of politics and diplomacy, 'she might have thought that it would be dangerous to execute a fellow monarch because it might serve to spur on others to do the same. Not only that; since in the end she was compelled to give way in order to save the state, it ought to serve to persuade Lord Essex to behave himself lest he meet the headsman one fine morning.'

'He's not clever enough to learn his lesson,' riposted Rafe with a grin, and they all began to laugh, so that to Martin's relief the table talk turned to other matters than death and treason.

'Let us talk of Christmas,' he proposed. 'I have had a letter from my father: a letter which surprises me. He has asked me to spend Christmas with him, bringing with me my wife and my immediate entourage. There are certain matters which he wishes to discuss with me.'

All his hearers stared at him. Aunt Jocasta was the first to speak. 'How very strange. In the last conversation I had with your father before I left Bretford House, he was adamant that he had no wish ever to see or speak to you again.'

'So he told me before I left,' Martin said. 'I would have thought that the sun would rise in the west if I set eyes on him before he was laid to rest in state in his coffin.'

'The question is,' Kate offered quietly, 'do you wish to oblige him?'

Martin was almost of a mind to say no. Instead, he said something which Kate thought was also strange. 'I shall have to consult Webster before I make a decision.'

Rafe, who was a trifle jealous of Webster, exclaimed, 'And Jacko, too, I suppose.'

'Why Webster?' queried Aunt Jocasta, who thought that all servants should know their place—always excepting Jacko, of course.

Martin shrugged his shoulders. He could not tell them of the great service which Webster had done him and that in the doing he had shown wisdom and judgement beyond his years. 'I have always found his advice to be worth having.'

'Do you want mine?' enquired Rafe belligerently over his syllabub.

'Always,' said Martin, 'and whenever you care to give it.' He had no wish to hurt Rafe's feelings, but his talents lay in other directions than those of Webster.

'Ask yourself what's in it for your father, that he so suddenly wishes to see you? Or for you, if you obey his wishes? Or if you don't?'

'Well said, but it doesn't advance the matter much, does it? I still have a decision to make, and a difficult one.'

Kate said suddenly. 'The past is dead and gone, except in our minds where it never dies until we do. Let us consider the present. Had you been your father's best beloved son, would you be happier than you are now—successful and well-respected, surrounded by friends? Your brother was your father's best-beloved—was *his* life so happy and successful?'

She did not add 'happily married', but the inference was there.

'Are you trying to say that he did me a favour?'

'No,' she told him, her eyes hard on him. 'Only to look at the consequences of his behaviour. Is it in you to be magnanimous, to forgive him, to think how he suffered when John died as he did? That he deserved to suffer is no matter. In the end we all make our own lives and die our own deaths.'

They all, including Martin, stared at her in wonder.

'You mean that we ought to visit him?'

'That you should consider it most carefully. You have now listened to our advice. By all means consult Webster—and then make up your own mind. He is your father, not ours.'

Her speech confounded Martin a little, but also told him something. That, he reflected, is why I love her, not simply lust after her. For it is love I feel, for her mind, as well as her body. By the gods, she equals the Queen in wisdom!

Aunt Jocasta twittered at them all, 'Your father was always wrong-headed, given to strange dislikes—and for no reason. I mind me he hated our cousin Rollo, and a kinder and better fellow never lived.'

'Perhaps he disliked him because he *was* a kinder and better fellow,' Kate suggested.

Rafe shook his head at this, but Martin stared at Kate as though she had suddenly grown two heads. Dare he believe such a strange explanation of his father's behaviour towards him? That he had been disliked because, far from thinking him a worthless wretch, his father had begun to understand that he was the stronger and better of his two sons and had decided that he would make up for John's deficiencies by favouring him and putting down his rival.

It was almost impossible to believe it to be true. It would be a perversity of such magnitude that anyone who held to it would be… Martin had no word in his vocabulary to describe such a man. And yet…and yet…if it *were* true he could never forgive his father, but he might be able to pity him—which was a different state of mind altogether if the theologians and the philosophers were to be believed.

Yes, he would speak to Webster, because he was the only person he knew, beside Kate, who would be able to follow such a convoluted argument. Rafe lived in the world of the here and now and would dismiss any such discussion as airy nonsense.

Meantime Bevis Frampton railed against Fate: Hadleigh still lived. His attempt to corrupt Webster by his black arts had been a failure. Either Webster had tricked him, or the power he had gained over him had worn away before he had met his victim. All was to do again. He bitterly recalled his early youth, when everything had been so easy. He had disposed of his first victim, Harry Grantly, so successfully that no one had ever suspected him.

True, he had failed with Oliver Woodville, but that had been an exception. All of his other victims, save only the Queen, his one other failure, had gone to their deaths unaware of who had sent them there. He would himself engineer Hadleigh's death, not leave it to others. If Essex, as he hoped, soon mounted an uprising against the Queen, he might, in the general mêlée which was sure to follow, find some way of ending Hadleigh's run of luck. While he waited on that he would keep watch on him and his minions.

Webster, when approached for his advice, and told of Lord Bretford's invitation and the response to it by Rafe, Kate and even Aunt Jocasta, thought carefully for some minutes, his eyes fixed on some horizon which Martin could not see. It was perhaps as well that Martin could not read his secretary's mind, for Webster was thinking, already? Has what I put in train succeeded already? Or has the old fool suddenly had a fit of wisdom, looked at what Martin has done and truly is, and come to the conclusion that, somehow, he must have misjudged him in the past?

Aloud, he said, 'I would give your father the benefit of the doubt, as it were. He is an old man, near

death, and he might be seeing the past in a different
light. Why he rejected you and why he now wishes,
so suddenly, to see you again—and at Yuletide, too—
remains a mystery which might be solved if you were
to visit him. Kate's suggestion that you allow the past
to die seems to me to be a wise one. You have nothing now to prove to him or to any man—what you
have done speaks for itself.'

'So I go.'

'That is my advice—but the final decision must be
yours.'

'Then I shall accept his invitation—if only to find
out why he has made it.'

'A most sensible decision—if I may say so.'

'You may, indeed.'

When Martin had gone Webster lay back in his
chair and contemplated the ceiling. He had been
tempted to make the decision for Martin, in order to
discover whether his own machinations had succeeded, whether the vow which he had made when
he had found John Chancellor's commonplace book,
to right the wrongs done to Martin, was obviously on
the way to fulfilment.

In the end, though, it had to be Martin's choice,
not his.

It was going to be a very interesting Christmas.

# Chapter Twelve

Interesting Christmas or not, stalemate reigned on the way to it, with Essex still besieged in Essex House and defying his Queen, and in the affairs of the Earl of Bretford. Martin had sent his father a letter accepting his invitation to stay with him over Yuletide, as Webster persisted in calling it, but the wording of his reply was cool in the extreme.

Martin and most of his family, for such was the name of everyone who worked for him and lived at Saxon Hall, prepared to move to the Strand on December the 24th. Festivities had already begun at court: it was apparent that, on the surface, at least, the Queen was not taking Essex's implied threat to her sovereignty very seriously.

Raleigh, who had warned her not to be too precipitate in dealing with Essex, but to allow him to destroy himself with his folly, told Martin that Sir Robert Cecil had made great, and secret, preparations in order to withstand any uprising which Essex might try to bring about.

'Cecil's as wily a young fox as his father was an old one,' he ended. 'Her Grace has had the most amazing luck in having around her such a collection of wits—and from the beginning of her reign, too. I am beginning to think that luck is the most important ingredient in success.'

'Exactly half, if Machiavelli is to be believed,' Martin countered with a grin. 'The other half being the cunning of the Prince—and both ingredients are needed.'

'That's what Essex lacks, cunning,' sighed Raleigh. 'If he were half as clever as he thinks he is, he would be one of Her Grace's chief ministers and generals by now. As it is…' and he left the rest of his sentence unfinished. 'I was his friend once,' he added, 'but no longer. He may be bent on a form of suicide but I am not. By the by, I hear that you are to spend Christmas with your father at Bretford House. Have you become reconciled with him?'

'That I don't know. After years of throwing me off, even when at last I became his heir, suddenly, out of the blue, as it were, he sends me this invitation. My Privy Council, such as it is, all seemed to think that I ought to accept it, so we shall be journeying to the Strand in a sennight.'

'By your Privy Council, do you mean the motley crew whom your father deplores?'

Martin laughed. 'Yes, joined by my wife since we

married. I truly believe that in wisdom and learning she is very like our lady, the Queen, was when she was a young woman. As to that, I don't think that Cecil has a better crew in his ship than Rafe, Webster and Jacko.'

'Particularly Jacko,' quipped Raleigh, laughing in his turn. 'I was most struck by him on my last visit to you. A murderous henchman who has a rare vein of common sense is truly a remarkable fellow to have at your back.'

'Most particularly since, by some miracle, he is a favourite of all the ladies, both gentle and simple, in Saxon Hall.'

'Not your good lady, surely.'

'My good lady, her aunt and all the women in the kitchens.'

Raleigh shook his head. 'I shall never understand women if I live to be a hundred. Anyone less like the gallant chevalier whom they are all supposed to desire than Jacko is, I have yet to meet. By the by, a little bird has told me that Essex will be mounting his grand assault on the Queen early in the New Year. If so, I would advise you to be prepared to withstand an attack on your property either at the Royal Exchange or at Saxon Hall: any such rebellion is likely to get out of hand if the mob joins in.'

Martin wondered exactly who Raleigh's little bird was—someone near to Essex, no doubt, probably spying for Cecil and anyone else whom he thought needed to be informed. Raleigh had never said anything to suggest that he knew of Bevis Frampton's campaign against him, so Martin did not question him about it.

That same evening he told the Privy Council of Raleigh's name for them and of his belief that it might be wise for them to make plans to resist a possible assault on Saxon Hall.

'And your father's home, too,' said Webster suddenly. 'Remember that Bevis Frampton is one of Essex's most fervent supporters. Who knows what he might try to do to you and yours?'

He had not forgotten that Kate was unaware of Frampton's constant attempts on Martin's life, as well as the failed bid to kidnap her which had been the result of one of them. He had always thought this decision to be a mistake. He put his hand to his mouth as though regretting a slip of the tongue, when Kate, who had been listening intently to everything that was being said, enquired, 'Who is Bevis Frampton, and why should we be worried about what he might be planning?'

Martin's look for Webster, whom he believed had just made a rare mistake, was a reproachful one.

'I will tell you later,' he said. 'For the moment let us begin our own planning. Rafe and Jacko will be responsible for readying us to withstand an attack, both here and at Bretford House. I shall oversee the guarding of our premises at Southwark. I would suppose that Essex's main aim would be to reach the court and try to take possession of the Queen herself, to compel her to carry out his demands. We must, however, be prepared for a general uprising which might engulf London.'

His hearers nodded their heads in agreement. Jacko said aggressively, 'We'll have to find firearms as well as some pikes, and if we do I'd like to offer Essex's head on one of them to Her Grace. He deserves that for his ingratitude for all she has done for him. Anyone else but him would already have lost it on Tower Hill.'

This earthy piece of savagery set them all laughing, even Kate.

Later, when they were alone again, she said to Martin, 'Now, what is all this about Bevis Frampton—and who might he be?'

He answered her wearily, 'I had hoped that you might not have to know about him, but Webster made one of his rare errors and let the cat out of the bag.'

'It deserved to be let out if you were keeping important matters from me,' she told him severely. 'I am your wife, I was nearly kidnapped and I deserve to know why.'

'*I* don't know why Frampton is trying to kill me, only that he is.' And Martin proceeded to tell her of all that had passed since the first attempt on him immediately before he returned to Bretford House, except that he did not tell her of Frampton's attempt to suborn Webster. He tried to make as light of it as possible, but he could not deceive Kate.

She shook her head at him. 'If the Queen could be

kept informed of the many attempts on her life, then I ought to know of those which might involve me. Do not talk to me of weak women,' she shouted at him, her usual calm composure broken for once.

Martin gave her a sad smile. 'Well, you know now.'

'And what sort of answer is that?' She glared at him, still furious. 'As for Webster making a mistake, I have the feeling that he never makes one. Perhaps he thought that I ought to know.'

'If so, he thinks a great deal too much,' said her harassed husband.

'Which is why you value him so highly, so you can't complain about that. In any case, in future, I expect to be told when your life—and possibly mine—is in danger.'

'So noted,' returned Martin, with such a rueful look on his face that Kate could not help laughing.

'I meant what I said,' she assured him when she could speak soberly again.

'I know, and that is what troubles me.'

'Am I mistaken, or would you have preferred to marry a fluttering creature, fit only to mouth, "It is as you wish, my lord and master"?'

This was such an accurate description of Mary's behaviour during their short time together that Martin was silenced. What would have happened if she had not died so early in their marriage? Would he have tired of her unthinking worship of him? Whatever Kate felt for him, it was not worship. She spoke to him as though they were equals, as the Queen would have done to any man who had dared to marry her. What would be the end of such a marriage? More to the point, did he want to be worshipped? Was not this give and take with her part of the joy of being married to her?

Was that why he loved her? He could not yet tell her so, nor could he allow her to repeat words of love to him, for still, at the back of his mind, was that he had loved once, had told his wife so, many times, as she had told him—and then had lost her, as well as the proof of their love which had lived so short a life.

'Come to bed,' he said suddenly. 'I think that Raleigh was a little surprised that you had joined my Privy Council, even though he thinks it fit that his Queen should rule one.'

'Are all issues between us to be resolved in bed?' Kate teased naughtily, twisting away from him a little.

'What better place can there be?' was his riposte. 'And if you do not agree to retire to ours immediately, I shall be compelled to carry you there.'

'Faced by such a threat, Lord Hadleigh, there is only one thing I can do. Which is to refuse, for so far no one has ever forcibly carried me to my bed and it is an experience which I should most like to enjoy.'

Martin's answer to that was to take her in his arms, throw her over his shoulder and begin to carry her upstairs. They were met on the landing by Webster, who could not stop himself from raising his eyebrows at them.

'Not a word, Webster,' Martin shouted at him. 'You have already said too much today, and this is your fault.'

Fortunately for Webster's peace of mind as Martin raced by, Kate lifted her head and smiled happily at him. So his own naughtiness in allowing Kate to discover about Frampton's villainy, had merely had the result of adding further spice to his master's marriage. As though it needed any more, he thought ruefully, contemplating his own celibate life. I suppose that if I ever found a jewel like Kate Chancellor I might be tempted to marry!

Kate had not told Martin that she loved him, ever since he had asked her not to. What was strange was that he behaved towards her as she had always believed a man who loved his wife would. Why, then, was he so reluctant to put his feelings into words? The way he had treated her after he had carried her upstairs to bed was that of a man who was either deeply in love, or deeply in lust—which never considered one's partner—with his wife, and she preferred to believe in the first explanation.

For some reason she thought that his unwillingness to admit her love for him, or his for her, had something to do with the portrait of the pretty young woman which was hidden away in the closet in his room. More than once she had tried to look at it again to see if there was anything in, or on, the painting which might give her a clue as to who she was, and why he treasured it so much, but she had always found the closet to be securely locked.

Her curiosity was further roused when one afternoon, rummaging through the library's bookshelves, she overheard Rafe and Webster busily talking about her husband, apparently unaware that she was nearby. Webster was commenting on Martin's unfailing good humour. Rafe gave a short laugh.

'Only since he married this one,' he told Webster. 'After he lost the other one he was like a bear with a sore head for years, but I still think this one's better for him than t'other.'

'And good for all of us, too,' was Webster's answer, after which they began to talk of other things.

Kate waited until they had left the library before she returned to the withdrawing-room, and while she waited she thought of what had been said. The only conclusion which she could come to was that Martin had been married before, a marriage of which he had said nothing to her or to anyone at Bretford House, although it was plain that Rafe and Webster knew of it.

A first marriage to a wife who was now presumably dead, for she did not think that Martin would commit bigamy, might account for his determination never fully to commit himself to her, and also to his hiding away of her portrait. It also explained a number of other mysteries. The woman in the portrait she had seen in his closet must have been his first wife. Did he still grieve for her? Was that why he had told her never to love him?

What began to trouble her while she stitched busily away beside Aunt Jocasta was how she could broach the matter with him. It was wrong—if her assumption was correct—that he had not told her that he had been married before, and that that was why he had been holding himself back from making her his true wife in every sense: one to whom he could tell the truth about his feelings for her.

On the other hand, for her to accost him over a possible first marriage meant that she would have to admit that she had heard Rafe and Webster discussing his private affairs. She would need to be cunning if she were to conjure up some other reason for raising the matter with him, particularly when he was going out of his way to be kind to her. Best, perhaps, that she say nothing. It might trouble him to talk of his dead first wife to his second live one—it was always wise to let sleeping dogs lie.

Christmas was almost upon them when Martin came home early one afternoon. He burst into the withdrawing-room where she sat with Aunt Jocasta, full of Christmas spirit, or, as Rafe dryly put it later, full of the sack which they had all been drinking with their customers to celebrate Yuletide.

'You must be up betimes tomorrow,' he announced, 'for I am taking us all to the Royal Exchange so that you may see it decorated with Christmas garlands as well as the holly and the ivy.

After that we shall eat at one of the ordinaries. In the afternoon the Waits will be singing carols in the square in order to entertain the shoppers and those who work to serve them.

'It will be our last excursion before we visit Bretford House early on Christmas Eve.'

Aunt Jocasta said eagerly, 'Am I to accompany you this time?'

'Indeed, and Rafe, Webster and Jacko, too.'

The following morning the weather proved as kind as they might have hoped. It was cold, but sunny, after a heavy frost the night before. Martin swathed Kate and Aunt Jocasta in furs before they left.

'Your first Christmas presents,' he said, and when the three of them climbed into their coach they found brass warming-pans already there so that the bitter December cold should not trouble them on their journey. As usual he had thought of everything. Rafe, Webster and Jacko were travelling in the other coach. Several armed grooms followed them on horseback. They had orders to guard Kate, Martin and Aunt Jocasta when they walked through the square, so that on this visit no one would have the opportunity to attack them.

Fortunately this time their trip was a great success. Aunt Jocasta bought material for a new dress from Martin's shop, and they admired all the jeweller's wares and enjoyed dining at the ordinary. All in all, as Aunt Jocasta said afterwards, the whole expedition was so unlike both her and Kate's previously sheltered lives that that alone made the day worthwhile. She did not add how much she had enjoyed being carefully watched over by Jacko, but that too, was a great part of her pleasure.

Kate did have one curious experience. She was standing outside Martin's shop, with Rafe and one of the grooms guarding her, while inside, Aunt Jocasta and Martin haggled with Peg over a length of brocade, when she suddenly became aware that she was being watched by someone whom she could not see. It was a curious sensation which she had only experienced once before. She could feel the man staring at her, before she turned to try to find him.

There he was, only a few yards away from her, on the rough road which surrounded the square. He seemed to be an insignificant little fellow, dressed in grey and silver. He had a large man in livery beside him—his guard, probably, but his stare was for Kate, and Kate alone, and did not take in any of the clusters of shoppers who came and went, carrying their Christmas trophies.

She shivered at the sight of him and turned back to say to Rafe, 'Tell me, Rafe, do you know that little man in grey standing directly behind me? He has been staring hard at us for some time. I do not like the look of him.'

Rafe peered over her shoulder, 'What little man in grey, Lady Kate? I can't see anyone answering to that description.'

Kate swung round again. The man had disappeared,

lost among the crowd which had begun to fill the square. The big fellow had gone, too.

Webster came out of the shop where he had been buying linen for a new shirt.

'What is it, Lady Kate? Why the worried look?'

Before she could explain, Rafe said, 'She is distressed because some little man in grey has been staring at her.'

To their surprise Webster, his face furious, thrust his parcel at Rafe. 'Hold that for me. Show me where this man is. When I find him I'll teach him a lesson in good manners.'

'He's disappeared,' said Kate. 'He was over there. Why are you so agitated, Webster?'

'Because I think that he may be someone dangerous. Keep hold of my parcel for me, Rafe. I'll try to track him down.' And he ran in the direction which he thought that the man might have taken.

Rafe, astonished, said, 'I have never seen Webster so worked up about anything. In fact, I've never seen him worked up before.'

'Nor I,' said Kate.

Martin, coming out of his shop with Aunt Jocasta and Jacko behind him, and overhearing a little of what had been said, exclaimed sharply, 'What's that about a little grey man, Rafe?'

Rafe explained, and was immediately surprised by Martin's reaction, which was as powerful as Webster's. 'Where is he, which way did he go?'

'We don't know,' explained Kate. 'Only that Webster has run off to try to find him.'

'And which way did Webster go?'

The moment that they told him, Martin started off in the opposite direction, calling on one of the grooms to accompany him.

'Where's he off to in such a hurry?' demanded Jacko, who had arrived in time to see Martin disappear.

Rafe explained. 'God knows,' he ended. 'The grey man might be anybody—or anywhere.'

'No need to wait for God to tell us anything. I only know of only one little grey man who might be staring at m'lady, and that's Master Bevis Frampton. You should have known that, Rafe.'

'I've never seen him, only heard of him,' was Rafe's tart rejoinder.

'Who is Bevis Frampton?' exclaimed a puzzled Aunt Jocasta.

'That, the master will have to tell you,' said Jacko, not obliging Aunt Jocasta for once. This time it was Rafe who said, 'He's one of Lord Essex's supporters.'

He did not add that because he had never actually seen Frampton—unlike Jacko, who seemed to have seen everybody while he had tried to gather information about Bevis—he had been unable to guess at the identity of the man who had been staring at Kate.

Jacko said, 'How the devil did Webster come to know him?'

Rafe shrugged. He liked Webster, but there was

something about the man which frightened him a little. He was beginning to think that devious was his middle name.

Aunt Jocasta still puzzled, asked, 'And why should he stare at Kate?'

Before anyone had time to answer her, Webster reappeared. He took his parcel from Rafe, saying, 'I'm sorry, but I couldn't find him. There were a number of coaches coming and going at the end of the street. He may have left in one of them when he grasped that we had seen him watching Lady Hadleigh.'

'Martin went after him, too. He might have had better luck,' offered Rafe.

But he hadn't. He returned shortly afterwards, having been unable to find his quarry. A pale-faced Aunt Jocasta immediately asked him, 'Who is Bevis Frampton, and why should he be staring at Kate? And why should you and Webster rush off to try to catch him?'

'I'll explain a little later, when we get home,' Martin said, putting his arm around her and, at the same time, assuring her that they were in no immediate danger.

'In fact,' he finished, 'I think that we should all retreat to the ordinary and try to forget little grey men who stare at my wife.'

'I wasn't frightened,' Kate assured him. 'Only curious. I'm still curious.'

'You're always curious,' said Martin before steer-

ing them all, including the grooms in the direction of
the best ordinary in Southwark—or so he claimed.

Even the excellent meal they ate in the ordinary,
and their subsequent jaunt to Cheapside, where they
found more Christmas decorations and a large crowd
who were loaded with Yuletide fare and provisions,
could not stop Aunt Jocasta from worrying about the
strange and violent way in which both Martin and
Webster had reacted to the news that her niece was
being watched by a little grey man.

Kate tried to forget the whole wretched incident by
watching the bear being baited. She didn't enjoy the
spectacle very much because she felt sorry for the
poor beast, but was amused when Aunt Jocasta threw
herself into Jacko's arms when the bear's master,
leading him on a chain, walked him into the crowd
immediately in front of her. Kate whispered in
Martin's ear, 'I don't like to see the bear being made
fun of.'

'Because you used to call me a bear?'

She drew away from him a little. 'You knew?'

'Of course, I felt rather flattered, particularly since
a bear is on my Martin coat of arms and my motto is
*Cave ursum*.'

'Which is Beware of the Bear, so you thought of
yourself as a bear before I did.'

'Exactly. And now I think that we ought to go
home before your aunt seduces Jacko.'

'And then you may tell me why, if you are all
aware that we are in danger from Bevis Frampton,

you don't report him to the Sheriff and his constables on a charge of attempted murder? That would surely result in his being sent to prison—and we should be safe from his wickedness.'

'Because I have no firm evidence of his guilt to put before a magistrate and, without it, I might be considered to be a vindictive fool. Two of his hirelings, who could have identified him, are dead.' He did not tell her of Frampton's attempt to control Webster in order to use him as his assassin, for he did not wish to frighten her too much.

He stopped, and then continued, his face and voice most earnest. 'Promise me that you will never allow him to come near you, and that if he does, you will try to leave his presence immediately.'

Kate said, 'I will do as you ask. Not only that, I shall not tell Aunt Jocasta about any of this. She is fearful enough without having to worry about Bevis Frampton, too.'

Martin put an arm around her and kissed her gently, 'Come my love, let us go home and try to forget Bevis and all his works—for a little time at least. As the apostle says, "Sufficient unto the day is the evil thereof." Tonight we may celebrate Christmas and tomorrow is another day.'

Celebrate they duly did, and afterwards they slept the deep sleep of the fulfilled.

# Chapter Thirteen

Christmas Eve arrived and they all set off for Bretford House, well wrapped up against the cold. Their procession was a lengthy one, for it included most of Martin's family, except the kitchen staff, the gardeners, his steward, and the guards whom he had hired to protect Saxon Hall, but also five more sturdy fellows who would do the same duty for his father's home while they were there.

The only thing which reconciled him to spending Christmas with his father was his desire to discover what had prompted his invitation. After a slow journey they arrived at the house to find no one waiting for them, and only a bemused footman to answer the door.

The moment that they all streamed into the house after the footman, Martin knew that something was wrong. It was extremely cold in the entrance hall, and the withdrawing-room, when they were shown into it, was no warmer and strangely dingy. A small fire, only recently lit, was sputtering in the hearth. A scuttle beside it was empty of coals.

'Master Gordon, m'lord's secretary, will attend to you in a moment,' they were informed. 'He is at present with m'lord in his bedchamber.'

It seemed quite plain that their arrival was not expected.

They all stared at one another. Kate thought that her second introduction to Bretford House was even odder than the first. The room was so chilly that she began to shiver. Martin, asked, 'Do you know this Gordon fellow, Webster?'

Webster shook his head. 'I have heard of him. He took the post which I left when I joined your family.' He hesitated. 'I do not wish to offer you a hasty judgement, but his reputation is not of the best.'

Time passed and the secretary did not arrive. Martin walked over to the bell and pulled it savagely. The footman entered. He still looked bemused.

'Inform the butler immediately that the fire needs more coal—you may take the scuttle with you when you leave.'

The footman picked up the scuttle, and said, 'Begging your pardon, m'lord, but the butler left to go to another household a week ago and he has not yet been replaced. I will fetch some coals for you myself.'

'No butler,' said Jacko, 'and, it seems, no secretary who cares to attend on us, either.' To Aunt Jocasta he said, consolingly, 'Put your furs back on, mistress, you'll need them in here. Let me help you.'

'What the hell is going on?' exclaimed Martin violently. 'I will go upstairs at once and try to discover what in the world has reduced Bretford House to such a state.' And he made for the door—to have it opened before he reached it.

The man who entered said smoothly, 'Forgive me for not offering you a formal welcome, but I was not aware that you were arriving today. I was attending on Lord Bretford in his bedchamber. He had been taken a little more ill than usual and I felt that it was my duty to care for him. I am James Gordon, his secretary and general factotum. What may I do for you?'

Martin stared at him, at his courtier-like clothing, at his lantern-jawed face and his general air of being in charge—but of what? Certainly not this uncared-for house, which was obviously quite unprepared to entertain a large party over Christmas.

'I am not in the least disturbed by not being offered a formal welcome, but I am by the state in which I find my father's home. Dirty, a dearth of servants and deathly cold. Pray take me to his room at once. I wish to speak to him.'

'Oh, I am not sure that that would be wise. Better to wait a little.' The secretary was even smoother when he came out with this.

Martin swung round and shouted, in his best quarter-deck voice, 'Jacko, please remove this fellow from my sight. Take him to the library and guard him there until I return to interview him and decide whether or not to throw him into the Strand—or the Thames, if I feel so inclined.'

'A pleasure,' grinned Jacko, showing his teeth. Grabbing Gordon by the shoulder, he bellowed, 'Let's be having you,' and marched him away, his prisoner protesting loudly the while.

Rapidly running up the stairs, Martin was not quite sure why he was feeling so angry. After all, it was only his unfeeling father who was being mishandled, and why should he object to that? He entered his bed-chamber to find him wasted, and grey in the face. He was leaning back on his pillows, breathing heavily. The room was nearly as cold and grimy as those downstairs. The bed-linen, like his nightshirt, was grey.

His father stared at him. 'You came,' he said feebly.

'As you invited me, yes.'

'I thought that you might not.'

'I always keep my word. It seems, however, that we were not expected—nothing has been made ready and the house is untended and neglected.'

Martin could scarcely conceal his shock at the sight of his father. He had always remembered him as a big man, sturdy and dominant, bellowing with anger at his younger son's supposed misdeeds. Now his frailty was so great that it seemed that he might not have long to live.

'If you intend to remain here for Christmas—and I hope that you will—perhaps you could help me to rid myself of that fellow Gordon, who has taken over my life. When he first came here, I thought him a blessing, but now I think of him as a curse. He has dismissed most of my servants, and refused to send for a physician. He says that I do not need one because he will look after me...'

He began to cough helplessly. There was a pitcher of water on his bedside table. Martin poured a draught into a mug and held it to his father's lips so that, after a moment, the coughing ceased.

'I think,' his father said, 'that when I am safely dead, he will loot the house of its treasures and all the money I keep here. He did not know that you were coming because I did not tell him that I had invited you for Christmas. I sent my letter to you by the butler without his knowledge and kept your reply secret from him. He dismissed the butler last week—for being insolent, he said. My valet was dismissed long ago.'

'If you will give me permission, sir,' Martin said—he could not yet call the old man father, 'I will mend matters here at once. First, though, I shall send for a physician, servants to build you a proper fire, and change your bedding and night clothes. How long have you been at his mercy?'

'Since Lord Clifton left. He was all that was proper until then.'

'I will have to leave you now,' Martin said, 'to set all this in train. Is Mistress Cray, the housekeeper, still with you?'

'Yes, but she has been sent to work in the kitchens. He appointed a new one whom I have never seen.'

Then he said, inconsequentially, 'I'm very hungry.'

'I fear we must wait for the physician before you eat,' Martin told him, before leaving. 'If Mistress Cray is still with us, I will send her up to you, for you ought not to be left alone.'

He ran downstairs and rapped on the housekeeper's door. It was opened by a tall buxom woman, well-dressed, with a knowing face.

'And who might you be?' she demanded.

'I might ask the same of you. I am Lord Hadleigh, your employer's son.' And he pushed past her into the first warm room in the house. A sumptuous meal for two persons, which included sack and fresh white bread, was set out on the table.

'I am Mistress Joanna Banks, housekeeper here.'

'Housekeeper no longer, Mistress Banks, and before I hand you your notice you must tell me where I may find Mistress Cray.'

'Cray? You mean Cray,' she replied insolently. 'She's in the kitchen, of course. And who are you to give me notice? I was employed by Master Gordon and only he can dismiss me.'

'You mistake,' Martin told her, without raising his voice. 'Since you are, I suppose, Gordon's doxy, you may join him in the library and wait to be turned off—unless I choose to send for the constables.'

He seized her by the arm—and well-built though she was, she could not resist him—and ran her down the corridor until he reached the library where Jacko, and one of the guards he had brought with him, were keeping Gordon prisoner.

'Here's his light of love and accomplice,' said Martin. 'You may look after her as well. She and he seem to be the only people in this house who are warm and well-fed.'

'We can soon remedy that,' grinned Jacko.

'True,' said Martin. 'Take the pair of them to the guardroom by the front door and lock them in. They're not to be fed, or released, until I decide what to do with them. No candles are to be put in there, either. As I remember it there isn't a window.'

The housekeeper set up a wailing protest against his cruelty.

'Why, madam, I do but follow your example—what more can I say than that?'

Now to find Rafe. He and Webster were building a large fire in the withdrawing-room. Candles had been lit, since the day was dark, and the footman was busy obeying them, a sullen look on his face. It seemed that he had not been working either. Kate and Aunt Jocasta were busily tidying the unkempt room.

'Rafe, I want you to find the nearest physician and bring him here as quickly as possible. If he demurs—then you know what to do?'

'And I,' said Webster, rising from his knees now that the fire was going well. 'What am I to do?'

'Visit the office off the library and go through my father's records there. Try to ferret out what Gordon has been doing. I'm sure that he's been swindling the estate. Among other things, he's almost certainly been pocketing the wages previously paid to the servants he has dismissed. I don't think that my father is aware of the extent of his villainy.'

'So noted,' grinned Webster, off to have some fun with the Bretford ledgers.

After reassuring Kate and a bemused Aunt Jocasta that all was well, or would be in a short time, Martin set off to find Mistress Cray. She, and only three other servants, were in the kitchen, eating a meagre meal.

'God bless you, Master Martin. I knew if you discovered what that villain Gordon has been doing, you'd come and stop him. It's the only reason I stayed here. They wouldn't let me go near your father.' They, no doubt, being Banks and Gordon.

'Well, you may visit him now. I would like you to look after him until we can hire a nurse once the physician has seen him. In his present condition he shouldn't be left alone. You can then take over as housekeeper again.'

Mistress Cray rose, and to his astonishment stood on tiptoe to kiss him on the cheek. 'You're a good man, Martin Chancellor, and your pa doesn't deserve you. Bless you for coming to care for him after all he did to you.'

What next? When Rafe returned with the physician he must send him with orders to transport most of the staff at Saxon Hall to Bretford House, leaving only a small one there. From what he had seen on his rapid tour of the place, a large and competent staff would be needed to restore it to its former glory.

By nightfall the physician had been and treated his father. Later he sent along two nurses to look after the old man. Rafe had brought back with him enough staff from Saxon Hall to keep the house going until the next day—the rest were to come along on the morrow—with extra supplies of food. Webster had untangled the Bretford finances so that Martin could finally confront the guilty pair with their villainy.

Several hours in the dark in the guardroom had stripped them of all their impudence. Released, and confronted by a grim Martin, they agreed, unwillingly, to allow their belongings to be searched. Among them were discovered many of the valuables which they had hidden away—presumably to sell. Not only that, a deal of money was recovered, which they had received from the sale of other precious objects which they had already stolen and sold, together with Gordon's profits from his swindling of the Bretford estate.

Thus having rendered the conspirators penniless, Martin did not send for the constables, but allowed them to collect their clothing and leave.

'And if I hear that either of you is engaged in this kind of villainy again, I'll make sure that next time you'll swing,' were his parting words. 'My friend, Jacko, will keep an eye on you in future.'

Later, after enjoying a good supper in a house

which was rapidly growing warmer, Martin and Kate were about to go to bed when Mistress Cray came in. 'Your father is asking for you, Master Martin—I mean m'lord. He grew agitated when I advised him to wait until morning.'

'You may call me Master Martin as often as you wish—and I will visit him immediately. Now that he has two nurses you ought to try to rest yourself.'

'I will that, Master Martin.'

He turned to Kate, saying, 'You may either wait for me here, or retire to bed. It is as you please.'

Kate's smile for him was a saucy one. 'Oh, bed, I think—we are all in need of it after a long and hard day.'

'Be off with you then,' he said, giving her a loving smack on her well-padded rear. 'I shall try not to be too long.'

He found his father sitting up in bed again. Mistress Cray had made him lie down until the physician had seen him. He did not look quite so ill, and one of the nurses was taking away a tray of food. The other was in the anteroom, where a makeshift bed had been set up for her.

'You look tired,' were his first words to Martin.

'But not so tired as you, sir. Mistress Cray said that you wished to see me.'

'Indeed, there is something which weighs heavily on my mind.'

He stopped and sighed, as though saying the words

were almost too great a burden for him. Martin remained silent and waited for him to go on.

'I know that I misjudged you when you were a boy. Your mother was never strong, and when she died after your birth... God forgive me, but I could not but think that, had there been only one child, she would have lived. I felt such anger against you—and I dealt with you cruelly, especially when I learned of your many sins. And now I learn I was mistaken. Documents have recently come to my hand which reveal that the misdeeds for which you were punished were committed by your brother John. Not only that, but later he led a life which I can only consider wicked, and for which, in the end, God punished him by inflicting on him the Great Pox. I cannot ask you to forgive the cruel way in which I treated you, since I do not deserve it. I may only ask it from God, who is the last, great judge of all men.

'I shall quite understand if, having heard this, you do not wish to remain at Bretford House with me. Furthermore, since, despite everything, you have saved me from Gordon and his light of love's persecution, my remorse has become the greater. I do not deserve your care, nor you.'

Martin said nothing immediately. Ever since he had fled Bretford House he had waited for his revenge: for the day to come when he could throw in his father's face the facts of his innocence, and then leave him, and Bretford House—for ever this time. That day had arrived, and the anger which had sustained him during the years in which he had created a successful life for himself had suddenly leached out of him. He thought that he knew why.

'Forgive me, father,' he asked, 'if I ask you a question before I answer you.'

Puzzled, his father replied, 'You may ask as many questions of me as you please. It is your due.'

'Only one: it is this. Did you ever know a man called Bevis Frampton?'

His father's face cleared. 'Frampton? Oh yes, I knew him. We were part of a group of young men who came upon the town together, long ago. We thought him a joke, a regular figure of fun. I remember that fellow creeping around after your mother, before we were married, staring at her and making her uncomfortable. He was a friendless creature, and no wonder. Why do you wish to know?'

Could that be the explanation? Bevis Frampton had carried his resentment against Martin's father and his mother into old age, allowing it to fester and corrupt his whole life. By killing him and John he was paying the Chancellors back for the pain he had suffered in his youth.

And what of himself? He would be little better than Frampton, if he allowed what had been done to him in youth to affect his behaviour in maturity so that he rejected his dying father, who had, mistakenly, treated him so cruelly. More than that—was he not allowing his unhappiness over Mary and his child's sudden death to cast a cloud over his marriage to Kate?

The past was dead. It could not be changed, but it ought not to be allowed to live on to sour the present.

He leaned forward and took his father's hand. The old man was looking anxiously at him, doubtless awaiting the storm of anger which Martin would have unleashed on him before maturity had taught him the pointlessness of such a revenge. Besides, strangely enough, it was he who had benefited by being rejected and John, the favoured son, who had been ruined by his father's indulgent treatment of him.

Instead Martin, his face and voice as grave as he could make them, replied with, 'All I need to say now is that I know Bevis Frampton to be a vindictive wretch. For the moment, let us forget him. To answer your question, I will, as best as I can, look after you in your old age. You are my father and you gave me life. What happened between us in the past is dead and gone; let us forget that, as well.'

Two tears rolled down his father's face. He pressed the hand which had taken his. 'You will stay with me then?'

'Yes, particularly since when I informed the physician that I wished to take you to Saxon Hall he advised against it, saying that that it would be dangerous to move you. So, if you are agreeable I, my wife and my staff will remain here until you are fit to be conveyed to my home.'

His father said in a low voice. 'I think that I could sleep now. I have not been able to do so since those documents were sent to me by I know not who. They are in the chest over there. Take them and read them.'

Martin rose and walked over to the chest. He took out the papers which he found there. He examined them briefly before saying, 'I have no mind to read them. I meant what I said when I told you that the past was dead. With your permission I will destroy them and allow no one but ourselves—and whoever sent you these—to be the only witnesses of my brother's perfidy.'

'There is a good fire over there,' said his father and Martin tossed the documents in and watched them burn. He thought that he knew who had ferreted out the truth and sent the proof of it to his father, but he would never speak of it to him—for that might revive the dead past. He would express his gratitude in other ways, for Webster had made him part of the Chancellor family again.

'How did you find Lord Bretford?' Kate asked him, when he came to bed. She had worried a little about what might have been said or done during the interview with his father. Martin had seemed so much happier lately that she did not want him to be disturbed or distressed by having to relive his unhappy youth.

'Better,' he said briefly. 'We had a short talk about Gordon's wickedness, after which we agreed that, since the past is dead and gone, it ought to remain so. He is my father again and I am his son. We are all to stay at Bretford House until the physician de-

cides that we may take him home to Saxon Hall,
where we shall be able to protect him from predators
like Gordon and his mistress.'

Kate sat sharply up in bed, her whole face aglow.
'Oh, I am so pleased for you, and for him. It could
not be right that you should be estranged.'

'No, and since he has admitted that he misjudged
me I can let the past go. It must not spoil the present.'

He nearly marred this pretty speech by adding, 'Oh,
and by the by, I love you,' but he thought that his
change of heart was too great and too important for
him to tell her, in passing, as it were. The day had
been a long one, and they could celebrate their mutual
passion tonight, without words: those could come on
the morrow.

After all, Christmas Day was a time of celebration,
and this year his celebrations would be the most important since he had fled the home where he was now
truly welcome again.

## Chapter Fourteen

Christmas came and went. Martin's staff, despite the short notice which they had been given by their hasty move to the Strand, managed to put on a show of food, drink and decorations which would have graced the Queen's court. After the Christmas meal was over, they brought in the Yule Log which should more properly have been placed in the hearth and lit on Christmas Eve. They then joined together to sing the carols which they had been practising before the invitation to Bretford House had arrived. Martin and Rafe accompanied them on their lutes, and Webster turned out to possess a fine baritone voice when he sang one of the verses of 'Joy to the World' on his own. Jacko was allowed to bang a small drum occasionally, since he claimed to possess no singing voice at all. Aunt Jocasta clapped in time with him.

Lord Bretford was carried downstairs in a litter to watch some of the celebrations, the first which he had enjoyed for many years, and was allowed by his physician to join in drinking the toast to the Yule Log with his new family before he was returned to his bed.

It was nearly midnight when Martin and Kate tumbled into theirs, full of food, drink and the kind of mindless happiness which a successful day's celebration of Yuletide always brings. It also encourages lovers to demonstrate their feelings by indulging in another ancient custom, always provided too much alcohol has not been drunk.

Together they climbed towards the greatest fulfilment which they had yet achieved. Kate was always to claim that their first child, Richard, was conceived on Christmas Day. Afterwards, when they were lying, sated and glowing, with sleep far from their minds after all the excitements of the day, Martin turned to Kate and murmured, 'Dear heart, I have somewhat to tell you.'

'Now?' she murmured in reply, twisting to kiss the hand which cradled her chin.

'Yes, now, what better time to tell you how much I love you, my darling heart, with a love so strong that it almost frightens me. Because of that I must ask your forgiveness for having refused to allow you to speak of love to me. The more so because I know that I have loved you ever since the first time we met but, because of the sad manner in which my first marriage ended, I felt that I dare not tempt Fate by confessing it, lest I should suffer again what I suffered then. I lost my first wife and our baby in childbirth while I was at sea. I came home to find them gone.

It dealt me a blow from which I thought that I would never recover. I could not believe that I would ever be able to marry again.

'This was the reason why, after we were married, I was unable to tell you how much I was coming to love you, nor could I allow you to confess your love for me. I felt that to do so would tempt the cruel Fates, who had already punished me once and might do so again.

'When I spoke to my father and told him that the past was dead and gone and should not be allowed to sour our present, I suddenly understood that I, too, must let go of my own past and live in the present, lest, by my cowardly refusal to accept your love, or reveal mine for you, I might destroy our marriage.'

Kate, tears in her eyes, kissed him again. 'Of course I forgive you. I knew that you had been married before, but I did not know that you had lost both wife and child at one fell sweep of death's scythe. I am not surprised that it made you bitter and afraid to love again for fear that you lost me in like fashion. Now that you have told me your sad story I understand you a little more. You lost not only your father, but your wife and child as well. A less strong man would have despaired of life.'

'So you forgive me, and for that generosity of spirit, I love you even more,' he murmured when she turned to offer him herself so that he might lie at rest in her loving arms. He had purged himself of the past, not once, but twice. He had found his father again and become reconciled to the loss of his wife and child—but he had also gained another wife whose loving kindness knew no bounds. Not only that, her shrewdness matched his own.

He could not stop himself from exclaiming, 'You knew that I had been married?' And when she blushed and turned her head away a little, he took her chin again and looked deep into her eyes.

'And you said nothing! You never cease to amaze me. No, do not tell me how you found out—leave that a mystery—but I can see that it will be difficult for me to hide anything from you.'

'Oh, nonsense,' she exclaimed. 'You kept Bevis Frampton a secret from me.'

'Yes, but the eye and mind of love had nothing to do with him.'

'Why do I never win an argument with you?' Kate complained, but her voice was such that he knew that she was teasing him.

'On the contrary, it is you who invariably win them,' he told her with a loving kiss.

'Say, rather,' she said, 'that we each win half of them, which is as it should be in a happy marriage.'

'True, and a happy marriage will be even happier, if we do this, and this.' And when, much later, they drifted happily into sleep, they shared the same thought: now that the past is over and done with, we are well and truly married!

If Martin and his family were enjoying Christmas, the same could not be said for many of those

living in London. The perpetual shadow of Lord
Essex and his feud with the Queen hung over them.
The Queen celebrated the birth of Christ at Whitehall
as though she had not a care in the world, but her
advisers knew as well as she did that this apparent
peace and harmony could not last.

'The longer she hesitates to deal with him the more
dangerous the whole business grows,' Sir Robert
Cecil told his secretary. 'His head should have rolled
on Tower Hill long ago. I have even been approached
by some anxious courtiers who wish me to persuade
the Queen to consign him to the Tower, try him, and
sentence him to death. After that she must designate
King James of Scotland as her successor, since so
long as there is no official heir to the throne, so long
might some adventurer like Essex benefit from the
uncertainty which it creates.'

Cecil was only saying what many thought. Again,
like many, he was angry and disappointed that as the
year wore on his mistress still prevaricated, as though
one more execution was too much to bear after so
many had been carried out.

'Were she a man,' he once exclaimed angrily to
Francis Bacon, 'Essex would have been dead and
gone long ago.'

'Aye, but would a man have done as well as she
did against Spain? We have to take the bad of her as
well as the good.'

And that was the trouble, Cecil wanted her to be
perfect—and only God was perfect, even though

some of his works took a deal of understanding when one surveyed the imperfect world which he had created. Well he, Cecil, could help God—and the Queen—a little, if the spies he had in Essex's camp were telling him the truth. The uprising, they reported, was timed for March and was intended, if successful, to make Essex Lord Protector of England. If this were true it would give Cecil and the Privy Council three months to prepare London and the court to withstand any assault.

Late in January, however, it was not one of his spies, but one of Essex's supporters, Sir Ferdinando Gorges, who helped Cecil the most. Those around Essex had begun to talk openly of killing the Queen— they included Sir Christopher Blount and Bevis Frampton—rather than simply capturing her when they had taken over London and the court. Frightened by the implications of this new development, Gorges told Sir Walter Raleigh of it. Raleigh immediately passed his message on to Cecil and the Privy Council.

Cecil responded by attempting to spur Essex into premature action by spreading the rumour that the Queen was ready to send him to the Tower: a rumour which was shortly to come true, since Elizabeth was finally beginning to grasp that to delay further might risk the safety of the Crown itself.

Martin was on the edge of all this plotting and counter-plotting through his friendship with Raleigh, who early in February called on him at Bretford House. At first Raleigh was his usual cheerful and lively self. Martin sent for sack and biscuits while his visitor gossiped away about this and that, and nothing much to the point until Martin wondered what the purpose of his visit was.

'We haven't seen you at the Friday Club lately,' Raleigh said, offering his goblet for refilling. 'Is this because you are so engaged with your new wife, or because you are now reconciled with your father and are, so I am told, running his estates?'

'Both,' said Martin with a smile, 'and perhaps, in a moment, you will tell me the real reason for your visit.'

Raleigh laughed ruefully, 'Am I so transparent?'

'To me, a little, because I have known you for so long. What is troubling you?'

'Everything, and nothing, since there is little that I can do which will mend matters. Essex is bent on destroying himself and those who support him. Her Grace, by delaying and allowing him time and room to move against her, is doing nothing decisive. She talks of summoning him to the Privy Council, and then, when at last she does, she allows him to prevaricate by sending word that he is too ill to attend. Which he was some time ago, but is no longer.

'To make bad worse, Southampton has given Gelli Meyrick enough money to persuade Burbage and Shakespeare to stage *Richard II*. They intend to show it on the evening before the uprising begins. That should provide a fine inflammatory start to it and no mistake.'

'The gossip was that Essex was planning to move in early March,' Martin said.

'That is out of date now—the sooner he acts, the better, the hotheads around him are saying. They're probably right, since he has given Cecil time to make ready to repel him. The word around the court is that the Queen will summon him to attend the Privy Council on a morning in early February, possibly the seventh. If so, the play will be staged that same evening. What everyone is afraid of is that, if Essex is right, and the citizens of London turn out in his favour, then he might well succeed—and if so, God have mercy on us all!'

'How, may I ask, do you expect me to help you?'

'You can't, but you can help yourself. If Essex does look like succeeding, London will turn into a battlefield like the one in Paris on the night of the massacre of the Huguenots. I am advising all my friends to be prepared for an armed mob to descend on their homes ready to rape, loot and burn.'

Martin grinned again. 'I am before you. I have extra guards posted here and at Saxon Hall.'

'Saxon Hall would be a better place to be than at Bretford House.'

'We can't leave yet, my father is not fit to be moved. No, I am ready for them—or as ready as a man might be, and I thank you for the warning.'

'You are my good friend—and that ass Frampton has been publicly railing against you lately. What in the world have you been doing to make him hate you so?'

'I? Nothing. It is an old tale and one not worth the telling. Nevertheless, I will bear your warning in mind.'

Once Raleigh had gone, Martin sent for Webster, Rafe and Jacko and ordered them to begin to prepare Bretford House to withstand a possible armed attack. He also told Kate the gist of Raleigh's message, which she received as staunchly as he might have hoped. He noticed that she was looking a little pale these days, but she was not complaining of illness so it was probably winter taking its toll. There was little more that he could do to protect her, and the rest of his now greatly extended family.

All they had to do was watch and wait.

To Cecil's profound relief, the Queen acted at last. He could only hope that her decision had not come too late.

On the morning of February the 7th—as Raleigh had hinted—she sent a messenger to Essex telling him to report at once to the Privy Council. His reply, after consulting his supporters, was to send the messenger back with an insolent answer from him: he could not obey her summons since he had been playing tennis, was sweating exceedingly and needed to rest.

The moment of decision had arrived for Essex, too. He had three possible courses of action. He could send the Queen a message that he would report on the morrow, or he could flee the country, or he could immediately raise the rebellion which he had been planning for so long.

Vainglorious as ever, and sure that London would rise in his favour, Essex decided on rebellion. He had, he believed, three hundred men of his own, armed and ready to follow him anywhere—or so they claimed. Events later proved this not to be true.

During all this commotion Bevis Frampton had been busy plotting on his own behalf. Many who had flocked to Essex House to support the Earl were petty criminals, as well as some who had lost their all in the harsh world of Elizabethan commerce. Under cover of following Essex on what was increasingly looking like a mad enterprise, he could take an armed gang of his own, drawn from these failures, to Bretford House and dispose of Bretford himself and his wretched son, Hadleigh.

The reward for the gang would be the looting of the house. The gang would, of course, begin by supporting Essex, but would break off to follow Bevis. They would thus avoid capture by the Queen's forces, should Essex fail, and the inevitable traitors' death which would follow, but might gain a small fortune instead.

That his own plan was as mad as Essex's never occurred to him. He had reached the last stage of mania, when the victim is unable to see the world as it is but only as he wants it to be. In that he was not unlike Essex himself.

\* \* \*

On that same morning of February the 7th, Kate wandered into Mistress Cray's room to ask if she might have a herbal drink made up for her. She had been feeling sick on rising and listless in the afternoons since early January and thought a herbal infusion might cheer her up a little.

The housekeeper looked hard at her. 'And how long, m'lady, have you been ailing like this?'

'Since shortly after the New Year.'

'And your courses? Are they still regular?'

It was Kate's turn to look hard at Mistress Cray. 'They never came in January but they have been late before; I have even missed them occasionally.'

'Did no one ever tell you, now that you are married, of a possible reason for that, m'lady? Of why your courses might suddenly cease?'

Kate shook her head. 'No, only that when they first appeared they would continue each month until middle age.'

Mistress Cray sighed. Oh, these poor young girls who were born into great families, no wonder that they sometimes fell into sin if they did not understand the workings of their own bodies—never mind those of men!

'Did no one ever explain to you that when a woman begins to breed, her courses stop?'

Kate's hand flew to her mouth. 'No, never! Is that what can be wrong with me?' She swallowed a little and her face changed from white to scarlet. 'No one ever told me anything. I did not even know how a man and a woman behaved in bed together after they were married.'

Mistress Cray sighed again. 'My dear lady, in the first months, nay weeks, of breeding, sickness and tiredness are commonplace for many women. And if your courses have ceased I would swear that is what now ails you. I will make up a potion of *nux vomica* for you to drink each morning immediately after you rise. Your only consolation lies in knowing how much it will gratify Master Martin to know that you are carrying his child.'

'And I, shall I be gratified?' This was asked with more than a touch of the usual lively-spoken Kate Chancellor.

'That goes without saying, although I know that it is hard to feel gratified while you are vomiting.'

'Very true,' Kate replied.

'Goodness, you look pale, child,' Mistress Cray exclaimed, forgetting all about ladyships when Kate showed every sign of being overcome again. 'Take this basin, while I go to prepare the *nux vomica* for you immediately. It is a little late in the day, but it might help you.'

Kate gratefully accepted the basin, and later, after she had drunk the promised potion and had eaten a small round of plain bread, found that she felt a little better—although her face was still wan.

'Now that I know what is wrong with me, I must tell Martin,' she said. She was not sure, knowing what had happened to his first wife and child, how happy he would be to learn that she was breeding, but he deserved to be told the truth at once, and not find it out through servants' gossip.

Martin had been spending the morning at Bretford House, putting the finishing touches to his plan for foiling an open attack on it. Webster, Rafe and Jacko had all been given their separate duties. Webster had protested at his, but Martin had said quietly, 'In some ways yours is the most important of all. I shall have enough bravos about me to try to conquer any major assault which might be mounted—you, on the other hand, are better qualified to take Lady Hadleigh and the women to safety if all goes awry here.'

Webster still looked a little downcast, but finally gave a grudging assent. After all, Martin, Rafe and Jacko had all been in battle, while his life had been spent in the study and the libraries of the great and famous.

At the same time most of Bretford House's large staff of menservants also had their duties assigned to them that morning. The guards whom Martin had hired would be, in essence, the officers who would steady the servants with no experience of war. He would be the overall captain-general.

'Why,' Rafe asked just before the meeting ended, 'are you so sure, that if an attack comes, it will come soon? Besides that, Frampton has never tried such an outrageous piece of villainy as this before.'

Martin did not tell him of Raleigh's hidden warning. Instead he said, '*Richard II* is to be staged today.
I am sure that it is meant to be the rallying cry for
an insurrection. As for Frampton, he is one of Essex's
noisiest followers, constantly urging him to stage an
uprising. What's more, I have reason to believe that,
all his smaller assaults on me having failed, he may
try a larger one under cover of Essex's piece of folly.
If he does not—what matter? We lose nothing by being armed and ready.

'I shall inform my father of our arrangements once
this meeting is over, but we must make sure that none
of the women know of our preparations for their
safety until it looks as though they have become necessary.'

'Not even Lady Hadleigh?' asked Webster.

'No. I might have warned her if she were in health,
but she is ailing these days and I do not wish to make
her condition worse. If an attack comes, you must
seek out her, and Mistresses Cray and Saville, at once,
Webster. Their safety must be paramount.'

He was still worrying about Kate and the women
when he entered the withdrawing-room to find her there,
looking pale and ill. She had a book open on her knee,
but was not reading from it. Aunt Jocasta was not present—she was upstairs having a nice lie-down—or so
she claimed. Since Jacko had also gone upstairs once
the strategic meeting was over, Martin was inclined to
wonder how nice her lie-down was being—she seemed
to have so many of them these days.

'Oh, I'm so glad to see you at last!' Kate exclaimed. 'When you said that you were not going to the Counting House today, I thought that we might spend it together.'

'Alas,' said Martin, 'I have been arranging other matters this morning—but now that they are dealt with, I shall be happy to oblige you. I might have suggested that we take a ride together to the Park, but, looking at you, I don't think that it would be wise.'

'No, indeed,' said Kate happily, for he had made what she had to say to him a little easier for her, 'seeing that I have somewhat to tell you, which I hope will not only please you, but your father also.'

'Now what in the world can that be?' he replied. Kate had made a friend of his father, but he found it difficult to believe in anything she could say which might please both of them.

'It is this. Today I have learned that my illness is not an illness at all. It is something which happens to many women when they are increasing. In short, we are to have a child. Mistress Cray has given me a potion which has already made me feel a little better.'

Martin's reaction was to sink on to the settle where she sat and put his arms around her. His face had gone even whiter than hers. What a time to learn that his second wife was breeding—a time when he was not sure what the coming days would bring! He said nothing, only hugged her gently to him.

'What is it?' asked Kate, surprised by his silent reception of her news. 'Are you not happy for us?'

'Yes, very happy, but, oh, my darling, you must be careful. Dear God, I cannot contemplate the thought of losing you and the child. Do nothing rash, I implore you.'

'Now as to that,' said Kate, who could feel his big body trembling against her slighter one, 'we must wait for the physician to advise me on what I may, or may not, do. I have asked Mistress Cray to send for one immediately.'

What Martin would dearly most like to do was to put Kate in a gilded cage, far away from London and the possibility of riots and worse. To settle her in a rural Arcadia where nothing evil could touch or harm her. The cage would be so large and splendid that it would not be a prison...

He told himself to stop thinking these wild and senseless thoughts. He loosened his grasp on her, replying, 'Yes, you are right. We must use our common sense, but, oh, my darling, I fear me that I cannot prevent myself from recalling the past...'

She kissed his troubled face. 'Dear Martin, you told me the other day that we must not dwell on the past—neither must we anticipate the future. Let us live in the hope that this time you will be lucky and see your child born.'

But she did not know what he knew, of what he had spent the morning planning, and it was now more than ever imperative that she should remain ignorant of it, for perhaps he was wrong and tomorrow would come and go trouble-free—which was, after all, the best that fallen humankind could hope for.

So Martin took her on to his knee, kissed her again, beginning to recover his usual buoyant spirits, and then placed his large hand on her still flat stomach, a look of awe on his face.

'My child—and yours—is there. God grant that all goes well with it and with you.'

He was so moved by her news that he could say no more, and they lay there until Kate, exhausted by her sickness, went to sleep in his arms as sweetly and peacefully as a baby herself.

At Essex House, however, the Earl and his followers were in a frenzy. Cecil had cornered them, they cried, but later that same night a letter from Thomas Smyth, the Sheriff of London, arrived. In it he pledged to support the Earl in any action he chose to take.

This, together with the belief that the citizens of London would join him in an attack on the Queen and the court, simply urged Essex, and the motley crew who were now gathered under any banner he cared to raise, on to further excesses.

'Come, my friends,' he shouted, 'we must act before Raleigh and his creature Cobham murder me. We must attack tomorrow, seize the Queen so that she may protect me from my, and her, enemies—and may God defend the right.'

His speech was greeted with wild enthusiasm by his hearers, who were very different in their nature from those who had first supported him when he had returned from Ireland. Once, many of the great lords had favoured his cause, but as Essex grew more and more extreme in his language and his conduct they had, apart from Southampton and Sir Christopher Blount, his most loyal friends, faded away.

Instead he was surrounded by a rabble consisting of the kind of adventurers and bully boys whom Bevis Frampton had persuaded to join him in his separate plot against Lords Bretford and Hadleigh. So the die was cast, or, as one of the cleverer among them said, 'The Rubicon will be crossed and like Caesar we shall conquer,' causing Bevis Frampton's chief lieutenant to mutter, 'Who the hell is Caesar and where the devil is the Rubicon? The Thames will do for me—and Whitehall!'

They could scarcely wait for the morning to arrive, the morning which might see them rule England—or die in the attempt.

Mid-morning on February the 8th, the inhabitants of Bretford House learned of the insurrection when one of Martin's clerks from his Counting House in the City hammered on its great front door.

Martin, who was comforting an ailing Kate in their bedchamber, ran rapidly downstairs on being informed of his arrival. He was joined by Webster, Rafe and Jacko when the clerk, who had been instructed to keep an eye on events in central London and report on them if anything untoward occurred, told them that Essex had at last moved against the Queen.

'M'lord, there is a great tumult in the City. It is said that Lord Essex has taken a party of men to attack the Queen and the court. Some of the mob have joined him. I heard tell that the Sheriff, Master Smyth, was one of them, but others say nay.'

'How are they armed?' asked Martin, all practicality.

The clerk shrugged. 'It seems that the lords have rapiers, while the lesser men have bludgeons. Some said his followers numbered over a thousand, others that they were barely a hundred. 'Tis said also that he murdered the men who arrived early to arrest him. Whatever the truth of the matter, it is certain that they are marching on Whitehall.'

'With rapiers and bludgeons?' Martin queried. 'Nevertheless we thank you, and now we must prepare to defend ourselves. Who knows how—and where—this might end?'

What he feared the most was that, under cover of Essex's reckless enterprise, Frampton, as Raleigh had hinted, might act. He began to muster his troops and their weaponry. Unlike Essex and his followers he had ready an assortment of pistols and hackbuts—a form of primitive musket—as well as pikes, broadswords and rapiers, with which to withstand an assault if the attackers succeeded in entering the house. Since it would certainly come from the front, the footmen were already dragging tables, wooden settles and chests into the great entrance hall, so that the way into the House would be hard once the front door was breached.

There was nothing to be done but watch and wait. He ran back upstairs to tell Kate. By now she had recovered from her earlier sickness and was sitting up in bed recovered enough to hear the news from the City. He sat by her on the bed saying, 'My darling, the Earl of Essex has begun his enterprise to try to seize the Queen. You are not to be afeared, for if trouble awaits us here, we shall, God willing, be ready to repel it.

'What I ask of you is that if that happens and Webster comes to you with orders from me which may sound strange to you, you will obey him immediately and without question. It will be for your own good. He will lead you and the women, who will be in the charge of Mistress Cray, down to the river to be rowed to where you will be safe if all goes ill here—which pray God it may not.'

'And you, what will you be doing?' she asked, her eyes wide.

'Defending this house so that if my men and I succeed we may have a life in it together. I fear that my father must remain here, for he is not fit to be moved.'

'But I may be moved. Not so—I would wish to stay with you.'

He went down on his knees beside the bed.

'No, you may not. If trouble does come, and we are not yet sure that it will, you must think first of the child you are carrying. You must act to save it, for if all fails here—which God forbid—but you have got safely away, you and the child will be able to survive. I dare not risk both your lives by allowing you to remain here. You do understand me?'

'Yes, would that I did not. I will do as you ask— and try to be brave.'

'Knowing you, I would expect nothing else. Now let us kiss.'

'And part,' she murmured sorrowfully. 'But not for long, I hope.'

'It may not come to that,' he told her, 'if we manage to repel an attack. My information may be wrong—but I fear it is right.'

They clung together for a moment, before he rose and walked to the door—to leave her. He did not look back, nor did she expect him to. Instead, once he was gone she ordered Jennie to dress her for the day in sturdy clothing, not her usual light indoor gowns. She also called for her warm fur coat and Jennie's warmest jacket to be laid out on her bed, ready if all went awry and they needed to escape from Bretford House. Aunt Jocasta was also sent for and told to make ready to leave if all went awry.

'Nothing will go wrong,' she announced firmly, while obeying Kate's orders. 'Jacko will see to that!'

Kate hoped that her aunt was right but, once

dressed, she could only watch and pray for Martin, for herself, for their child—and everyone in Bretford House.

Bevis, despite his constant urgings for Essex to act, had no real belief that an insurrection led by him would succeed. Once the Councillors who had come to arrest Essex that fatal morning, were arrested themselves and imprisoned in the library, Essex had ordered his followers to join him in a direct attack on the Queen and her court.

It was afterwards disputed how many obeyed him, but the number certainly ran into the early hundreds—although there were not as many as he had hoped. Martin's messenger had correctly reported that they were armed only with rapiers and bludgeons, and with the belief that the Londoners who had always loudly supported him in all his recent troubles would rise *en masse* to install him as England's Lord Protector.

Alas, as Bevis had suspected, their support was vocal: they had no intention of actually taking to the streets and risking being cut down by the Queen's troops. Even the Sheriff, once the rising began, bolted from his home in Fenchurch Street, so that when Essex arrived there, it was to find him gone.

Bevis was also long gone by then. He had never meant to join Essex and risk a traitor's death: he was only using him in order that, in the confusion which followed, he would be able to take his grand revenge on the Queen and the Chancellor family. He and his gang of misfits, thieves and mercenaries, all prepared for the rich pickings which a successful attack on a Lord's mansion might bring them, made straight for Bretford House in the Strand, secure in their mistaken belief that their task would be an easy one since they would have the advantage of surprise.

Like Essex's makeshift force they were armed mainly with swords and bludgeons, although a few had pistols, but their main and first weapon was a balk of timber from the dockyards which they would use as a battering ram to destroy the front door in order to make their entry through the gap which they had created.

He might be their leader, but Bevis had no intention of joining in the actual fighting. Instead he would stand back and direct operations from the rear. The real captain was the fellow who had jested about Caesar and the Rubicon.

Martin's supporters all agreed afterwards that the anxious time of waiting was worse than the actual assault when it finally arrived. One of the guards had been posted in the street to act as a sentry who would run into the house to inform them when Bevis's troop came in sight.

Martin, his breastplate on—Rafe and Jacko were similarly equipped—had immediately ordered all the men to take up their arms and assemble in the entrance hall. Webster and several sturdy oarsmen were in the kitchens, where Kate, Aunt Jocasta, Mistress Cray and the women servants had been gathered. If things went ill, Webster was to lead them out of the back door and down to the river so that they might escape by it. Fortunately, although cold, the weather was fine.

The hackbuts and pistols were loaded and Martin's troops were arrayed behind the hazards which had been placed in the would-be invaders' path. He had divided those who possessed firearms into two. The first group would fire when the door was breached, and the second group would then take over, giving the first group time to reload their weapons.

He had instructed those who were carrying swords and pikes to remain in the rear until those in front of them ran out of ammunition, when they must be prepared to join in the general mêlée which might follow once the attackers came streaming in, in force.

At this point the sentry ran in, shouting, 'There are a large number of men approaching along the Strand!'

Martin shouted back, 'Stay here and keep watch at the right front window. Tell me immediately if, and when, they begin to advance up the drive.'

The sentry did so, remaining silent until he shouted again, 'They've turned into the drive, there's about fifty of them, as far as I can tell. The front men are carrying what looks like a battering ram.'

The sentry was right. The advance party, led by their captain, on reaching the front door, immediately began to attack it, fired by the knowledge that they were not only about to enrich themselves when they sacked the house after the door was destroyed but that rape and murder might also follow.

All those in the entrance hall drew a collective breath when the assault began and the door started to shatter.

Martin immediately rallied his troops, shouting, 'Ready and steady now. Do not fire until I give you the order, nor move until I order you to do so. Hold fast and all will be well.'

He had chosen to arm himself with the pistol which he had captured from the assassin who had been killed when he had dived into the Thames. It would, he thought, be a fine piece of revenge if he were able to use it on Bevis himself.

It did not take long for the door to give way and for the first men to scramble in over its shattered remains. As they entered Martin raised his own pistol, shouting, 'Fire!'

A fusillade of shots thus greeted the captain, who was leading his troop from the front. He, and the three men who followed him, had no time to be shocked by the discovery that their prey was ready and waiting for them, for they were all either killed or badly wounded immediately. Their dead and dying bodies lay in front of the barricade which Martin had caused to be erected. He had the grim satisfaction of disposing of the leader with his first shot.

He, and those who had fired the first volley, immediately stood back in order to reload their pistols, while the second group of defenders made ready to dispose of the next band of attackers when they entered—which they duly did, and were immediately replaced by Martin and his men.

Bevis, on hearing the noise of gunfire, grasped at once that the advantage of surprise, on which he had pinned his hopes, had disappeared. He watched with growing despair when it became apparent to him, and to the rest of his makeshift force, that they were being shot down as fast as they tried to enter Bretford House, instead of entering it to kill their unsuspecting and unarmed prey at will.

The other disaster which Bevis had not foreseen was that Martin and several of his small force were battle-hardened veterans who knew the best way in which to withstand an assault, unlike his own men who, lacking discipline, had charged recklessly through the small opening of the door, and continued to do so long after it was plain that their assault had become suicidal. It was, Jacko afterwards said, the best target practice he had ever taken part in.

After the third wave had been disposed of as easily as the first and second, the men behind it broke. They turned and fled like the cowardly and indisciplined rabble they were. They ran off in all directions, their pretence of being a genuine fighting force having been destroyed along with their leaders. None of them had the stomach required to continue once they saw what had happened to their fellows.

One of them turned on Bevis, who was shouting at them that if only they would be patient they might yet seize the house. 'You said that it would be easy,' he bellowed, 'and you lied. Now this is easy, for I'm damned if I'm going to hang for you,' and he ran Bevis through with his rapier.

He fell, his erstwhile supporters running by him, all bent only on saving themselves and damn any insurrection. Which was exactly how Essex's men behaved when some of them were shot down by the militia which Cecil had ordered to be ready to withstand any attack from them.

Inside Bretford House a terrible silence fell. Three dead bodies lay on the floor and four other men were feebly crawling their way towards the door, too far gone even to groan, their few comrades who, on entering had escaped death, or had not been seriously wounded, having fled with the rest when they grasped that a general retreat had begun. Martin, lowering his pistol, stepped over them and walked through the ruined doorway to find that the attackers had gone. The last remaining remnant of the force which had arrived with such high hopes was Bevis, who was lying half on and half off the drive.

Martin bent down. His enemy was still living, but only just: he was covered in blood from his haemorrhaging wound. Bevis looked up at him and managed to mouth feebly, 'Damn you, Hadleigh, you have all the luck which I never had,' before his eyes rolled upward and he fell back, dying.

It was over. The shadow under which Martin had lived since he had returned home had been lifted. Now all that remained was to shore up the hole left by the missing front door, and inform the parish authorities and the constables of the attack and its consequences so that the dead and injured might be removed.

Until that was done, the women in the house were to use only the backstairs so that they might avoid the scene of carnage which the entrance hall had become. Martin also had a duty to visit his father to tell him, and the guard who had been posted in his bedroom, that all was safely over.

Much later, Kate was seated in the withdrawing-room when Martin came down from his father's bedchamber. She had removed her fur coat, and was warming herself before the blazing fire which one of the footmen who had taken part in the skirmish had replenished.

Martin had divested himself of his breastplate, but he still looked like the fighting man he had once been and not the smooth nobleman of his recent transformation. He sat by her and took one of her hands in his.

'You're cold,' he said. 'Let me warm you.'

'Let me thank you, my Lord Hadleigh, for saving us.'

His answer, she thought, was typical of the man he was.

'It is not only I whom you must thank, but all who stood with me in the hall.'

'That, too,' she said, 'when Bretford House is itself again.'

From where they sat they could hear the noise of the entrance hall being cleared of its burden of dead and wounded men and misplaced furniture, as well as that created by those who were closing up the hole left by the destruction of the front door.

'Oh, it's itself again,' he told her with a grin. 'I understand that your aunt and Jacko have gone somewhere private to celebrate our small victory.'

'Not small—but let us hope that their celebration will be large. One thing which you have not told me, and that is what became of Bevis Frampton. Did he escape?'

'No, one of his own men killed him in the rout which followed their failure. We need fear nothing more from him and may walk abroad again as we please.'

'Thank God for that. There is one other thing, Lord Hadleigh...' Kate paused dramatically, 'if I am free of sickness this evening, I trust that tonight Aunt Jocasta and Jacko will not be the only ones celebrating.'

'Depend upon it, and if I were not expecting to be involved in all the business which will follow this— and Essex's rebellion, which has also almost certainly failed by now—I would be happy to join you in an immediate celebration, but...'

A knock came on the door.

'You see,' he told her, and shouted, 'Come in.'

It was Rafe.

'I'm sure that you would wish to hear the latest news from the city. It seems that Essex was driven back by the militia after he had been publicly proclaimed to be a traitor. He, and the few followers he had left, fled back to Essex House, which is being besieged by troops loyal to the Queen. They say that the Earl of Nottingham is in charge.'

'One thing's certain,' Martin said. 'Essex, and what remained of his small army, will not be able to defend Essex House from an attack by experienced troops. We were lucky in that all the trained soldiers were on our side.'

'Trained seamen, rather, but I suppose that's the same thing,' riposted Rafe with a grin. 'We were repelling boarders, after all. Well, I'll leave you to your good lady, now.'

'For the moment,' sighed Martin. 'I have much to do.'

As soon as Rafe had gone, he kissed Kate gently on the cheek. 'Until tonight, then, since for the present I must leave you.'

Kate watched him go to do his duty, secure in the knowledge that this time, all danger over, she knew that he would return safely to her so that they might begin their life together in peace and raise the family which they both wanted so much.

# *Epilogue*

*October, 1601*

'A toast,' said Martin proudly, 'to my son, Richard Chancellor, the Bretford heir, and to his mother,' and he waved his goblet towards Kate, who sat in the great chair at the top of the table, his child in her arms—a sight which he had long hoped to see.

Kate's morning sickness had not lasted very long, and her baby's birth had been an easy one. Richard was a month old, and this was the first time he had been taken into company. His grandfather was seated beside him, a look of pride on his old face. He had been determined to live until his son's heir was born, and had succeeded so well that he had been able to move to Saxon Hall in London's suburbs, far away from smelly central London.

'May I also propose a toast?' he asked. 'It is to Her Grace, Queen Elizabeth, to whom we must give thanks for saving us from adventurers both from abroad and at home.'

'Amen,' said the company with one voice. They were all remembering the earlier part of the year of Richard's birth, when Robert Devereux, Earl of Essex, had tried—and failed—to overthrow the Queen's government, and Bevis Frampton had suffered a similar fate when he had attacked the Chancellor family at Bretford House.

Now, in this cold October, all was quiet again, although both at home and in the court, change was in the air. Bretford House was being rebuilt and refurnished after its years of neglect under Martin's father. Webster had recently learned that a distant cousin of his father's had died and that he was now heir to the barony which his father had inherited. He was about to return home to help him to run his new estates and to consider beginning another career. Rafe was betrothed to a young lady of good dowry and would succeed to Webster's post.

Jacko's new life was the strangest of all. Six weeks ago he had learned with some shock that Kate's Aunt Jocasta Saville was expecting his child. He was not as surprised as Aunt Jocasta herself, who had thought, or rather hoped, that in her mid-forties she was safely past the age of childbearing.

'No child of mine will be born a bastard,' he had declared belligerently to Martin. Without waiting for any man's permission he had proposed marriage to her and, despite the difference in their station, she had accepted him.

'For if,' she declared loudly and often, 'one of the Brandon family's great ladies could marry her groom and remain respectable, then I am entitled to marry Jacko, whose status is better than that of a groom, being one of Lord Hadleigh's right-hand men.'

Martin had been approached by Sir Robert Cecil, through Sir Walter Raleigh, to become one of *his* right-hand men at court. It could, Cecil had said, lead on to even greater honours. He had refused this offer, as he was later to refuse many others. He had seen what happened to men who came too close to the ultimate seat of power in the court.

He remembered the Earl of Essex's end. His rebellion having failed, trapped on the roof of his own home, he had drawn his sword and shouted down to his would-be captors that he would kill himself rather than give way to the Queen and Cecil. Whereat Lord Nottingham had threatened to blow the house and all its occupants up, if he, and his companions, did not agree to surrender themselves immediately.

He did so and was tried and executed, privately, on Tower Hill. It was reported that he met his end bravely. Lord Southampton, his most faithful lieutenant, was also sentenced to death, but the sentence was later commuted to imprisonment for life in the Tower of London. The players whom he had bribed to stage *Richard II*, had been lucky enough to escape punishment because they were thought to be mere pawns in

the great game of politics as played out under
Elizabeth.

Bevis's accomplices who had survived the attack
were also never brought to book, although, later on,
some of them were caught and hanged for other
crimes which they had committed. Bevis's death had
been put down as an accident which had occurred in
the temporary anarchy of the Essex rebellion. The distant cousin who inherited his meagre estates turned
out to be an amiable fellow, every man's friend—a
joke which only Martin and his immediate cohorts
properly appreciated.

All was thus set fair at Bretford House and Saxon
Hall. The black sheep had come home, to a father
who had discovered that his fleece was white after all.
Not only that, by using his strength and courage he
had been able to overcome an enemy who had dogged
the House of Chancellor for many years—and then
provide it with the long-wanted heir.

The only fly in the ointment was the Queen's great
age. It was inevitable that her death could not be long
delayed and many said that after Essex's execution
she had lost the zest for life which had sustained her
for so long. All informed men believed that the next
monarch would be James VI of Scotland, but no one
seemed to be welcoming with any great enthusiasm
the prospect of his becoming James I of England.

Nevertheless on this happy day at Saxon Hall such
considerations were far from the minds of the revel-
lers. 'The first of many,' Lord Bretford had whispered

to his son when he had first been allowed to hold his grandson.

'But not too many,' Martin replied, 'for Kate's sake,' having seen what constant childbearing had done to the wives of some of his friends.

'But enough,' said Lord Bretford, handing the babe back to his father.

To mark the christening, Sir Walter Raleigh had sent a large silver urn and had asked his parents to celebrate the day by filling it with the best sack so that each of the guests could drink a goblet-full from it.

Later, the feast over, the baby in his crib, and the urn emptied Kate and Martin sat alone among the remnants of the feast.

'You see how wrong you were to worry, my darling,' she told him. 'The babe and I are still with you, even though you have declared your love to me these many times: the curse has been lifted.'

'True,' he replied, 'and the proof of your love for me lies in his bed upstairs.'

'So you have had your share of luck, at last.'

'And long may we live to enjoy it,' was his answer to that. 'My family is my rod and staff and to the devil with kings, queens and courts: they are for other men, not me. My love and mine own acres are enough.'

'And for me, too,' was her answer, and thus it was for both of them through the long years to come, and for their children, too.

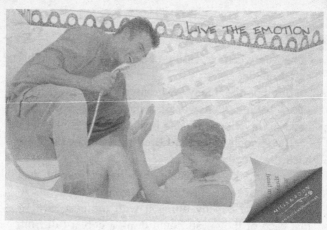

LIVE THE EMOTION

**Modern Romance**™
...international affairs
– seduction and
passion guaranteed

**Medical Romance**™
...pulse-raising
romance – heart-
racing medical drama

**Tender Romance**™
...sparkling, emotional,
feel-good romance

**Sensual Romance**™
...teasing, tempting,
provocatively playful

**Historical Romance**™
...rich, vivid and
passionate

*Blaze Romance*™
...scorching hot
sexy reads

*27 new titles every month.*

*Live the emotion*